MERE MORTALS

Books by Erin Jade Lange

The Chaos of Now
Rebel, Bully, Geek, Pariah
Dead Ends
Butter

MERE MORTALS

ERIN JADE LANGE

HARPER TEEN

An Imprint of HarperCollinsPublishers

HarperTeen is an imprint of HarperCollins Publishers.

Library of Congress Cataloging-in-Publication Data
Names: Lange, Erin Jade, author.
Title: Mere mortals / Erin Jade Lange.
Description: First edition. | New York : HarperTeen, 2022. |
    Audience: Ages 13 up | Audience: Grades 10-12 | Summary: "Two
    teenage vampires are turned mortal and must face the greatest
    nightmare of all—high school"— Provided by publisher.
Identifiers: LCCN 2021058435 | ISBN 9780063219113 (hardcover)
Subjects: CYAC: Vampires—Fiction. | High schools—Fiction. |
    Schools—Fiction. | LCGFT: Vampire fiction. | School fiction.
Classification: LCC PZ7.L26113 Me 2022 | DDC [Fic]—dc23
LC record available at https://lccn.loc.gov/2021058435

Typography by Chris Kwon
22 23 24 25 26   PC/LSCH   10 9 8 7 6 5 4 3 2 1
❖
First Edition

To Dad, the original storyteller. Thank you for the walks in the woods.

And to Mom, who still takes care of me. May I be half the mother you are.

ONE

BLOOD & PICKET FENCES

It was a place of nightmares surrounded by a white picket fence.

"Home sweet home," Reg muttered beside me. His lips tightened over his fangs, and I could almost smell his disdain.

"More like a prison," I said.

We stood side by side on the edge of the property, unwilling to step forward but not daring to run away—not with Elders present. This place, with its hideously cheery fence glowing in the moonlight, was where we would serve our sentence. Our *life* sentence.

I felt a claw of panic scraping its way up my throat and spit it at Reg.

"This is your fault, you know," I said.

His face, always an elegant mask of cool detachment, cracked ever so slightly. "*My* fault?"

"If you hadn't confessed—"

"To a crime *you* committed."

"Because you tried so hard to stop me?"

"Enough!" Reg spun to me with a speed no human eye could

follow and flashed his fangs, nearly as white as the fence.

"Ew. Put those away." I flicked a pale hand toward the offending teeth.

Rude.

He tucked his fangs back, and when he spoke again, it was with his usual lazy lilt. "It could be worse. It could be the stake."

There was a shift in the air behind us as the two Elders, who had been conversing in low tones to the side, now stood at our backs. Elder Adante cleared his throat—a totally unnecessary action for our kind, *the drama queen.*

"Charlotte and Reginald Drake, House of Drake, Clan of Bone, you are hereby sentenced to life."

Humans got sentenced to things like life in prison or life on parole.

Vampires? Just *life.* That was punishment enough.

"A stake would be better," I said, the panic scratching at my throat again. I forced it down. "At least then we could avoid the wrinkles."

"You never know," Reg said. "You may not grow old at all. You may get lucky and get hit by a bus."

"Do you fear death, Charlotte?" Elder Adante asked.

I refused to turn and face the Elders, to let them search my expression for any hint of fear.

"Please." I scoffed. "The only thing I'm afraid of is being *bored* to death. And don't call me Charlotte. It's Charlie."

Reg took my hand and squeezed it with all the strength he would soon lose—enough to grind granite into dust.

"My sister fears nothing," he said.

It was a lie, and he knew it. He couldn't read my mind, of course—mind manipulation took a hefty dose of vampire venom—but after a century, we didn't need to hear each other's thoughts to know them.

"It would be a reasonable fear," Adante mused. "Life and death are inextricably linked for humans, part of the same cycle, each defined by the other and unable to exist without its counterpart."

I dragged my gaze beyond the white picket fence. We'd lived so many places in the last hundred years—mansions, penthouses, beach bungalows, and even, in the best of times, castles. I thought we had lived everywhere and every way one could live. But we'd never lived in a—

"What is this?" I whispered.

"Don't be dense, Charlie," Reg said. "It's obviously a cottage."

"It looks as old as we are," I complained.

"Older, in fact," Adante said. "This cottage has been here since before you were born . . . the *first* time."

Reg forced a thin smile onto his face. "It's . . . quaint."

I wasn't sure why he was bothering to be polite at this point. Why show respect to the Elders when they hadn't shown any to us—constantly treating us like children, no matter how long we lived.

"And what is this supposed to be?" I swept an arm to indicate the fence that stretched out before us. It circled the cottage yard and was made entirely of wooden posts—each one thicker and narrower than your typical fence slats and sharpened to a severe point at the top. "Is this some kind of joke?"

Reg eyed the fence and forced a wry smile. "Ah, yes. A fence made of wooden stakes. Very clever," he congratulated the Elders.

Elder Adante sounded ever so slightly exasperated. "It is a fence, nothing more. Well . . . not *quite* nothing more."

I turned, finally. "What is it?"

"It is your punishment."

Reg gulped. "So it is for— You do mean to— We are to perish, then?"

"Die." I crossed my arms. "Not perish. Really, Reg, watch some TV, why don't you."

"Hardly the time to correct me," he huffed, "when we're about to be staked."

"I doubt we're going to be staked."

"I tire of this," the second Elder said to Adante. I couldn't remember her name. Mary or Madelaine or something. Until today, Adante was the only Elder we'd really spent any time with, since he was assigned to House Drake. Each house—dozens of them within the four clans—had an Elder representative, a diplomat of sorts. But if Adante was a politician, then this other Elder was the muscle. Power radiated off her in a way that would have chilled me if my body wasn't already ice-cold.

"You are not to fall upon the posts," Adante said.

Reg let out a loud sigh of relief.

"But the fence is your end, nonetheless," Adante continued. "It is the end of this life and the beginning of, well, *life*. We wish you well."

It sounded so final, I half expected the Elders to turn and

leave, but they stood there as if waiting for us to do something.

"Um, thank you?" Reg tried.

Adante lifted a stiff arm in response—his bony hand a shade darker than ours, but just as bloodless—fingers pointing ominously toward the small gate in the white picket fence. He meant for us to cross through it.

Instinctively, Reg backed away a step instead. But a single step was as far as he got. The other Elder was behind him in an instant. If I had blinked, I would have missed it. She was faster than both me and Reg, and I was certain that her sole job tonight was to make sure we passed through that suspicious gate.

I resisted the urge to expose my fangs. I didn't want to give them the satisfaction of seeing any fear. Instead, I summoned up all the attitude I could and pointed at the pile of luggage filling the sidewalk and spilling into the street. "And just who exactly is going to carry our bags? I assume there is no bellhop?"

Adante's arm still hung in the air, pointed at the gate. He could stand there for a decade and never get tired. "Your bags are not my concern. Now it's time to go. We've said our goodbyes."

"Yes." I smiled. "And what warm and fuzzy goodbyes they were. Thanks ever so much for your hospitality over the last century. Do tell everyone back home we said, 'Bite me.'"

Reg grabbed my arm and pulled me away from the Elders, who remained as still as statues but now had their fangs bared. "Stop it, Charlie."

"Get it?" A hysterical laugh bubbled up from my throat as

Reg dragged me backward. "*Bite me?*"

"Be quiet!" Reg gave me one final yank, and I stumbled right into the gate. He caught me a split second before I fell through, but my rear end bumped the gate, and it swung open with an ominous creak like a tree swaying in a storm.

As if to complete the scene, a slight breeze swam up from the cottage yard, rustling fallen leaves and blowing my long dark hair across my cheeks.

"We're going, okay?" Reg called back to the Elders. "We're going."

He set me upright, and our eyes locked. At first glance, his eyes were so much like my own—as tar black as our hair. But Reg's eyes were the kinder pair, always. There was fear in them now, but also a softness. "Let's make the best of it, shall we?"

"Will we," I corrected.

"Right." Reg put on a big fake smile and grabbed my hand tight as we faced the cottage, the tips of our toes right on the threshold of the open gate. "Here we go, then."

"All your fault," I breathed. But I squeezed his hand hard, grateful to have at least one part of my life I could still hold on to.

Then together, we stepped through the yawning gate, past the stupid white fence, into the yard.

And our world turned upside down.

TWO
THIS IS NEW

The second we entered the yard, the breeze that had teased my hair became a roaring wind, whipping up a cocoon around us. For one delirious moment I thought we were running. It felt just as wild as the wind we created when moving at top speed, slicing through the air with a power greater than any man-made engine. But our feet were planted on the ground, and the wind tangling my hair was not a natural one.

I pressed my face to Reginald's chest, and he wrapped his arms around me. The closer we drew together, the tighter the tornado around us closed in, until it was pressing down on us so hard we couldn't breathe.

Air. I need air!

The sensation was nothing like the need for blood that I had known for so long. This was more urgent, more all-consuming. It eclipsed all other thoughts and— *Oh God, I need air!* Panic rippled down my body, and the need for air caused an actual pounding in my chest.

No, wait. That pounding wasn't need. It was something else.

Something I hadn't felt in a century—something I couldn't remember *ever* feeling, because it had been erased from my memory the day I turned vampire. It was my heart. My heart was pounding for the first time in one hundred years.

Just when I thought I might pass out from shock and lack of oxygen, a force more powerful than the wind blew me backward off my feet. I felt Reg's body ripped from mine with the same energy, and for a split second I was flying, until I landed with a painful thump on my back.

Pain. That was new too.

I gasped, desperate for the air now filling my lungs. Slowly, it came, and after a few moments, I didn't even have to try to breathe. My body—this new aching thing with a beating heart—breathed for me. I opened my eyes, and a new terror set in.

I can't see.

"I can't see!" I called out. "Reg, help! I'm blind!"

"Hush," Reg said from somewhere across the yard. I heard a rustle and a groan, then his voice drew closer. "Give your eyes a minute to adjust to the dark."

I did as he said, lying still and keeping my eyes open until one by one, tiny pinpricks of light pierced through the darkness. Stars. A whole sky full of them. Reassured, I sat up, testing my sight. I had to squint to make out Reg crawling toward me through the grass and leaves, clutching his side. Behind him, the white fence glowed, and I followed the line of stakes until it reached the gate, where the Elders stood ever stiff and impassive just outside the fence.

Elder Adante tugged on the ends of his shirtsleeves, making tiny adjustments to his cuff links. He could not have looked more bored.

"The transition is complete," he said. "I trust you'll have all you need here."

I scrambled to my feet, a sudden rage eclipsing all my pain and fear. "That's it?! You're just going to drop us here without telling us where to go or what to do?"

Adante indicated the cottage behind us. "You go there. What you *do* is up to you."

"As if any of this is up to us," I snapped.

"Charlie," Reg warned. "Be calm."

"Don't tell me what to—"

"They bicker like children," the second Elder muttered as if we weren't there.

"They *are* children," Adante replied. "It is precisely the problem. Of all the things we shed when we turn—our memories, our illnesses, our physical imperfections—we cannot lose the essence of who we are. If we are children, we are doomed to remain children."

"Excuse me, *we*"—I pointed back and forth between myself and Reg—"are standing right here. And we're not children."

Adante's answer was a cold stare. "You are now."

The other Elder attempted something like a smile. "It's for your own good."

Her patronizing tone set my skin on fire. I felt my face burning from my cheeks all the way up into my hair. I forgot for a moment how powerless I must be—forgot how slow and weak and practically blind I was, and in that moment of amnesia, I rushed toward the Elders, opening my mouth to show them my fangs.

Except I had no fangs, and "rushing" felt like wading through thick honey compared to how fast I could move only minutes ago. I had to pass through the gate to get to the Elders, and for one irrational moment, I wondered if that would restore my powers. But as I crossed the white picket threshold, I felt no change. My heart was still beating, my lungs still pulling in air. Disappointment caused me to stumble. Either that or my toe catching on the edge of the sidewalk.

I tripped and fell, my knees skidding a few inches on the concrete before I landed ungracefully in a tangle at the Elders' feet. How humiliating. I had never had a clumsy moment in my whole long life.

Adante gave the slightest shake of his head. "A pity."

"For your own good," the other Elder repeated.

Then they were gone. Just like that. One moment they were standing above me, and the next, they vanished.

I stood up, ignoring the throbbing in my knees, and spun around on the spot, trying to find the Elders in the dark. But all I could see was the cottage, with black hills cutting a curving line across the night sky on either side of it, and across the road, a wall of something—probably corn—waving and whispering in the dark.

"They— Where did they . . . ? How did they . . . ?" I turned in a new direction with every stutter, still searching the shadows, but all I saw was Reg.

He was on his feet now, leaning against the fence and still holding his side. His mouth was hanging open in a shell-shocked expression that only amplified my fear.

"Reg, they disappeared! Did you know they could do that?"

He shook his head slowly. "Even the Ancients can't disappear. How can Elders?"

"They can't," a voice like gravel said from behind Reg.

I had to squint to make out the shadowy figure on the front porch of the cottage. "Who's there?" I called. I stepped back into the yard, flinching a little as I passed the picket fence, but there was no wind this time.

"Vamps can't disappear." It was a man—an old one by the sound of it. "They just jogged off—same as they always do. Only you can't see it now. Little too fast for your eyeballs to follow." The old man chuckled, and it sounded more like a cough.

"Who are you?" I demanded. "What are you doing here? This is our . . . *cottage*." I waved a hand miserably over the tiny building. It wasn't much, but if it was all we had, I was ready to fight for it.

The shadow on the porch lumbered down the few steps to the lawn. I could make out his outline now, and it was large and strong, making him seem younger than his rasp. I wasn't great at guessing human ages, but I pegged him at about sixty. The raspy chuckle came again.

"On the contrary. This is *my* cottage, and you are my

guests . . . for the time being. Think of me as your caretaker."

"Sir." Reg gave an embarrassing little bow, and I stomped on his toe. "Ow!"

"We don't need taking care of," I said.

"If you say so." The old man's hand stroked his chin, and I could see a beard and mustache taking shape in the dark. "But way I see it, you do need a place to stay, so let's just start there, huh?"

"And the way *I* see it, we've been taking orders from Elders for too long," I said, propping a hand on my hip. "Look where that got us—a shack in the middle of nowhere."

The man coughed. "We're actually just outside of Nowhere, and I'll thank you not to call my home a shack or me an Elder. I'd venture to say you're a fair bit older than I am, little lady, though it may not look that way."

"You're not vampire?" Reg asked.

The man's hand stopped pawing his beard and became a fist at his side. "'Course not. And lucky for you two, neither are you anymore."

"Lucky?" I breathed fire. "Lucky?! This is the worst—"

Reg squeezed my arm. "Perhaps we are getting off on the wrong foot. My name is Reginald. This is my sister, Charlotte."

"Charlie." I pouted.

Reg crossed the yard with his hand out toward the man, but at least he didn't bow this time. "You may call me Reg."

"And you can call me a recluse. All the kids do." They shook hands, and Reg looked like he might break in the old man's powerful grasp.

12

"We're not kids," I said, still lingering back by the fence.

"You've been kids for a very long time, I suspect," the man said. "But you won't be for much longer. Enjoy the few years you've got left. One day you'll be wishing you *were* kids again."

"Spare me the teachable moment."

The man spread his arms wide. "Look, it's way past late. You're welcome to sleep out here if you like, but I, for one, am going inside. If you choose to stay in my *shack*, there are rooms made up for you."

"We'd like that very much," Reg nodded hastily. "Thank you for your hospitality."

"Speaking of hospitality," I said, "we have a lot of luggage."

Reg gestured to our mountain of suitcases out on the sidewalk. "Yes, is there someone . . . ?" He trailed off.

The old man eyed the bags. "Best get to hauling it in, then." He was chuckling again as he made his way back up the porch steps.

I waited until he was inside the cottage to fix Reg with my most withering stare. "*Sir*? *Thank you for your hospitality*? Since when are you so polite to humans?"

"Since we *became* them," Reg said. He strode across the lawn until he was right in my face. It seemed to take ages. "And since the first person we've met is strong enough to rip my arm off with a simple handshake."

"Don't be so dramatic."

"Don't be so stubborn." He marched past me and stood at the center of the pile of luggage. "This is all we have. Everything we own, save for whatever Drake House put in our trust." He pointed toward the cottage door. "Our lives are in the hands of—of—"

"Some old guy?"

"Precisely. So I simply want to weather this ordeal with what little bit of dignity we have left and hang on to our few remaining worthless belongings."

"Excuse me, Prada is not worthless. It's priceless. It's—"

"Enough, Charlie!"

The cornstalks across the road swayed as if leaning away from Reg's outburst, and I swayed with them. It wasn't like my brother to lose his temper. That was usually my role, and he was upstaging me.

I stepped over a suitcase and joined him in the middle of the mess.

"You okay?"

It was a ridiculous question. Of course he wasn't okay. None of this was okay. But it was Reg's job to be the levelheaded one, and I needed him to snap out of it right about now.

"I am . . . unsettled." Reg collected himself. "But look on the bright side."

"There's a bright side?"

"They didn't stake us. Perhaps that's a sign this is only temporary, and the Elders are attempting to teach us some sort of lesson."

The idea that the Elders would go through this much trouble just to play games with us was as ridiculous as asking Reg if he was okay.

"Like an elaborate trick? Can you just imagine?" I smiled, even though I didn't mean to, and my voice took on a high pitch alarmingly close to a giggle. "It's almost kind of funny, right? Isn't it kind of funny?"

Reg took my hands as they started to tremble.

The tremble rippled up my arms and into my chest until my whole body was shaking and my legs were Jell-O. I collapsed onto a mound of duffel bags and hatboxes. A strangled sound like a hiccup escaped my throat. Reg knelt in front of me and wiped something wet from my cheek. We both stared at the moisture on his hand in wonder for a moment, then my hands flew to my face.

Tears.

New again.

I felt another one slip from the corner of my eye, and all at once it was a flood. I collapsed into Reg's arms, letting the tears come. I don't know how long we sat like that in the dark, with my eyeballs leaking all over Reg's shirt, but I was vaguely aware of him carrying me into the cottage, huffing and puffing the whole way, and settling me into something soft and warm. My last thought, as sleep finally stole the tears away, was that Reg was dead wrong.

This sentence was far from temporary.

We were permanently, infuriatingly, hopelessly human.

THREE

SUNLIGHT & THE ASSASSIN

I woke up to something warm but intangible coating my skin and a glow behind my eyelids. My eyes fluttered open, seeking the source of the heat and light. I found it immediately, but it took me a moment to process the sunlight pouring through wide-open curtains.

Wait. Sunlight?

My brain snapped awake as my eyes snapped shut.

Sunlight!

I yanked the covers over my head and scrambled away from the window, seeking out the edge of the bed in the darkness provided by the comforter.

"Sunlight!" I screamed. "*Reg!*"

Mercifully, my hand found the edge of the mattress, and I tumbled over the side, away from the deadly rays. The covers tumbled with me, and I was tangled beneath them screaming.

"Sunlight! Reg, help! I'M BURNING!"

"Charlie?" Reg's voice was weak and distant at first, then louder as he threw open the door to the room. "Charlie?!"

"I'M BURNING! I'M BURNING!"

I thrashed under the covers, trying to untangle myself and shimmy underneath the bed at the same time—all my instincts telling me to get to the darkest place possible.

But the covers fought back, and I only bound myself up tighter.

"I'm burning," I said again, but this time it came out as an exhausted sigh.

"Charlie." Reg again, quieter now. His hand pressed through the covers to cup my head. "Daylight can't hurt you."

It took a second for his words to sink in. Ever so cautiously, I stretched out one hand until it escaped the blankets and hit the naked air. I winced in expectation, but there was no pain, no burning. I pulled back the rest of the covers, which stopped fighting me now that I wasn't moving like a maniac.

The first thing I saw was Reg, standing above me, absolutely bathed in the sunlight. He held his arms wide and did a slow spin.

"See? It's fine."

I tossed the rest of the covers aside and stood up, brushing wild hairs from my face. "Well, of course," I said. "I was—um—having a nightmare, obviously."

"Obviously." Reg smirked.

I marched over to the window and pushed the curtains open even wider, determined to prove I wasn't afraid, but I couldn't help but squint as the full blast of sun hit my face. Slowly, slowly, I opened one eye and then the other. I had to blink a few times before my eyes adjusted to the brightness. Then the scene outside the window came into focus. The hills around the cottage, so black the night before, were now waves of the brightest green I had ever seen. The occasional patch of wildflowers popped bright purple or yellow against the long blades of grass, which eventually gave way to hay-colored cornfields on all sides.

"Beautiful, isn't it?" Reg asked, joining me at the window.

I humphed in response. I wasn't ready to get chummy with the scenery.

But of course it was beautiful. Any moron could see colors brought to life by sunlight were more spectacular in person than in pictures. No movie or TV show I'd ever seen could do this justice. A sigh escaped my lips before I could catch it, and I hastily tried to turn it into a yawn.

Reg tipped his face toward the sun. "Perhaps this punishment will have its silver linings."

More like golden, green, and gorgeous purple linings. I pressed a hand to the window as if I could reach out and touch the wildflowers. I wondered what they smelled like. I actually sniffed the air, but the scent that reached my nose was definitely not floral.

I turned away from the colors outside the window and wrinkled my nose at Reg.

"Is this what you smell like now? Oh God." I lifted my shirt to my nose and took a whiff. "Is this what *I* smell like?" But the aroma wasn't coming off us, and once I realized it wasn't human, it wasn't half bad.

Reg laughed. "It's food."

Food. Of course. But what food? Why didn't I recognize it?

I sniffed the air again. "It's . . . different."

"I suppose a new kind of nourishment shall take some getting used to," Reg said.

"Oh, *shall* it?" I parroted. "You *suppose*? If we have to do this, try to at least talk like you belong in this century. You sound ancient."

"I *feel* ancient."

"You're barely one hundred. Ancients are at least a thousand." I moved to push past him and stopped, startled by a thought. "Wait, Reg, how old *are* we? I mean, how old will we be now?"

He cocked his head, thinking. "Hm. Sixteen, maybe?"

"Maybe?!" I sucked in a breath. "We can't *not* know how old we are. And can we really be the same age?

"Calm down," Reg said in his bored, *Charlie is panicking for nothing* voice.

"No, we are completely unprepared for this," I raged on. "It's cruel. It's cruel and unusual punishment, and we have no idea what's next."

Reg smiled. "Next is breakfast."

As he said the word, a fresh wave of that aroma rolled into the room, and my stomach responded with a disgusting noise like it was popping bubbles.

We followed our noses into an airy kitchen made entirely of wood and stone. Every surface was polished and sparkling in the sun that poured in from two walls of windows. It may have been a simple cottage, but at least it was clean.

As if reading my thoughts, the old man spoke from where he was hunched over a stove.

"A little more shiny than shack, don't ya think?"

I sneered at his back in response and yanked an intricately carved wooden chair out from the gleaming table at the center of the kitchen.

"Careful with that," the old man said, turning around with a heavy skillet. "Made it myself."

I fingered the edge of the chair, feeling the carefully made ripples and ridges. It was impressive—something we would have paid high dollar for in our former lives.

"The chairs are spectacular," Reg said, selecting his own seat and handling it with the utmost care.

"They're okay," I said. "What is that smell?"

"Eggs, of course," Reg said as the old man scooped food from the skillet onto plates.

Eggs. Right. I recognized the scent now, but it was much stronger—and more appealing—than I remembered it ever being.

"I don't understand," I said. "Did our sense of smell get . . . better? I thought all our senses were superior to humans."

"You *are* human," the old man corrected. He dropped the skillet back on the stove and passed around the steaming plates. "And superior is a matter of opinion."

Reg leaned over his plate and licked his lips. "She's right though," he said. "The aroma is much more powerful now."

"Same as it ever was," the old man said. He dropped into a chair across from us and dug a fork into his own pile of eggs.

"It's what you *don't* smell now that makes it seem stronger."

Reg and I shared a quizzical look, then I saw Reg's black eyes—*no, wait. More brown today than black. Odd*—as he caught on first.

"Blood," he said.

"Oh." I sucked in a breath, tasting the air. He was right. Sitting this close to a human, we should have been overwhelmed by his scent. I couldn't remember a time I'd been around food without humans. And the smell of their blood always eclipsed every other aroma.

"It feels as though we should recall a scent this strong from our time as humans," Reg said. "Perhaps it was taken when our human memories were erased?"

I rolled my eyes. "They don't take *everything*. We still know how to walk and talk and go to the bathroom."

Our caretaker grinned. "Vamps don't do that."

"Well, no," I said, an unfamiliar warm sensation in my cheeks. "But we remember how."

"Good, because that's a handy skill for humans." He winked at Reg, who grimaced.

Clearly he hadn't considered *every* aspect of our new lives.

The old guy scooped up a forkful of eggs. "Look, Charlotte—"

"Charlie."

"Right." He talked through a mouthful of food. "I don't know if they actually erase your muscle memories or if that kind of thing just disappears over time, but I wouldn't put it past them. Who knows what logic vamps have for what they've stolen from you."

Stolen. I rolled the word around in my head. I hadn't really thought of the memory fade as stealing—more of a courtesy to newborn vampires, to help them transition. If we remembered our humanity, we might fight the urge to feed, and without blood, vampires starved down to shells of themselves. Worse than dead; they were eternally dying. The fade was a gift, really.

Wasn't it?

"Why did they not perform the fade on us, I wonder?" Reg said.

"That one I can answer," the old man said. "Humans with amnesia spend too much time poking around in their own past, trying to dig up a history. It's better if they're in on their own punishment."

"Fascinating," Reg said.

Oh, please.

"It's hardly fascinating."

"Well, there, *Charlie,* maybe you'll be fascinated by the taste of those eggs." The old guy pointed his fork at my plate. "Give her a shot. I'm kind of proud of that recipe."

I crossed my arms and leaned back, but my stomach gurgled again, arguing with me.

Reg gave an apologetic smile. "Charlie and I have forgotten what hunger feels like. But we certainly haven't forgotten our manners." He aimed the last bit at me and made a point of lifting his fork and stabbing at the eggs.

"Had manners once, did she?" The old man asked, letting out one of those raspy laughs.

Reg stuffed a forkful of the eggs into his mouth. His eyes

closed almost immediately, and he moaned as he swallowed. "Wow."

"Told ya. It's my secret recipe."

"It's . . . it defies description," Reg raved. "Thank you so much . . . er, I don't believe we caught your name."

"I kind of like it when you call me sir."

"I'm not calling you that," I said. "What's the big mystery? Just tell us your name."

"You want my name?" His fork clattered to the plate, and he cracked his gnarled old knuckles. "All right, then, let's get on with it. Good a time as any."

He looked each of us in the eye. "My name is Salvador Sicarius."

No!

Reg and I were out of our chairs in an instant, our backs pressed against the kitchen's stone wall.

"Assassin!" Reg hissed.

"Slayer!" I cried simultaneously.

Our heads tilted back in identical motions, mouths open to expose our fangs, but of course we had none.

The old man—*no, the slayer*—collected his fork, waving it in our direction. "You're going to want to break that habit. You look pretty silly making those faces without your pointy incisors."

I sucked my lips back over my teeth, feeling foolish, yes, but mostly afraid. Next to me, Reg's eyes darted right and left, looking for an escape route.

"You lied to us," Reg said.

"Did not."

"Did too," Reg insisted.

I managed an eye roll, despite my fear. "Really?"

"We know your name," Reg said, never taking his eyes off the assassin. "Every vampire from here to Transylvania knows your name. And we know what you can do."

Salvador Sicarius went back to shoveling eggs into his mouth. "I suspect I can do a heck of a lot less than you think I can. But yeah, I get that a lot."

A little piece of egg dribbled down his chin and caught in his beard. The sight of it stifled some of my fear. He didn't *look* like the Sicarius slayers of legend. He didn't look like any kind of vampire hunter at all. He just looked like a messy old man.

I frowned, almost disappointed he wasn't living up to my nightmares. "I never thought I'd meet a Sicarius," I said. "You're . . ."

"Not what we expected," Reg finished.

I crossed my arms. I would have come up with something more colorful, but Reg was probably right to play it polite.

Salvador dragged a napkin across his chin, knocking the egg bit loose. It landed with a little *splat* on the table. "You expected a warrior? Someone in armor, maybe? Waving a stake?" He flipped the fork in his hand, so he was holding it like a weapon and stabbed the air. "Shouting, 'I shall smite thee!' or some nonsense?"

We cringed away from the fork until he aimed it back at the plate and continued to inhale his breakfast. "Well, sorry to disappoint. My days of wielding a pointy stick are done."

"You don't need a stake," Reg said. "All you need are your hands."

"That's right. So maybe you know more than most." Salvador carried his now-empty plate to the sink and came back to the table holding up the offending hands. "But do you know what these hands can do?"

"Kill?" I tried to say it with a *duh*, but it came out as more of a *peep*.

"Some vamps may see it that way." He sat and gestured for us to do the same. I pulled my seat as far away from the table as I could and sat on the edge, ready to run if I needed to.

"My touch doesn't kill," Salvador said. "It brings you back to life."

"Oh yes," I said. "The healing touch of the slayer. That's the fuzzy bedtime story I remember."

He laughed like I'd made a joke on his behalf and not at his expense. "No, I'm sure you heard a much different version."

"I understand," Reg said.

"You do?" I cocked my head at Reg, but he kept his eyes on the man across the table.

"I've read about it in some of our older texts. Your touch can make us mortal."

My eyes fell on the slayer's hands, and I couldn't keep the awe out of my voice. "Really?"

"Really."

"But you didn't touch us," I said. "You didn't do this."

"I did, in a way." He nodded out the kitchen window to the white fence outside.

"The fence?" I asked. "But how?"

He shook his head. "That's about enough for now, I think. You kids ought to eat those eggs before they go cold."

But even Reg had lost his appetite in the presence of a slayer. I protested, "You still haven't told us—"

"I told you my name," he said. "That's what you asked for. Now, if that name gives you the heebie-jeebies, you can just call me Sal."

"Sal," I echoed, testing it out.

"Yes, Sal it is, I think," Reg said, recovering from his shock and once again filling his face with food.

"At least around the house here," Sal said. "But if you want to avoid questions you can't answer, I suggest you call me Grandpa at school."

"What?" I spluttered.

Reg choked on his eggs. "Did you just say—"

"School?!" I finished.

Sal laughed himself into a hacking cough that drowned out our protests, and he was still howling when he got up from the table and lumbered out the front door.

Reg pushed his plate away, finally losing his appetite, and we stared dumbfounded at each other for a long minute.

"School," Reg whispered.

I dropped my head into my hands. "Maybe he's trying to kill us after all."

FOUR

THE GIRL IN THE MIRROR

"This one?" I held up a black Gucci turtleneck.

"Eh." Reg shrugged.

I tossed the turtleneck aside and yanked a black lace mini-dress out of my open suitcase. I checked the label. Prada. Perfect.

"This one?"

"It's okay." Reg yawned and stretched out on my bed—or more accurately, on the mountain of clothes that now covered my bed.

"Reg, this is important." I stomped a foot and added the dress to the pile.

"It's exhausting," he said. "Don't you own anything that isn't black?"

I pouted, inspecting a pair of stretchy black jeans. Sal had given us all of a day to get used to the idea of going to school, and twenty-four hours later, I'd barely had time to unpack, let alone find the perfect thing to wear. I had an outfit for *every-thing*—ball gowns for impressing the sons of foreign dignitaries at important political galas, one-of-a-kind jackets to catch the eye of aloof rock stars, ultrashort shorts and tall boots to draw in the cowboys. And yes, most of it was black, because black was better for hunting. But an outfit for a first day of school? Now that was something I had simply never needed.

I held the jeans out for Reg to see. "What do these say to you?"

"They don't say anything. They're trousers."

"Reg."

He sighed. "What do you want them to say?"

"'Fall in line, bitches. Your new queen has arrived.'"

"The leather skirt," Reg said, pointing to the summit of Mount Wardrobe.

I dug back into the pile, pushing Reg out of the way.

"Careful, Charlie," he teased, rolling off the bed and to his feet. "One might get the impression you're almost excited to go to school."

"Don't be ridiculous," I said, but I didn't meet his eye.

"I must admit, Queen Bee is a role you were born to play."

I conceded that with the tiniest of smiles.

"So why the dressing drama? You know you'll look divine in anything you choose."

I pounded a fist into the nightstand next to the bed and winced, annoyed that my hand felt dented instead of the hardwood.

"Reg, you can't talk like that."

"Like what?"

"Divine. You have to sound like a teenager."

"I am a teenager, according to the Elders, and this is how I speak."

"You have to talk the way teens talk *today*. Real teens. Human teens."

"How am I supposed to learn to speak like the mortals when we've spent so little time among them?"

"Please. We are around humans constantly."

"Hunting. Feeding. Not . . . mingling."

"Television has been around for half your immortal life," I pointed out, "and the internet for decades."

"I'd rather read a book." He grinned at me. "And I'd say the fact that I read at all means I'm probably going to be better at this school thing than *you*."

"I read," I huffed.

"Fashion periodicals don't count."

"They're magazines, not periodicals. I swear, Reg, if you embarrass me with your old-fashioned lingo, I will pretend I don't even know you. I will—"

"Relax." Reg grabbed hold of an arm I hadn't even realized I was flailing. "I'm just having a little fun with you. Even *I* call them magazines. If I didn't know any better, I'd say you're nervous."

I scoffed. "Nervous about what? You think I can't handle a few small-town teenagers?"

"On the contrary. I'm certain *they* won't be able to handle *you*. That's why I can't figure out— Oh, I see." His face lit up in that annoying way it did when he thought he was the smartest person in the room. It was extra irritating that he usually turned out to be right.

"You see what?"

I propped my hands on my hips, not an uncommon pose for me, but it had the added bonus of preventing my arms from any further waving about.

"Charlie, you can absolutely control a bunch of middle-America adolescents."

"I know."

"No doubt, you will charm even the teachers into following your command."

"Naturally."

"And maybe all of that will make you feel a little less helpless about our situation."

I opened my mouth a couple of times, searching for words. Reg didn't have it—not exactly.

"I'm not helpless," I said, convincing myself as much as him.

"Then why all the fuss?"

I massaged the hand that had pounded the table, wondering at the way it still pulsed with pain—a mocking reminder that actions have consequences. As if I didn't already know.

The ache in my hand, the way colors screamed in the sunlight, the strange smells . . . after a century of certainty, I was unprepared for the barrage of new and unfamiliar. I would never admit it to Reg, but it was all a little overwhelming.

"I just feel like we're trapped inside a kaleidoscope and I need something . . ."

"Black?" Reg held up the leather skirt.

"How can you be so calm?"

I vastly preferred this familiar, unflappable version of my brother to the rattled stranger I'd seen on our first night, but could he at least be a *little* disturbed by all this?

Reg waved a hand. "I've given it some thought, and I suspect this whole thing may be a bit of a ruse . . . a show of force, to ensure we learn our lesson. When the Elders decide we've been in time-out long enough, they'll come back for us."

And how long is a time-out to an Elder? A year? A decade?

A shiver ran through me. *A century?*

Reg interrupted my thoughts before I could consider the full weight of that possibility.

"Perhaps when we're of age."

"We're over a hundred."

"In human years," he said. "Likely only a year or two away."

It may as well have been a century.

I shuddered as I realized Reg might be right. Laws had changed since we were first made vampire, and it was no longer legal to turn children, thanks to the Treaty of Annis. According to the treaty, humans could not be given immortal life until they reached adulthood. The decision was validated over the years by scientific advancements and studies of the human brain and hormones. Not that the Elders needed validating. They only had to look at stories of the Ancients—some of them just small children when they were turned. Ten thousand years of temper tantrums were enough to prove the point.

Did the treaty rules apply to us now?

Reg caught the distress in my face and sighed. "Look, there's nothing we can do about it right now, so we might as well enjoy ourselves."

"You make it sound like a vacation," I said.

"It is, in a way."

"In that case, I want a refund."

"Bah. Brooding is boring," he said with a sparkle in his brown eyes.

Yes, definitely brown now.

I gasped and leaned in. "What's happening to your eyes? They're not black anymore."

"Oh. Yes, they're changing," he said. "Same as yours."

"Mine?"

"Of course. You don't know? Charlie, haven't you looked in a mirror?"

"No."

What for? It's not like my reflection was anything new. Vampires could see themselves in mirrors just fine, but the only reflection I'd ever needed was in the eyes of my victims . . . *er, admirers.*

Reg stood and held out a hand to help me up. "Come on. There's a mirror in the washroom."

I followed Reg, mumbling "bathroom" under my breath. I kept muttering until he practically shoved me in front of the mirror over the sink.

The eyes staring back at me were not my own. They were the palest blue and enhanced by a soft pink in the cheeks just below.

"Who is she?" I whispered, reaching out to touch the girl in the mirror.

Reg appeared in the mirror behind her. "Wonderful, isn't it? It must be what we looked like before we turned."

I blinked, and the girl in the mirror blinked as well. It *was* me, though I barely knew myself. Reg and I both had the same black hair, the same paper-white skin, but there was something else now too—a sort of light that wasn't there before.

"Just when I thought it wasn't possible for you to admire yourself anymore," Reg said. "I think I've just lost you to your own reflection."

"I'm not admiring myself." My skin felt hot again, in that new unfamiliar way, and this time I saw the change, as the me in the mirror went from white to bright red, the rosy color in my cheeks spreading all over my face.

I stumbled backward.

I had seen many colors in the skin of vampires, all faded by the lack of blood flow but as varied as humans'—pale echoes of who they must have been in their first lives. But I had never seen anything like this warm the cheeks of our kin.

"Why, Miss Charlotte, I do believe you're blushing."

I swiped at Reg, but he dodged and slipped out of the bathroom. I chased him back to my room, where he held up the black dress like a hostage.

"Touch me, and the Prada dies!"

I tutted. "You're an imbecile."

"Oh, Charlie," Reg corrected in his best impression of me. "Nobody says 'imbecile.' I'm a *moron*."

"Yes," I laughed. "You are."

"And you're stuck with me." He tossed the dress at me. "For life."

I caught the dress, fingers curling tight around the fabric.

"For life." An uncomfortable lump formed in my throat, and

I whispered, "Reg, what are we supposed to do now? Besides school . . . what's next? If the Elders don't come back for us . . . what do we do for the rest of our lives?"

Reg held out his hands, still bone white and delicately smooth.

"I, for one, plan to get a tan."

An hour later, I met Reg and Sal in the kitchen, where they were picking over a pile of food.

"Are you guys eating again?" I asked. "The buffet never ends around here."

Sal had fed us a smorgasbord of meats and vegetables the night before, to give us a taste of everything and gauge what we liked. Judging by the way Reg had stuffed his face, he loved it all. Personally, I had only nibbled on a piece of chicken and an ear of corn, which tasted fine enough but didn't seem worth the hour I spent afterward picking kernel skin out of my teeth.

I was much more enamored of my new sense of smell than taste. The aromas that had been dulled down to nothing by the powerful scent of blood were now assaulting my nostrils at every turn. I had spent my first full day of sunlight walking the meadows around Sal's cottage, literally following my nose. I collected one of every flower I could find, amazed that the smell never waned from the petals, no matter how much I sniffed them. When I'd brought the bouquet back to the cottage, Sal had made a snide remark about half the flowers being weeds, but he'd given me a glass vase to put them in and showed me where to set the vase on the windowsill to catch the most light.

I didn't want to follow any instructions the old man gave me, and I definitely didn't trust a slayer, but I had to concede he probably knew more about keeping things alive than I did.

On this morning, the sunshine beckoned us outside once again, but we were doomed to spend the day indoors pretending to be high schoolers. Fortunately for me, I thought with some superiority, I watched every teen show on TV. I knew exactly how to talk, how to dress and how to rule a school. But Reg? Now that was just hopeless.

"Is that what you're wearing?" I asked, eyeing the flannel shirt and jeans he had on now.

"Yeah. So?" he said through a mouth full of bacon.

"So . . . it's plaid," I said. The problem was self-evident.

"I borrowed it from Sal," Reg answered. "I'm trying to blend in until we can go shopping."

"Dressing like some old farmer is not how you blend in with students."

"I'm not a farmer," Sal spoke up from the end of the table. "But I'll give you old."

He pressed a hand over a wooden box next to his plate and slid it toward us.

"What's this?" I asked.

Sal gestured for me to open it.

"Your future."

FIVE

MEET THE SMITHS

The box had the same intricate carvings as the kitchen chairs. Sal obviously had skilled hands, but I also remembered him saying his hands had something to do with the fence that had ruined our lives, so I wasn't about to open Pandora's box. Reg did the honors instead, and I peered over his shoulder.

"Cell phones," Sal said. "I assume you know—"

"How to use a phone?" I interrupted. "Yes. Vampires are allergic to sunlight, not technology."

Sal let out a long sigh, but I also thought I saw the corner of his mouth twitch up just a hair. "My number is in the contacts. And you'll have each other's numbers in there too. Under the phones you'll find your new IDs."

Reg and I each pulled a phone and a card from the box. "IOWA" was stamped on the top left of the stiff rectangle and below it, photos Sal had taken of us the day before. Driver's licenses.

"We can't drive." Reg sounded almost apologetic.

"We didn't need to," I said. "We could always outrun a car."

Sal was unsurprised. "Well, it won't be the first time I've

taught one of your lot to press a pedal and spin a wheel. But it would be suspicious for you to not have a license at your age." He nodded at the cards in our hands. "You'll see I guessed you around sixteen and seventeen. That'll make Charlie a junior and Reginald a senior."

"Excellent." Reg plastered a smug smile on his lips.

"Why am I younger?" I complained. "I'm obviously more mature!"

"Obviously." Sal's bushy gray eyebrows shot up. "I think we can pass you off as siblings, but making you twins would draw too much attention. Best to keep a low profile."

"Pass us off?" I repeated. "You don't think we're really brother and sister?"

"A hundred years ago? At your age? For all I know, you two were lovers."

"Ew!" I shrieked, as Reg coughed up a "Gross!"

Sal looked amused as he stood and moved to the sink to wash the breakfast dishes. "You never know."

"It's highly unlikely," Reg said, "given my personal proclivities."

"I'm not his type," I translated.

Sal glanced back at us, eyes wide with understanding. "I see."

"I trust that won't be a problem?" Reg asked.

Sal returned to the dishes. "The folks here are small-town, not small-minded."

"Good," I said. "Because if anyone so much as looks at my brother sideways, they will answer to me."

"Of all the things to worry about . . . Most folks who come

through here just carry on about death." He paused. "And wrinkles. I hear a lot about the wrinkles too."

"Sorry if our concerns are boring you," I said.

"Refreshing change of pace, actually. Gets a little tiresome hearing them wail about dying like it's right around the corner. I suppose it must be your age. Think you're invincible and death is light-years away—just like human kids."

"Eternally teen," I muttered, quoting the Elders. I'd heard them say it a hundred times.

Eternally teen. Trapped in immaturity. More educated with age, but never any wiser.

It was something they talked about a lot when the clans signed the Treaty of Annis.

By the time Reg and I were made vampire, turning children was already out of fashion, but teenagers were still fair game. Reg and I were among the last teens turned before the treaty, and all we'd heard about every day for a century is what a big mistake *that* was.

If you asked me, the treaty was a form of discrimination. Maybe the Elders were jealous of our forever youth. Whenever they complained about our antics, it always just sounded to me like Reg and I were having a lot more fun than the old folks.

"Charlotte and Reginald Smith," Reg read from our licenses.

Smith? I squinted at the name next to my photo. "But we're Drakes!"

For a century, I had used that name like a key to open doors into social circles all over the underworld. The House of

Drake held a place of honor not only within the Bone Clan but among all vampire-kind. It hadn't occurred to me that losing our immortality meant losing our noble name. A fresh wave of injustice rolled over me.

All for one tiny mistake.

"You're not a Drake anymore," Sal said without turning from the sink. "Smith is the name I go by in town, and I think the easiest story is that we're family. Plus, you'll find it's a tricky one to google if any curious kids want to look you up. Too common."

"Well, it's boring," I said after a moment. "But it's better than Sicarius."

I spit out the slayer family name as if it tasted bad on my tongue.

Sal froze at the sink, fingers gripped tight on a dish hovering halfway to the drying rack. After a moment, he rolled his shoulders, cricked his neck, and settled the plate into the rack.

"On that, we agree."

I was too stunned to respond. So far, I'd found Sal easy enough to spar with, but agreeing with the old guy? That would take some getting used to.

"It's almost time for school." Sal's gruff tone returned as he dried his hands and faced us. "I know you're not too keen on the idea, but a couple of kids running around not going to school would draw too much attention."

"What if we're eighteen?" Reg suggested. "Perhaps we've already graduated high school, and we're taking a break before college."

"Yes!" I squeezed my brother's arm in congratulations for his stroke of genius.

"Oh." Sal's face fell. "Hadn't thought of that. I've never had teenagers here before—the last one to come through was before my time. Mostly, I get older vamps I pretend are girlfriends or old army buddies visiting. I get them jobs and send them packing. Easy. But you two . . ."

"It's not too late," I said, waving my fake ID. "Just change our ages."

"It *is* too late," Sal said. "I already enrolled you—a week ago, when I got the word from the Elders."

Reg ran a hand along the back of his neck, as if working out a knot. "A week? Is that how long we were in our coffins awaiting sentencing? Seemed shorter."

"Well, this part will seem like an eternity if we have to sit it out in some dreary school," I said.

Sal frowned. "If you don't go now, people will notice. People will talk."

"We're new kids," I pointed out. "People will talk anyway."

At least, that was always the case on all my TV shows.

"And what are we to tell them?" Reg asked. "When people ask who we are and where we're from?"

"Well, now, I've given that some thought." Sal leaned on the table, his broad weathered hands spread on the wooden surface. "You're from New York—a suburb, not the city. Don't want to be too interesting."

I stifled a sigh. As if I could just *stop* being interesting.

40

"Your parents died, so you came to live with me, your grand-father—"

I interrupted with a grunt of disagreement, and he tried again.

"You came to live with me, your . . . uncle Sal?"

He paused while I considered. When I offered no noise of protest, he went on.

"You're sad and you don't want to talk about it. Most people won't press."

"That's it?" I said when Sal fell silent. "That's our whole story?"

"It does seem a bit . . . slim," Reg said, and for once he sounded more pained than polite.

"The best cover stories are simple. And boring. All anyone 'round here knows about me is that I come from a big family on the East Coast—which is a lie—and that I'm retired." He looked down at his hands pressed against the table and curled them into fists. "Which is true."

I yawned. "You're right. That is boring."

"You're free to fill in the blanks." Sal stood up straight. "The good news is, you arrived in time for the first day of school. Fewer questions that way. Mind you, you'll still get *some* questions, so keep your answers short and stick to the cover story."

"And you?" Reg asked. "People might give me and Charlie some space if they think we've lost parents. But questions are sure to come your way."

"I get a lot of strays through here. People have learned to stop asking."

"What's the name of the town anyway?" I asked.

"It's more village than town," he said.

"Town, village. Either way, it's nowhere."

"Exactly right."

"What?"

"The name of the village. It's Nowhere."

My mask of disdain was shattered by the drop of my jaw. "You have got to be kidding me."

Sal met my eye and held it. "It's a quiet place, but don't mistake quiet for dull. You two might find you're not even the strangest or most exciting people here."

"Oh, Sal," I said, shaking my head and smiling at the old guy for the first time. "I am *always* the most exciting thing happening *anywhere*."

Twenty minutes later, Sal shooed us out of the kitchen with new backpacks, directions to school, and the promise of a short walk. And twenty minutes after that, I was dripping sweat and cursing his name as we finally reached civilization.

If you could call it civilization.

The path from the cottage into town was a straight line of country road with more dirt shoulders than sidewalks, walled in by cornfields on either side. Eventually, that endless tunnel of corn gave way to rows of houses with sharply peaked rooftops and colorful shutters. Maple and oak trees leaned over the streets to shade our path, and a cheerful-looking sign welcomed us to "Nowhere: No more, no less!"

Reg paused, reading the words aloud. "I wonder what that could mean."

"Who cares?" I said, stomping past the sign.

He shrugged and jogged a few steps to catch up.

"I am soaking wet," I complained. "Sweating is the absolute worst part of being human."

"Maybe you shouldn't be wearing a sweater in September."

"Says the guy in flannel."

"I'm not the one who's melting."

"Well, I'm not apologizing for Prada." I lifted my chin and picked up my pace, despite the fresh line of perspiration I felt slide between my spine and my furry black top. "It's the best sweater for this skirt, and this skirt screams first day of school."

Reg pulled at the hem of my leather mini. "Didn't you wear this to an AC/DC concert, circa 1985?"

I smacked his sticky fingers away. "Yes, and now it's vintage."

"That was a good night, hunting that crowd," Reg mused.

"And we'll never do it again."

"Of course we will. Just be patient."

"When have you ever known me to be patient?"

"Fair point."

We walked in silence for a bit, then Reg said, "Can you believe Sal thought we might have been something other than siblings? The possibility that we were . . ."

He shuddered, unable to finish the thought, and we both

made gagging faces that dissolved into laughter.

"He did make me wonder about the night we were turned," Reg said. "Where might we have been? On a road like this one? Were we attacked and I failed to protect you?"

"*You* protect *me*?" I scoffed. "Just because you're the guy?"

Reg was wise not to answer, but his questions still rattled me. As a vampire, I'd never thought twice about physical danger, but now, as a human, I was hyperaware of my soft skin, my breakable bones, my dependency on a beating heart.

"Reg, we're not the hunters anymore," I said. "We're the prey. The mouse instead of the cat."

He clucked his tongue in disagreement. "I don't think anyone will ever accuse you of being a mouse, and no magic fence can take the catty out of either one of us."

Laughing again, we turned from the residential street onto the main road, and the high school rose up immediately before us, a tower of red brick. I stopped short at the sight of it, my breath catching in my throat. I'd seen more imposing buildings. I'd *lived* in more imposing buildings. But for some inexplicable reason, I was on edge.

I ducked down quickly to check my face in the side mirror of an SUV. My new blue eyes looked back at me, surrounded by thick black eyeliner and lashes heavy with mascara. I said a quick thank-you to the gods of fashion and beauty for waterproof makeup. Everything was in place, even my hair, which I'd wisely slicked back into a ponytail. I had seen what humidity could do to human hair over the years and didn't want to risk frizz.

Reassured by the mirror and sweating a little less, thanks to the shady streets, I straightened up with renewed confidence. I felt every bit the queen bee, and this sad little school could probably use one. I tossed my head back as we crossed the street, passed under a "Hope High School" marquee and scaled the steps to the school's front doors.

I look amazing.

Reg and I pushed on the doors simultaneously, and they swung open too fast, slamming into the interior walls with a crash. A hundred pairs of eyes in the grand front hall looked up at the sound, then stopped to stare.

At me.

Because I looked ridiculous.

SIX

AS SEEN ON TV

Everything was wrong, from my Prada to my pumps.

I stood out like a black leather weed in a garden full of denim and cotton.

Where were the slinky sundresses? The thigh-high boots? The hair extensions? The students surrounding us looked nothing like the kids I'd seen on TV. Most of them were in jeans or shorts with sloppy T-shirts, and a few had pulled on sweatshirts to combat the building's over-powerful air-conditioning. Here and there, I saw a pair of wedge sandals to break up the monotony of flip-flops, but mostly the fashion train had skipped this stop.

For a moment, I wondered if I was at the center of some practical joke—a trick played on the new kids. After all, I'd seen a version of this episode on almost every teen TV show: the main character attends what they think is a costume party, but they're the only one in costume; or they have a nightmare about showing up somewhere naked. I wondered which scene I was in—what part I was supposed to play.

"Sorry," Reg said with a wave to the crowd and a great big grin.

I flinched, thinking he was apologizing for me, his strangely dressed sister, but as he tugged one of the giant doors closed, I realized his apology was for the noise.

The hallway wasn't exactly silent, with its slamming lockers and the sound of friends reuniting after a long summer apart, but it did seem like it had gone a little quiet after our entrance. Or maybe that was just the ringing in my ears. I closed my eyes, a wave of dizziness washing over me as my newly beating heart pumped double time.

When I opened my eyes again, most of the staring had stopped, but a few gazes lingered. A girl who had been eyeballing my skirt now turned to whisper something to a friend, and I pulled self-consciously at the hem of my vintage leather.

How could I have gotten this so wrong?

Okay, so Reg and I had spent most of the last century in big cities, and sure, we hadn't had any experience inside *actual* high schools, but we'd spent enough time with teenagers. Hell, it was a teenager who got us into this mortal mess! And that teen was just like all the others we'd known, from Beverly Hills to Dubai. Sure, they wore ripped jeans, but those holes cost hundreds of dollars and were straight off the runway. Could small-town Iowa really be this out of touch? I glanced at Reg in his plaid flannel shirt. *Or maybe I'm the one out of touch here.*

The only thing I had in common with the rest of these students was the backpack strapped to my shoulders, and I had

Reg to thank for that. He'd convinced me to leave my Birkin bag at home, saying it might split at the seams if I tried to stuff it full of textbooks. I realized now that he'd just said it to protect me. He knew—or at least, he suspected—what we might find here. And while he'd never be able to talk me out of my designer duds, he'd done what little he could to keep me from looking foolish. Maybe Sal was right to make him the older one. In that moment, he *did* feel like my big brother.

"Pardon me," Reg said, touching the shoulder of a passing student—a not-unpleasant-looking boy with sun-kissed skin and shaggy blond hair. "We're new and in need of guidance. Perhaps you could come to our aid?"

My really *embarrassing* big brother.

"Oh, okay." The boy looked surprised to be addressed by strangers—*or maybe to be addressed so strangely*—and when he stopped, it was with some reluctance. "What, uh—what can I help you with?"

While Reg asked for directions to the main office, I took in the rest of the boy. Over his tan freckled skin, he wore the same T-shirt and jeans that seemed to be the uniform at this school, but I could tell right away he wore them better than everyone else. His shirt was pure white with no splashy slogan, and his hair was extra messy where it nearly touched his shoulders, like he'd spent the day in the ocean and then dried out in the sand . . . if there were any salt water or sand in Iowa, that is.

"And you are?"

The question hung out there in space for a few seconds before I realized it was directed at me. The boy's green eyes caught mine, and I was struck dumb. Was he asking for my name? Had he said his? I wasn't really listening, or maybe it was that the buzz in my ears hadn't quite gone.

"This is my sister, Charlotte," Reg said.

When I still said nothing, the green eyes slid from my face to my ensemble. "Guess they got fancier stuff where you come from, huh?"

"Charlie," I choked out. "I go by Charlie."

And then the floor opened up and swallowed me whole.

Or no, wait. That's what I *wished* would happen. In reality, no such portal appeared to spare me this humiliation.

"Uh, right." The boy lifted one eyebrow and took a step backward as if to distance himself from my crazy. "Well, the office is at the east entrance, down this main hall."

I winced as Reg held out his hand like some kind of politician. "Thank you."

Tall, Tan, and Blond shook my brother's hand. "Sure thing. Good to meet you guys."

But judging by the way he sped off, it didn't seem like it had been that good at all.

The next half hour was a blur. Reg and I managed to find the main office and collect our schedules, then we wove through crowded hallways where more students either stared or whispered. Reg insisted they were only interested in the new kids, but I knew better. I didn't need my old superpowered hearing to tell they were laughing behind my back.

I straightened my shoulders as we passed one pack of giggling girls. If they wanted a real laugh, they could just open the latest edition of *Vogue*. My sweater was on page three.

Reg headed for the senior section of the school with a quick promise to meet me out front at the end of the day, and all too soon I was sitting in the back of a classroom, tapping a number two pencil against my desk and wishing I could stake myself with it.

At least in the back of the room, fewer kids could ogle my outfit. The boy in front of me did turn around to look though—some things never change. I sat up and pursed my lips.

"Stare much?"

But the look he was giving me wasn't a lusty one. He reached an arm around, his hand closing over mine—squeezing just hard enough to stop my incessant pencil tapping.

"Do you mind?" he asked, then he faced forward again without waiting for an answer.

I quietly seethed. *I do mind. I mind that no one here seems to appreciate designer labels or mysterious new kids. I mind that I have to play the part of kid at all, when I'm old enough to be your mother's mother's mother . . . or something. And mostly I mind that I came here expecting to collect minions, and instead all I have is a collection of embarrassing moments.*

But I put the pencil down anyway.

At least now I wanted to use it to stake someone else.

The end of the day couldn't come fast enough. After seven periods of subjects I either already knew or never was interested in and one lunch hour spent in the girls' bathroom trying to wipe off my eyeliner, I was done. I paced back and forth at the bottom of the front steps, impatient for Reg to come out. No doubt he was inside sucking up to some teacher half as educated as he was. I hoped he wouldn't bore me to death talking about his fabulous day all the way home.

"Watch it!" someone cried from the top of the steps.

I looked up in time to see students scattering to the sides like pins, and the bowling ball behind them was Reg. He leaped down the stairs, two at a time, and without breaking stride, he grabbed my elbow and dragged me away from the school.

"We are done here." He spit the words.

"*So* done," I agreed.

He was still pulling me by the arm when we hit the tree-lined street that led back to farmland, and I had to dig my heels in to make him stop.

"Reg!" I pointed to my feet. "This footwear is not suitable for jogging."

"Incompetent imbeciles," he muttered.

He let go of my arm and continued walking. I hurried to catch up.

"And judgmental jerks," I added.

When Reg spoke again, his voice was a high-pitched imitation of someone else. "'We raise our hands in this school, Mr. Smith.' 'Give others a chance to answer, Mr. Smith.'"

I kicked a rock out of our path. "Whispering behind my back instead of telling me what they think to my face."

"What happened to the free flow of discussion?"

"When did everyone start wearing flip-flops?"

"And you make just one *tiny* suggestion about altering the

reading list because it might be a *little* pedestrian . . ."

"Wait." I looked at my brother in disbelief. "You actually said that? To a teacher?"

"Charlie, you didn't see this list—"

"You insulted your teacher's course plan on the first day of class? That's pretty pretentious—even for you."

Reg hissed and pulled back his lips before he remembered he didn't have fangs.

"Wow." I cringed. "That really does look ridiculous."

Reg said nothing, still fuming, but I noticed a slight pink to his cheeks as he covered his mouth with his hand.

The sidewalk gave way to the muddy shoulder of country road, and we emerged from the canopy of maples and oaks into full sun.

"I get it," I said, squinting against the sudden brightness. "All day I just wanted to rip out someone's throat and bleed them dry."

"Like you did that boy?" he snapped.

This again.

"He lived."

"No thanks to you."

"That's right!" There was only room for one bad attitude in this sibling relationship, and Reg knew damn well that was my job. "It's thanks to *you*. Thanks to you leaving him outside that emergency room door. Thanks to you for confessing. Thanks to *you*, we're in this mess. If you had just let me—"

"Let you what? Let you turn him? Let you leave him there to bleed until he died?"

I took a deep shaking breath. "I was going to say, if you'd just let me handle it, I could have come up with . . . something."

"Handle it." Reg shook his head. "When you take that much of their blood, the only way to 'handle it' is to turn them, save them, or bury them." He ticked the options off on his fingers. "If we'd done anything but save him, the punishment would have been worse."

"Like there's anything worse than this." I pouted.

"If you had violated the treaty and turned one that young, a stake through the heart would surely be your punishment. Better sunlight than a stake."

I glared at the sun—or rather, since that was unreasonably painful, I glared instead at everything the sun touched, which was everything, period. It winked off golden corn tassels every time they swayed in a breeze; it caught the flat edge of worn rocks in the road so they glowed white; it shimmered in the distance like water that wasn't really there.

The sun, if you asked me, was awfully full of itself. I preferred the subtlety of night.

"I'll take the stake," I said, my voice growing shrill. "Over the sun. Over Iowa. Over *school.*"

Reg slowed his pace, and the anger slid out of his voice. "You don't mean that. High school may be hell, but it's only a year—"

I shot him a look.

"Okay, two for you," he amended. "But then we'll both be adults, officially. Perhaps then we can renegotiate our immortality."

"I can't do this for two more days, let alone two more years,"

I complained. "Reg, the way those kids looked at me—I just wanted to climb into a dark hole, curl up, and die."

As soon as the words left my mouth, their meaning became something literal.

"I'm serious, Reg," I said. "Darkness. Death. That's what I want. I want to be vampire again."

"Well, you can want that all night long, Charlie . . . and, come to think of it, all *day* long now . . . but that won't make it happen."

A quiet rage boiled up inside me. I'd already been told no too many times in the last few days—no to immortality, no to skipping high school, no to anything resembling fashion. After one hundred years of yes, I wasn't accustomed to hearing no.

"This is the worst part of being human. This—this—negativity!" I shouted, breathing heavily. I pulled at the damp neckline of my sweater. "That and all the stupid sweating!"

"Well, what do you suggest we do about it?" Reg said.

The cottage was in view now, its sun-drenched stone walls twinkling at us. I scowled in return.

"I *suggest* we take back our lives," I said. "Our *immortal* lives."

"And how do we do that?"

I set my jaw. "Together. And at any cost."

"Sounds diabolical." Reg smiled for the first time since we'd left school and nudged my shoulder. "But until we're all-powerful immortals again, maybe put away the Prada."

SEVEN

THE SLAYER'S SECRET

Sal was hulking in the doorway, leaning on the frame and smoking a pipe, when we got home, like he'd been waiting for us. I hesitated when we reached the gate, my hand hovering just above the white wood. Not flat and wide like other fence slats but thick and narrow. If the posts had been rounded like poles instead of squared off, they would be indistinguishable from stakes—clearly a slayer's version of a picket fence.

Had it really been only days since we'd first passed through this awful gate? If I'd known then what I knew now—if I'd known pain, known fear, known shame—would I have walked into my doom so easily? I thought I had put up a fight, but that was nothing compared to the fit I should have thrown.

"We should have run," Reg said, his eyes also on the gate.

"We couldn't have outrun the Elders."

Sal called out from the porch, "Come on, that fence don't bite."

"Could've fooled me," I shouted back.

Sal's laugh turned into a hacking cough as he puffed on his pipe.

I refused to be a source of amusement for a slayer—retired or not—and stormed through the gate before Reg could open it for me.

"How was the first day?" Sal asked, a smile still stretched above his grizzled beard as if he already knew the answer to his question and delighted in it.

I lifted my head as I passed him on the porch. "The students here are severely deprived. They could use an atelier. Or at the very least a mall. It's sad."

I glided into the house before he could respond, but I heard him behind me chuckling.

"So, I guess you'll be borrowing some of my flannel tomorrow too?"

That night, Reg and I gathered at the heavy wooden table in the kitchen, our dinner plates pushed to the side and our heads bent low over a sheet of parchment and an inkpot.

"Is all of this really necessary?" I gestured to the paper and ink. "Can't we just shoot the Elder Seat an email or something?"

My attention was half on the parchment and half on Sal at the other end of the table, where he was whittling a length of wood that looked suspiciously like a post for his fence. I guess we didn't have any reason to fear wooden stakes anymore, but after a hundred years of being afraid of something, it was hard to just shake it off, so Sal's project was making me squirm.

"Charlie, please," Reg said. "Let's be appropriate for once. This is the most formal letter we have ever written, and parchment shows respect. It's just fortunate that I had the good sense to pack my calligraphy kit. Besides, I am sure the Elders do not have email." He said *email* with disdain, like electronic communications were somehow beneath him.

I hoped, for his sake, that we did manage to appeal our sentence, because he was never going to survive in the modern human world without embracing technology.

"They do, you know," Sal said, glancing up from his pointy stick, "have email."

My head whipped toward Sal, half suspicious and half in awe of this information. I supposed he must have high-up connections if he helped carry out life sentences like ours, but I still had a hard time reconciling the idea that a slayer of the infamous Sicarius line could be working so closely with the governing body of all vampire-kind.

"They have a clerk with an email account, in any case," Sal said. "But Reg is probably right that no one has ever submitted a digital appeal. I imagine they'd find that kind of informality . . . distasteful."

Well, this letter was certainly formal enough. I turned my gaze back to our draft.

> Dearest Sirs and Madams of the Elder Seat,
>   We write today to beg your favor and beseech you to reconsider our mortal punishment. We recognize and apologize for our recent transgression . . .

Blah blah blah.

I pushed the letter toward Reg. The rest of it detailed our

overeager feeding on a teenage boy and the shame we suppos-edly felt over risking exposure for our kind. It did not explain how tasty this particular boy was and how all vampires got a little carried away sometimes without being punished and that the Elders only used this as an excuse to exile us for being young. Reg assured me that adding those details would not help our case.

"I wish I could remember all the bylaws regarding appeals," Reg said, tapping his calligraphy pen against his lips.

"They didn't spell all that out for you at your trial?" Sal asked.

Reg and I responded in unison. "What trial?"

"Reg confessed," I added.

"And had I not, they would have pulled the memories from our minds anyway," Reg said. "I thought a guilty plea might at least show some goodwill and regret."

Sal snorted. "Goodwill. Guess you see how far that got you."

"Well, what do you suggest, then?" I asked.

"Me? I suggest you stay human." He held the piece of wood at eye level, squinting as he inspected his work. "But if you're set on an appeal, you'll need a sponsor."

"What kind of sponsor?" Reg asked.

"A representative from one of the clans to stand for you. It's a minimum requirement for appeal. No sponsor, no dice. Best bet is to get someone from your own house."

"Yeah, right," I muttered.

Reg and I had asked every last member of the Bone Clan, from House Drake to House Archibald, to testify to our good character, in hopes of receiving a lighter sentence. Every last one had refused. If they weren't willing to help us when we had been kin, I highly doubted they would help us now that we were mere mortals.

So much for family.

"But technically, the sponsor doesn't have to be Bone Clan?" Reg asked.

Sal shook his head. "Any vamp will do."

Reg fidgeted with his pen and inkpot. "So, we look to the other clans."

I wrinkled my nose. "But nobody likes us."

"That's because the Bones are elitist," Sal said. "Can't go around looking down on everyone, then expect them to come to your rescue."

I sat up stiff in my chair. "Excuse me, but we are not elitist. Some vampires are just better than others."

Reg cleared his throat. "What Charlie means to say is that the Bone Clan has been wise over the centuries about cultivating and carefully maintaining wealth and does not feel it should be responsible for the financial support of other clanships."

Well, that wasn't *exactly* what I meant to say, but close enough. I narrowed my eyes, daring Sal to argue, but he didn't. He just ran his blade down the edge of his stake-like fence post, shaving off a thin curl of wood.

"Can you watch where you are pointing that thing?" I snapped.

Sal obliged, aiming the pointy end toward the floor.

"We don't have to be BFFs with everyone to get a sponsor," I said to Reg. "I'm sure we can find someone to take pity on us. Maybe a member of the Blood Clan."

Reg disagreed. "They don't take pity on anyone."

"But they hate the Elder laws," I argued. "If it were up to them, vampires would feed on humans without limits. They might be sympathetic to our cause."

"You don't want to get mixed up with the Blood Clan," Sal warned. He blew a layer of sawdust off the flat side of his post. "Nastiest bunch of vamps I ever had the displeasure of meeting. Vicious."

"Forgive us if we don't rely on the opinion of a slayer," I said.

"What about the Starlight Clan?" Reg asked.

I had to laugh. "No way. Do they even drink human blood?"

"Of course they do," Reg said. "But not without permission. They ask mortals to make an offering."

"Well, we didn't exactly ask permission for what we did," I said. "I doubt the Starlights would approve. And wasn't the Treaty of Annis their idea? You know they think it's wrong for anyone our mortal age to be vampire. I'm surprised they're not lining up outside this cottage to become human again themselves."

"They may not like the hunt," Sal interjected. "But they still like the immortality."

A dark cloud seemed to gather over him—eyes hooded and a deep frown creasing his face. "Some vampires won't give it up for anything."

He dropped his wooden post on the table with a loud clatter

and turned to stare out the window, the darkness on his face clearly taking over his thoughts.

Reg and I exchanged a questioning look, not sure where Sal's gloom had come from.

Finally, Reg spoke. "Well, that just leaves the Shadow Clan, then. Mysterious group."

"Very," I agreed. "So mysterious that I don't think we even know any of them."

"What about that Jonathan guy we met in Belize a few years ago?" Reg suggested. "Wasn't he a Shadow? I think he had a crush on you. I bet he'd do us a favor."

"I bet he would," I said. "If he hadn't fed on that over-intoxicated girl on the beach, gotten drunk from her blood, and stumbled off a pier."

I shuddered at the memory. If Reg had seen it with his own eyeballs like I had, he would not have forgotten so easily. As for me, I could never forget the visual of Jonathan dropping chest-first onto the sharp wooden post holding up a "No Swimming at Night" sign. He had immediately turned to black smoke and been carried away by the wind.

"What about you?" I asked Sal, snapping him out of his trance. "You got any Shadow Clan pals who might sponsor us? Maybe you could put in a good word—"

"Vampires are not my *pals*," Sal snarled, wrenching his gaze from the window and whatever far-off memory he'd been watching. "And if they were, I still would not help you become one."

He snatched up his post and spread his arms wide. "What exactly is it you think I'm doing here?"

I tried not to flinch as the pointy end of his stick swung in our direction. "Well, excuse me for—"

"And anyway, you are wasting your time," he said. "Every former vamp who comes through that gate tries to appeal to the Elder Seat, and no one—*not one*—has ever succeeded."

He kicked his chair back and stormed out the front door, my narrowed eyes burning holes in his back.

No one ever?

Challenge accepted.

EIGHT

ETERNALLY YOURS

A few hours later, our bellies full of barbecue (some human things were nearly as good as blood), Reg and I moved to the fields behind the cottage to finish our letter—three letters, actually. On Sal's information, we had decided to table the formal appeal to the Elders until we could secure a sponsor. Instead, we had drafted identical messages to the heads of the Blood, Shadow, and Starlight Clans, politely begging them to share our request for sponsorship with their vampire houses.

We sank into long, soft grass on the crest of a hill overlooking endless fields of corn and smaller plants that Sal told us were beans. A cluster of lilac bushes nearby showered us with tiny purple flowers every time the breeze blew.

"How perfectly pastoral," Reg said, spreading his arms toward the valley below.

"If you say so."

"And the air!" He took a deep breath. "You can almost taste it."

"I'd rather not." I made a point of holding my breath against the offending reek of manure wafting up from the fields. It was bad enough to smell cow dung. I had no interest in tasting it.

Gingerly, using only my fingertips so as not to smudge the still-wet ink, I laid our three letters out on the ground for a final inspection, but Reg didn't even glance at them. His eyes were on the horizon, where the sun was starting its slow, sleepy descent. He rested his elbows on his knees and pulled a long blade of grass back and forth between his fingers.

"It's almost enough to make you want to stay, isn't it?" he asked.

I leaned away, alarmed. "No, it's not. And don't say things like that."

"Like what?"

"Like you're thinking of staying human."

He sighed. "I'm not, it's just . . . being vampire was getting a little boring—always the same thing, night in and night out. Eat, sleep, hunt, repeat." He gave me a look of mock disapproval. "Or in your case, eat, sleep, hunt, shop."

I didn't disagree.

"After a century of the same, I'm ready for something—*anything*—new." Reg said. "Being human could be that new adventure."

"But we've been human before."

"Not that we can remember. At least this *feels* new." He held out a hand to catch a fresh flurry of lilac petals dancing in the air around us. "And it's not all bad. If it wasn't for that wretched school, it could even be fun . . . not forever, of course. But for a little while."

In the distance, the sun had now formed a giant orange dome over the fields, and Reg tilted toward it, soaking in the final blaze of day. I wanted to tell him it wasn't *that* spectacular, but the words died on my lips as I watched the changing light alter everything it touched. The lilac bushes went from lavender to royal purple to dusty pink to ashy gray. Every inch the sun slipped on the horizon, the world was painted anew. It was a power I had never witnessed before. In contrast, darkness seemed only to steal color away.

"No doubt this has been a shocking punishment, but . . ." Reg spoke so quietly, I had to lean in to hear.

Stupid human eardrums.

"But it could also be an opportunity."

"An opportunity for what?" I asked.

"To enjoy scenes like this." He thrust an arm toward the sunset, as if he wanted to punch it now, rather than soak it up. "To see a clear Caribbean Sea with my own eyes. I've only ever seen it under a night sky or in photos. I have endless curiosities about taste and smell and desire beyond blood. There are so many things in the world that humans go on about that we don't understand. Sunsets versus sunrises, chocolate versus vanilla, the obsession with smells like coffee and gasoline."

"Gasoline?"

"Apparently, some people love the aroma. I want to know why."

"So, we'll find out, okay?" I touched my brother's arm, a gesture that would have been uncomfortable with any other immortal. Despite the structure of houses and clans we formed to protect us from slayers and other hunters, vampires were loners by nature. But I had never been alone, thanks to Reg, and I couldn't get through this without him. "We'll smell gasoline and eat chocolate and get up early and stay up late so we can pick a side on sunrises versus sunsets. We'll do all of it—and then we'll get the hell out of here and back in the world where we belong."

Reg hesitated a moment, sighing into the setting sun, then he nodded once. "Okay, Charlie."

I exhaled.

"Now, get your filthy paws off my Prada," he joked, pushing my hand off his arm.

I looked down my nose at his flannel shirt. "If that is Prada, then I am the queen of England."

"Ah, the queen!" Reg tipped his head back. "So tasty. I do miss a good royal feeding."

"Stick with me. I'll have you back to drinking royal blood in no time."

"I believe it," Reg said. "You're better at it, you know—being vampire."

I ticked my head to the side, trying to figure out if he was teasing still.

"Better at the hunt. Better at the bleed."

"Except when it mattered most," I said, my thoughts on the boy we had nearly killed.

"I didn't say you don't get carried away sometimes, but you're still good at it. I thought I might be good at this."

"At being human? You are," I conceded, eyes on his plaid flannel. "Not that I would brag about it."

"I'm certainly better at *interacting* with humans than you are," he said.

"Why, because you get along with Sal? He's hardly human."

66

"Slayers are human," Reg argued. "But I was talking about Dexter."

"Who is Dexter?"

"The boy from school—the one who was so helpful this morning. At least I didn't go mute when we met him."

I was about to say that I couldn't recall anyone being helpful at all, but then a flash of green eyes filled my vision.

Tall, Tan, and Blond.

"His name was Dexter?"

Reg laughed. "So, you went mute *and* deaf. Wow, he really made an impression!"

"I have no idea what you are talking about." I sniffed.

"Please! The way you were ogling him . . ."

"Reg, I was so distraught over the hideous fashion train wreck in those hallways, I could barely remember my *own* name, let alone some human boy's. And in any case, I do not ogle." I tossed my hair and let the last of the sun's rays warm my face. "It's not a good look."

"No," he agreed. "It wasn't."

I pushed him over, laughing.

But as Reg rolled in the grass, I let myself picture the tall boy with the green eyes once more. If I had to endure being human a while longer, I might not mind another face-to-face with this Dexter to see just who ogles whom.

Reg settled with his back on the hill, staring out at the empty pink sky where the sun had been only seconds ago.

"I wonder why they didn't take our immortal memories," he said.

"Probably to torture us."

It was a time-honored ritual to perform a memory fade on new vampires—a courtesy that apparently could not be extended to us.

"I'll bet they want us to remember exactly how fabulous our lives were before," I said. "Make sure we know what we've lost— *Ouch!*"

I looked down at a sudden stinging sensation and spotted a skinny-legged, skinny-winged insect perched on my shin. I waved it away and scratched, with mild curiosity, at my first-ever mosquito bite.

"Perhaps in time, the memories will wash away on their own," Reg said. "If we are human long enough, we may forget our immortal lives."

Another sting, this time on my upper arm, and I managed to slap the spot in time to squash the mosquito. I brushed my hand off in the grass, satisfied by the kill.

"We won't be human long enough for that to happen," I said with confidence.

Reg sighed. "You're probably right. We would die long before our memories fade."

"Wow, depressing much?" I smacked my neck. Another mosquito attack. "That's not what I meant."

"Or we could get Alzheimer's. Then we might forget."

"We're not going to get— *Ouch!*"

Reg sat up straight. "What is it?"

"Mosquitoes! They are attacking me!" I swatted one away from my face and another off my leg. "Damn little bloodsuckers."

"So you have that in common, then." Reg said, and my next swat was toward him.

I scratched the first sting on my shin, which was turning into an ugly red welt. "Bug bites may be the worst thing yet about being human."

"Not all bugs bite," Reg said. He nudged my arm and motioned for me to look up.

All around us, hundreds of fireflies were blinking on and off, their bioluminescent bodies lighting up the quickly gathering dark.

"Exactly the kind of critters I like," I said. "The kind that look best at *night*."

I snatched up our three letters from the grass before we lost all light and held out a hand for the calligraphy pen. Reg passed it over, and I signed each one with as much flourish as my unskilled hands could manage.

> Eternally Yours,
> Charlotte and Reginald Drake
> House of Drake, Clan of Bone

Reg helped me fold the letters and stuff them into envelopes. As he pressed a wax seal onto the final message, I felt the sharpest sting yet behind my left ear.

I slapped the mosquito and scratched the fresh wound.

PS: Hurry up!

NINE

DEAD POETS & LIVING BOYS

"This fabric itches." I yanked on the hem of my shirt, trying desperately to force it into some kind of shape. "What is it, cheap wool?"

"It's cotton," Reg said. "And it's perfectly comfortable."

We were walking the dirt path between the cornfields, on our way to day two of the hideous torture humans called high school. Sal had suggested we try a little harder to fit in, and Reg and I agreed, knowing it would only help our appeal to be on our best behavior. But wardrobe remained a problem.

I had managed to find a pair of non-designer jeans, but it was harder to find a casual top. Reg ended up loaning me one of his T-shirts, and I had accepted, only because the baby blue matched the hue of my new eyes. Or my old eyes, I guess, since I probably had them before I was vampire. It was getting tricky to say what was old and what was new. The immortal version of "the chicken or the egg."

In any case, I still didn't feel like the girl in the mirror was me, but I noticed her hair was fading to a nice chestnut color, and I had decided it wouldn't be entirely awful to live in her skin for a while. I might even buy her some more blue clothes to go with those eyes, if I could find a decent place to shop within a hundred miles of Nowhere.

At the thought of shopping, I turned to my brother. "Reg, where is our money? Not the cash from House Drake that we stashed in the suitcases, but the rest of it. You said it's in a trust. Is that like a bank account? Do I need a new credit card?"

"You need a trust*ee*," Reg said.

"What's a trustee?"

"Not 'what.' *Who*."

I groaned. "Sal."

We reached the spot where dirt became pavement, and the beating sun and blue sky turned to a leafy canopy punctuated by steepled rooftops. I sneered at the welcome sign and its inexplicable *No more, no less!* slogan.

"So . . . what?" I asked as we moved down the shaded street. "I'm supposed to ask the old guy for permission every time I want to buy something?"

"I imagine it will be more like an allowance. Frankly, I'm surprised it's taken you this long to ask. I anticipated shopping withdrawal symptoms to set in sooner."

"Very funny," I said, tugging on the itchy shirt again. Who knew cotton could be so uncomfortable? "But I am not begging at the bank of Sal every week."

I have my pride.

Reg shrugged. "It's either that or get a job."

Pride is overrated.

I made a choking noise. "A job? These hands have never worked a day!"

As I held out my hands, I noticed they looked a little rough around the nails, and I wondered if I *had* worked in my former life. Few vampires knew their human origins. In addition to the memory fade, vampires were given new last names and typically relocated immediately. Modern technology made it trickier to shield new vampires from their past, but most were so focused on their thirst, they had little curiosity about their human lives. It was funny that I should wonder about it now. Here I was mortal once again, and my first human history still felt so far out of reach.

I pulled my fingernails closer to inspect them. "Looks like I'll have to start getting manicures," I said.

"Manicures cost money."

"Fine. If Sal wants to be our personal ATM, then—"

"Hey, new kids!"

Reg and I both stopped in unison, pulling up straight as if we'd walked into an invisible wall.

We'd reached the end of the tree-lined street, and the brick school building had come into view. We were earlier than yesterday, and the doors must not have been open yet, because a few hundred kids were milling around outside. One of them was waving at us from the opposite sidewalk.

Reg and I looked at each other, then behind us, then back to the boy. Yep, definitely at us.

Something in our expressions caused his arm to droop.

"Uh . . . you are the new kids, right?" he called.

Slowly, slowly, as if on the hunt, Reg and I crept forward toward the boy. He met us halfway across the road with his formerly waving hand now outstretched in a greeting.

Reg took it, and they shook. A perfectly normal human interaction. *Well done, Reg.*

I gave myself a few points as well, for not going catatonic this time.

"I'm Charlie."

"I know," the boy said, pushing a pair of chunky black glasses up the bridge of his nose. The glasses were expensive and perfectly on trend.

I decided I liked this human and would have to ask him where he shopped.

"You're Charlotte and Reginald Smith. I was supposed to find you two yesterday, but I guess you got here a little late. I'm in student government—on the Hope High welcoming committee. So, it's my job to say . . . welcome!"

"Thank you," Reg said. "And you are?"

He stood nearly a foot taller than the boy, which would intimidate most humans, but not this one, who seemed to have a big presence despite his short stature.

"I'm Poe," the boy said. "As in Edgar Allan."

I stiffened, and next to me, Reg covered up his shock with a fake cough.

Was this some kind of test? Edgar Allan Poe's death was no secret in the vampire world, but the Elders had managed to keep humans thoroughly in the dark for over a century. Could this mortal boy possibly know the truth?

A vampire by the name of Reynolds had tried to turn Poe but accidentally overfed instead. A shame, really. By all accounts, Poe would have made a fabulous immortal. Reynolds was famously banished for the crime—never to be heard from again, other than as a cautionary tale for new vampires.

Now that I thought of it, the circumstances were disturbingly similar to our own crimes. Maybe Reynolds had been exiled to Iowa too.

This new Poe looked nonplussed by our silence.

"The poet," he said. "You know him?"

"No," Reg said too quickly. "Never met him."

"He died before our time," I added.

Poe looked back and forth between us. "Yeah . . . pretty sure he died before everybody's time."

Of course. Idiots.

Hope High: 2, Reg and Charlie: 0.

"Right!" Reg let out a loud laugh, and I worried the boy— Poe—might actually run away from our crazy at that point, but instead, he started laughing too.

"You had me going there for a second! Thought you were about to say you'd never heard of 'The Raven.'"

"Of course we have," Reg said. "Though I'd venture to guess half the students in this building have not."

I wanted to kick Reg for his old-timey talk, but before I could even lift a foot off the ground, the bespectacled Poe lifted his chin and answered, "More of an astute observation than a guess."

"Indeed," Reg agreed. "And I've made a few observations of the teachers as well. For instance, I doubt many of them are fans of Poe."

"They're fans of *this* Poe." He stuck out two thumbs and aimed them at his chest. "And I gotta say, I'm not that into the other guy either. I prefer manga to macabre."

Reg smiled. "Fascinating."

And so it was that here, in a tiny village in the middle of Iowa, surrounded by cornfields for miles, that Reg found a human who spoke his language.

Poe winked. "Just don't tell my English lit teacher."

"Your secret is safe with me," Reg promised.

Safe with *me*? Was I invisible?

Even in a boring shirt and jeans, I didn't think I could possibly be invisible, but Reg and Poe were doing a good job of making me feel like I wasn't there. They walked together toward the school building, chattering on about the evolution of literature and the layout of Nowhere interchangeably, while I shuffled like a shadow behind them.

Once the Hope High doors opened, Poe led us to his locker, where he pulled out a stack of materials for each of us, rapidly naming off items as he piled them into our arms. "Student handbook, discipline policy, dress code . . ."

"Oh, they have a dress code here?" I quipped. "What is it, farmer chic?"

Reg shot me a warning look, but Poe agreed.

"I know, right? My kingdom for a Barneys."

He dove back into his locker. "Extracurriculars, photo release, campus map . . ."

Could have used that yesterday.

"And a little school swag to keep it all in." Poe topped off each of our stacks with a folder featuring a drone's-eye view of the school and an enormous football field stretching out behind it, surrounded by tall walls of the same red brick on the school's exterior, as if the building had grown long, skinny arms and wrapped the football field in a hug. Emblazoned over the image, gold letters proclaimed the school: "Hope High, the beating heart of Nowhere. No more, no less than academic excellence!"

Well, at least when the school used the town's motto, they turned it into something that made sense. As Reg and I stuffed all the papers we would never look at again into our folders, we were joined at Poe's locker by two girls who looked shockingly similar. He introduced them as Sydney and Sophia and informed us—totally unnecessarily—that they were twins. If it weren't for the fact that Sydney had dyed her pale blond hair bright pink, they would be utterly indistinguishable.

"Are you also on the welcoming committee?" Reg asked the girls.

Sydney twirled a lock of pink hair. "No, but we're a lot more welcoming than Poe."

Both girls giggled, and Reg smiled politely as if he didn't understand her meaning. He managed to keep his face passive even when he caught sight of the smirk on my face. These girls would learn soon enough that Poe was more my brother's speed.

"We're happy to show you around," the blond one, Sophia, said earnestly to both of us. "Oh! You guys should come with us to All Hours."

"All Hours?" I said. "What's that?"

"It's a coffee shop," Sydney chimed in, her words wrapped around a wad of chewing gum. "Everyone goes there after school . . . and before school . . . and on the weekends and late at night and basically all the time. It's the only place in town open twenty-four hours."

All Hours. Got it.

"It's the only place in town, period," Sophia added. "Sorry to tell you, you haven't moved to the most exciting place in the world. It's pretty much school, All Hours, and the mall."

"There's a mall?"

Thank the Ancients. I might survive this after all.

Sophia looked apologetic. "It's a couple of towns over, and you probably won't be impressed. I saw your outfit yesterday, and I can tell you are used to better stores."

I was liking Pinky and Blondie better by the minute.

"There used to be a movie theater," Sydney said, with a pop of her gum. "Forever ago. But it burned down on opening night. Total disaster. All Hours is pretty cool though. And the coffee's killer. You want to come?"

"I don't think so," I said, as Reg simultaneously answered, "We'd be delighted!"

We looked at each other, a silent conversation held entirely through our eyeballs.

Charlie, we need to fit in.

That doesn't mean make friends.

You promised we could smell coffee.

You promised to stop saying things like "delighted."

"Who's going to All Hours?" someone said. "I'm in."

Tan arms corded with lean muscle appeared in my peripheral vision.

"This is my buddy Dex," Poe said.

"We've met." Dexter nodded at Reg and turned to me. "Hi again."

"Hello," I said.

But it came out sounding too aloof or snobby somehow, so I tried again.

"Hi."

His eyes held mine for a second, then tilted upward. "Your hair is different."

"What?" I touched my hair self-consciously. "Different bad?"

"It was black yesterday. It's brown now."

"Oh. Oh yeah, I uh . . . it was a temporary dye. I washed it out."

I silently patted myself on the back for this quick thinking.

"It looks better," he said.

Excuse me?

"Was something wrong with it before?" I propped my hand on my hip.

He looked amused by my pose, and I was suddenly unsure of how to stand or where to put my hands.

"It's just better now, that's all," he said, smiling.

I felt a heat creep into my cheeks, and I knew it meant my human face was turning all red under Dexter's gaze.

"So, you're going to All Hours after school?" he asked.

"Yes," I said, and Reg said, "No."

Another eyeball conversation.

Reg, I thought you wanted to smell coffee.

I thought you weren't interested in human boys.

I hate you.

Reg winked at me and then said to the group, "We'd love to. Thanks."

TEN

ONE DOWN, TWO TO GO

Two things were waiting for us outside school at the end of the day, and I didn't know which repelled me more. At the bottom of the front steps, to the right, our new acquaintances stood chatting. I'd had all day to reconsider our decision to hang out after school, and I was now convinced it was a total waste of time. Sure, we needed to be on our best behavior if we wanted the Elders to hear our appeal, but we didn't need to get chummy with the locals. It would just make things super awkward when they went back to being food.

I swung my gaze to the left, where another unpleasant sight was parked. Sal's filthy gray pickup coughed and growled from the unmuffled undercarriage. Sometimes it belched out a little puff of smoke, just in case the noise alone wasn't drawing enough attention. I could not recall ever having parents, but I imagined this is what it felt like when they embarrassed you.

Sal himself leaned out the driver's-side window, craning his neck in every direction. Finally, he spotted me glowering from the top of the steps and waved me down. I glanced once more at Poe, Dexter, and the twins, letting my eyes linger longer on

Dexter than the rest. Then I tried to ignore the group watching me as I walked to the pickup.

"What are you thinking, coming here?" I demanded. "So much for keeping a low prof—"

"This came for you," Sal interrupted.

He lifted a slim white envelope up to my face, as if he could physically stop my talking.

"Is that—"

"Appears so."

"But it's so soon."

"That's not unusual."

He was barely holding the envelope, balancing it casually between two fingers as if it were a piece of junk mail and not my lifeline. I snatched it from his fingers, and the truck was roaring away before I could say thank you.

Not that I was *going* to thank him, but he could have had the decency to wait two seconds to find out.

I waved off the exhaust and clutched the envelope to my chest, marveling again at Sal's inexplicable connection to the immortal world. Last night, as Reg and I had quibbled back and forth over how much postage we would need to send our letters to the other three clans, scattered across the globe, Sal had finally gotten fed up and given us a better option.

He'd instructed us to place our letters, unstamped, in the mailbox just outside his white picket fence, but instead of turning up the little red flag to alert the postal carrier of mail, he had turned up a black flag and sealed the mailbox shut. By morning, the letters were gone.

"That's our uncle Sal." Reg's voice floated over to me, and I looked up to see him flanked by Dexter and Poe on one side, Sydney and Sophia on the other. "You ready, Charlie?"

I forced a casual smile onto my face and joined the group.

"Actually Reg, can you hang back a minute?" I waved the envelope quickly, then rolled it between my hands, so none of the writing would be visible. "Sal—Uncle Sal—brought us something. It's about Mom and Dad's estate."

The lie fell easily from my lips. A hundred years of hunting had taught us that much at least. How many lies had we told to lure our victims? How many lies had we planted in their minds after the feeding was done?

"Okay if we catch up?" Reg asked the others.

They gave us directions to the coffee shop, which were literally "turn right at the one stoplight," and walked ahead. Reg and I waited impatiently for them to get a solid distance out of earshot before we unrolled the envelope.

The return address read simply:

Clan of Starlight

"Not our best hope," Reg pointed out.

He was right, but hope I had anyway, and I ripped the envelope open in one pull. A quick scan of the letter, and my face fell. As expected, the Starlight Clan had refused our request. The letter claimed all clan members had been queried and none had stepped up, but I suspected they'd been advised *not* to step up, given the tone of the message. It was polite enough, but a final paragraph made the clan's position clear.

As you may know, the Starlight Clan helped draft

the Treaty of Annis and has long supported minimum age limits on immortality. The young can be so impulsive—more likely, for example, to overfeed without considering the consequences.

"Oh, we're well aware of the consequences," I grumbled.

Reg shushed me as he read over my shoulder.

We hope, in time, you will see this change as a gift and can begin to enjoy this second chance at childhood. Dance in the sunlight, as the sun is yet another star. Best of luck to you.

"Well, at least they are staying true to themselves," Reg said diplomatically.

I let him take the letter from my hands. "*Hmph.* Hippies."

Reg tucked the letter away in his backpack, and we hustled down the sidewalk to catch up to the group. They were half a city block ahead of us already . . . if this were a city and if the stretches of unmown grass and single-story buildings between side roads could be called blocks.

One down, two to go. At least Blood and Shadow hadn't shot us down right away. Maybe that meant they were considering it. The thought lifted my mood and lightened my step.

"Who needs those Starlight tree huggers anyway? You know what I always say, Reg."

"Sometimes ugly things happen to pretty people?"

"No, the other thing."

"We may not know our history . . ."

"But we can write our destiny," I finished.

ELEVEN

THE TRAVELER

All Hours Coffee House was an explosion of color bursting from the seams of an otherwise dull "downtown"—a generous term for the patch of pavement that housed all of Nowhere's storefronts. If Main Street, anchored by the high school, was the town's major thoroughfare, then this was its hub of activity. On either side of the street, a row of faded brick buildings hugged the sidewalk, sharing outer walls like one long unit and stretching two stories tall, almost like the village hoped to grow into an actual town someday.

All Hours was crammed into a small space between a laundromat and a post office, their drab storefronts making the coffee shop all the more vibrant. Bright turquoise awnings stretched out over the sidewalk, beckoning people in, and under the awnings, the wooden window trims were painted a bold shade of purple, while a sunshine-yellow door stood propped open by a giant burlap sack of coffee beans. If the colors didn't draw you in, the smell wafting out of that front door surely would.

"I guess humans were right about this one," I said to Reg,

taking a deep breath of the mouthwatering aroma.

"It is pleasant," he agreed.

We were standing shoulder to shoulder just outside the shop, staring through the open doorway at the band of teenagers waiting for us.

I looked up at Reg. "You sure this is a good idea?"

"It's an excellent opportunity to examine human behavior up close, in the light of day. Study the prey—better serve the hunt."

I bit my lip. It was true that we could take some observations back with us when this was all done, but as I tracked Reg's gaze to where Poe sat at the table, wiping a smudge off his glasses with the sleeve of his shirt, I was pretty sure my brother had ulterior motives.

Next to Poe, Dexter leaned back in his seat, constantly shaking a disobedient lock of hair out of his eyes. It was hard to blame my brother for wanting to sample the local flavors.

"Interacting with our peers also demonstrates acceptance of our punishment. That shows maturity." Reg tapped his head just above his temple. "Something the Elders think we lack, with our forever-adolescent brains."

The injustice of the Elders' opinions washed over me in a bitter wave, and I threw my shoulders back. "Let's prove them wrong."

Then I marched through the happy yellow doorway, partly because I wanted to make a point to the Elders but mostly because I just could not keep myself from the intoxicating scent of coffee for one more second.

The coffeehouse was as eclectic inside as it was outside, with an odd collection of mismatched tables and chairs, and coffee mugs in every color. Exposed-brick walls were plastered floor to ceiling with framed photos—some as small as a postcard, others big enough to fit over a fireplace—each one a capture of breath-taking scenery from across the world.

"Cool, right?"

I didn't realize I had stopped right next to the table of our new classmates until I looked down and saw Dexter smiling up at me.

He gestured at the walls. "The owner took all of them. She's been everywhere."

And she really had—more places than even Reg and I had been. Here, a cluster of photos taken on beaches in Indonesia, Tahiti, and the Caribbean. There, a poster-sized shot of Mount Kilimanjaro. Mostly, the pictures were empty of humans, save for a woman who appeared in a dozen or so shots. A photo behind the cash register showed her perched on an elephant in what I believed was Thailand, and in a large frame near the front door, she stood beaming in the arms of a man before the Great Pyramids of Giza.

I leaned toward the picture, drawn to the woman's long mane of blond hair blowing wild in the wind and the tall, dark-haired man with the strong arm looped around her waist. A bright sun beat down on them, so they almost seemed to glow.

"That one's my favorite." Dexter was next to me now, hands in his pockets, eyes on the pyramids. "Egypt is definitely on my someday list."

"I've never . . ." *Seen it in the daylight*, I nearly said. Instead, I finished, "Never been there."

"But you've traveled?"

"A little." *Keep it vague.* "Europe, mostly."

"Nice," he said. "I went to France when I was a kid, but I don't remember much about—"

"This isn't an art gallery, Dexter O'Shea!" A woman called out from behind us.

I spun at the sound and saw the elephant-riding, pyramid-gazing blond beauty pointing at us from behind the counter. She wasn't quite as flawless in person, but she was definitely pretty in that looks-good-for-her-age kind of way. I guessed her to be in her midforties.

"Are you two going to order or not?" Her words were commanding, but her smile was playful.

"Aw, Lina, you know what I want!" Dexter called. He leaned in close to whisper to me, "I bet she already has it made."

His breath tickled my ear, and I felt a pleasant little shiver run from the hairs on my neck all the way down to the tips of my toes. I had never experienced anything quite like it in my immortal memory, and it was the first physical reaction in this new human body that I'd enjoyed. I wondered what other sorts of things this Dexter might be able to make me feel before I turned vampire again.

"I heard that." The woman, Lina, interrupted my thoughts.

She reached behind the cash register and slid a tall glass across the counter. "One iced mocha, no whip. Yawn."

"Told you," Dexter said to me as he stepped up to retrieve his drink.

"And what about your friend?"

She looked at me now, and I felt pinned under the gaze of dark eyes that seemed incongruous with her blond hair, piled in a messy bun.

I stepped back, pretending to study the menu, but really, I was struggling to remember how to order a coffee. I had heard humans do it countless times, and I knew it wasn't as simple as asking for a cup. Words like "venti" and "dolce" and "skinny" rattled around in my brain, but I wasn't sure how to string them together.

I cast my gaze around for my brother and found him planted in Dexter's abandoned chair, leaning in toward Poe. "Reg, what do you want?"

"A coffee." He waved a hand in my direction without looking up.

It was all I could do not to pull my lips back and threaten him with the fangs I no longer had.

"One *plain coffee*," I said. At least now, anything I ordered would be impressive by comparison. "And I'll have a large iced non-coagulated vanilla latte."

I smiled, proud of myself, but a beat later, I knew I had said something wrong.

Lina narrowed her eyes, almost imperceptibly, and they seemed to pierce right through me. "You mean non*fat*?"

I lifted my chin, to keep myself from sinking into the floor.

"Obviously. That's how everyone orders it back east. It must be a New York thing."

"Uh-huh." Lina looked from me to Dexter and winked. "How would I know? I've only been a few places."

She busied herself with the complicated contraptions behind the counter, pulling levers and sliding tiny silver cups in and out of giant machines. As we retreated to our table, the Lina in all the exotic photos seemed to be giving me that same squinty-eyed assessment.

"Don't mind her," Dexter said as we joined the others around a large oak barrel that had been converted to a table. "She likes to haze new kids. But she's like a second mom to us."

Sophia propped her elbows on the barrel table, her blond hair swinging around her shoulders. "If she challenges you, it means she likes you."

"Totally," Sydney agreed, chomping her gum. I wondered if it was the same piece from earlier. I wondered what gum tasted like, what made it last so long. Was it food or something different?

"When I dyed my hair," Sydney said, "Lina put a sign on the door saying 'No Pink Allowed,' but when I came in, she had made me a special pink latte."

"She did charge you double for it though," Sophia pointed out.

My eyes tangled in Sydney's pink tresses. For a century, I had wondered what it would be like to try out new hair colors. When humans transitioned to vampires, many physical imperfections improved, and disease disappeared, but other things were unchanged. Height and weight stayed roughly the same, and skin maintained its general tone, fading from peach and copper and ebony to cooler shades. But for reasons absolutely nobody could properly explain to me, immortality made hair black as midnight—no exceptions—not even a teensy little highlight. I curled a lock of my new brown hair around my finger, wondering what I could do with it now.

A moment later, Lina dropped off our drinks, and I was sure I didn't imagine the way she hovered a moment too long, wiping her hands on her apron and looking back and forth between me and Reg. But if she had something to say, she swallowed it and walked away.

Reg and I exchanged a glance over the tops of our drinks, a silent "cheers" before sharing our first-ever sip of coffee. Then we were both gagging and retching in unison.

"Too sweet," I said, holding the icy concoction away from me.

Reg lifted his own mug. "Too . . . bitter?"

There was a pause, then laughter from the group as Reg and I swapped drinks.

He declared mine delicious, as I took a tentative sip of the hot black liquid he had passed to me.

Nirvana.

If this was bitter, I wanted bunches. Impossibly, coffee tasted even better than it smelled, and it wasn't just one flavor but an evolution that started with something—yes, bitter, as it slid over the tongue but then turned sweet as I swallowed and left a spicy aftertaste. What magic was this liquid that could change flavor even after it was gone?

"What do you think, princess?" Lina called from the counter.

When I looked up at her, I got the unsettling feeling that she had been watching me the entire time.

"It's delicious," I said. And then, because I was feeling generous, I added, honestly, "It's the best coffee I've ever tasted."

Lina's sudden roar of laughter took me aback. Had I accidentally said something wrong again? But when I looked around at our new acquaintances, they appeared as puzzled as I was.

"I bet it is, princess!" Lina said, doubling over the counter in hysterics. "I bet it is."

Poe eyed Lina over the rim of his thick black glasses, then pushed them up his nose and said seriously to the rest of us, "One day, I intend to be as fabulously eccentric as her."

"We basically all want to be Lina when we grow up," Sydney explained.

Sophia nodded in agreement. "She's a little off her rocker, but she's ours."

"And what can we say? The coffee is exceptional." Poe lifted his mug in Lina's direction, a tribute, and she responded by waving him off and disappearing into the kitchen, still snickering.

Dexter flashed me a bright white smile. "Some days she's a little more *off* than others."

TWELVE
BIGGER THAN PROM

Reg and I spent the next hour chatting up the humans and managing not to embarrass ourselves. Just as Sal predicted, whenever a question was hard to answer, we had only to refer to our fictional dead parents, and the group backed right off.

Our new classmates gave us the full verbal tour of Hope High, from sports (Sophia played soccer; Sydney feigned illness on a regular basis to avoid gym) to fine arts (the fall play was Shakespeare's *A Midsummer Night's Dream*, and Poe was apparently a shoo-in for Puck). Dexter was a member of something called Future Farmers of America, which should have sounded painfully boring but, coming from him, seemed terribly interesting.

He explained that he was raised on a farm but his parents had sold the land to move him closer to town so he wouldn't be so isolated from his friends and civilization. I liked the way he put air quotes around the word "civilization" and winked when he acknowledged that a city girl like me probably didn't see it that way.

Who knew farm boys could be so charming? In fact, I was surprised to realize that we had been in the coffee shop for over an hour and not one of these humans was boring me. We'd encountered plenty of not-boring humans over the decades, but it was strange to discover them here in Nowhere. Or maybe it was just the fact that I was actually able to focus on what they were saying now that I was unburdened of the desire to drink their blood.

"But why Hope High?" Reg asked at one point. "I thought high schools were usually named for the town."

"Would you want to go to *Nowhere High*?" Sydney asked.

"It was named by the guy who paid for it," Dexter said. "Some alum who got out and hit it big and wanted kids in his hometown to have a little *hope*."

"That big brick box is supposed to give us hope?" I asked.

Dexter held his hands up in a "beats me" gesture.

"I just can't believe the town actually built something new," Poe said. "The school is only a few years old. Before that, the last time anyone in this place tried to open something new, it went up in smoke. Literally!"

He pointed out the coffee shop window, and I followed the angle of his finger to a set of boarded-up windows, across the street and a few doors down. Above the windows, an empty marquee jutted out, bare and dark.

"A theater?" I asked.

"Shortest business ever to operate in Nowhere at less than twenty-four hours," Poe said.

"What happened?"

"A fire. Opening night. Gutted the whole place, and it never reopened."

"Perhaps it still will," Reg said. "How long ago was the fire?"

Poe locked eyes with Reg. "When our grandparents were our age."

"Oh."

"My grandad was there," Dex said. "He and his buddies almost didn't make it out."

"Why didn't they rebuild?" I asked.

Poe shrugged. "Apparently the owner's insurance wouldn't cover it for some reason. So he abandoned the place and sold it to some development company that never did anything with it. My mom says it happens all the time."

"Poe's mom is on the town chamber," Dex said. "He thinks it makes him a big deal. But it mostly just means he knows a bunch of boring information nobody cares about."

"Knowledge is power, my friend," Poe retorted.

"If we're going to have anything new, I'm glad it's a high school," Sophia said. "Kids used to have to bus out to a school an hour away, and they treated anyone from out here like hicks."

Sydney added, "Now that school begs for away games so they can play on our fancy football field or shoot hoops in our gigantic gym."

"Have you seen the gym yet?" Dexter asked. "It's way too big for a school with just a few hundred kids. We can actually fit the entire population of Nowhere in there. That's like a thousand people!"

"And we do fit them in," Poe said. "All the time. Hope High is HQ for all festivals, carnivals, productions, and events."

"The biggest of which is right around the corner," Sophia chirped. "Only two months to the Halloween Hoopla!"

I was glad I had my coffee mug to my lips so they could not see my involuntary grimace. My eyes met Reg's over the rim of my mug.

A hoopla?

Be nice.

As if sensing my judgment, the twins launched into a sales pitch.

"It's a party."

"It's a parade."

"It's both."

"It's bigger than prom!"

I perked up at that. "So it's like a dance?"

For all the events I'd attended in the last hundred years—from frat parties to formal galas—I had never once seen a school dance anywhere but on TV or in movies. I may not have a bucket list like Reg, but I had my own list of "never haves," and high school dance was on that list. As long as I was stuck in this human skin, I was absolutely going to take it to a party.

"Kind of," Sydney said. "It started out as a parade and exploded into a whole big thing."

Sophia chimed in. "The Nowhere Halloween parade has been around forever—like fifty years. It's so old."

If fifty years was old, I was downright antique.

While fifty was young by vampire standards, I still had to wonder how a town that had been around long enough to have a fifty-year-old parade still barely had fifty buildings, other than houses. Why did some places on earth grow old yet never go away? It was as though towns themselves could be immortal.

Poe held his hands in front of him, palms a short distance apart, and spread them wider as he said, "Over the years, parade turned to costume party turned to festival turned to . . ." He spread his arms as wide as possible. "*Hoopla*. It's ridiculous," he concluded, with a shake of his head.

He dodged a swipe from Sydney.

"Keep talking like that, and we'll kick you off the committee," she said.

Poe dropped out of his chair to kneel on the floor before Sydney, hands folded as if in prayer. "Oh, *please*. Please release me from your wretched committee."

"Committee?" Reg asked.

"Hope High Halloween Hoopla planning committee," Sophia said.

"Say that three times fast," Dexter joked.

Not that funny, but still cute. Still very, very cute.

"The hoopla is a whole-day event," Sophia continued. "Starting with the parade and ending with a big street party outside the school that night. There's a barbecue and bands and prizes for best parade floats and best costumes. Everyone in Nowhere goes. *Everyone*. Since most of the fun happens at the school, Hope High students get to plan the whole thing."

"Translation—free labor," Poe interrupted.

Sophia ignored him. "We sell parade entries and take a cut of all the food sales to raise money for charity. So, yes, it's volunteer work, but it's great for college applications."

"Charity, college applications, blah blah blah." Sydney flipped her bubble gum hair over her shoulder. "Soph, you always leave out the best bit. The hoopla kind of replaced our annual homecoming dance, so now we have a faux dance in the gym at the end of the night. It's more like an after-party, with everyone in costumes, so all the kids from school dress up in formal wear, but with a horror theme."

"Like a zombie bride," Sophia added.

"Or a mummy in a tux."

"Or a sexy vampire."

A warning look from Reg stopped me from announcing that they were looking at a sexy vampire. I hoped I was still the former, if not the latter. I kept my mouth shut and stuck my face in my coffee instead. It was my third cup, and my hands were shaking a little—an unpleasant but tolerable side effect.

"I like the dressing-up part," Poe admitted. "Not so much the intolerable planning meetings."

He looked hopefully at me and Reg. "I don't suppose one of you wants my spot?"

"Well, you're not exactly selling it," Sophia admonished Poe. To me and Reg she said, "Being on the committee has its perks. You get to ride on the school float."

"Oh, get real," Sydney said. "The only perk for Soph is that she gets to boss people around."

"Not all people." Sophia poked her sister. "Just you."

"But seriously," Sydney said, "it's pretty cool to ride on the float and help throw the year's biggest party. Trust me, I'm not a joiner. I leave that to Soph. But this is one extracurricular activity that's worth it."

It sounded like work, and I was not interested in work. However, I was acutely interested in parties and not against the idea of waving down at people from a parade float.

"How do you get on this committee?" I asked.

Sydney slung an arm over her sister's shoulder, and they put their heads together, pink and platinum hair intertwining, identical conspiratorial grins on their faces.

"You kiss up to the committee chairs," she said.

I looked up at Dexter through my eyelashes. "Are you on the committee?"

He shook his unruly lock of hair out of his face. "Nah, but I'll be at the party. I'm hoping a nice girl will ask me to dance."

"Oh, a *nice* girl?" I said, lifting my coffee to my lips. "That's a shame."

Sydney and Sophia giggled in appreciation, and I rewarded them with a wink. Maybe I could teach these girls a few things before I left them in the sunlight.

Dexter still wore a confident, lazy smile, but I noticed a blush had crept into his cheeks. My little flirt had knocked him off-balance. The poor guy. I'd had a century to master this skill. He'd had, what? A few years? It really wasn't a fair fight.

"It's okay, Dex," Poe said. "I'm not that into nice *girls* either."

Reg set his empty cup on the barrel table and leaned, almost imperceptibly, closer to Poe.

"Nor am I," he said.

Sydney and Sophia exchanged a look, eyebrows arching high into their foreheads. Realization had dawned. Their eyes flitted from Poe to Reg and back again. They both smiled.

"So, you're a junior?" Dexter asked me, his blush quickly fading. "You look younger. How old are you?"

"I'm a hundr—uh, sixteen?"

He laughed. "You're not sure?"

I opened my mouth a couple of times like a hungry koi fish, until I caught sight of Reg imitating me from across the table. I snapped my jaw closed.

"I'm sure," I said to Dexter.

Now I was the one off-balance.

"I'm a junior too," he said. "Too bad we don't have any classes together. But at least we're in the same wing."

"I guess I'll be seeing you around, then."

He smiled, the tip of his tongue caught between his teeth in a delicious way. "I know I'll be seeing you."

Maybe it was a fair fight after all.

"Looks like somebody's already lining up their date for the dance," Sydney said to Sophia, loud enough for all of us to hear.

I didn't know if Dexter was destined to be my date to this Halloween sock hop or whatever it was called, or if we would even still be human by then, but one thing was for certain. If I did go to the party, I would be wearing Prada.

THIRTEEN

PRETTY UGLY

"I'll thank you to keep me informed of your general where-abouts," Sal greeted us when we returned to the cottage.

He was hulking in the doorway again, for who knows what reason. Maybe he was watching the corn grow.

"Don't you have anything better to do than creep around on the porch waiting for us?" I retorted.

"It's my house, and I'll creep around wherever I damn well please."

I smirked.

"*Stand* around. You know what I meant." The flustered look on his face was a prize. "So, where were you?"

Reg pushed past me up the steps to the porch. "We were at a coffee shop frequented by the local youth. Perhaps you've heard of it. It's called All Hours and—"

"I know it," Sal snapped.

Reg hesitated at Sal's agitation. "We made some friends. We're attempting to fit in, per your sage advice."

I rubbed my nose and made exaggerated kissing noises, because words alone would not be enough to express to Reg what a traitorous suck-up he was.

"Look, it's simple." Sal turned away from us, and we followed him into the cottage kitchen. "If you go missing, I'm bound to report it. It's part of the deal."

"Report it to whom?" Reg asked. "The Elders?"

I shrugged my backpack off and dropped it on one of the carved wooden chairs around the kitchen table. "How much are they paying you to babysit us, anyway?"

"Not enough," Sal muttered.

"And if you report us to the Elders for running off or misbehaving, what do they do, come give us a superpowered spanking?"

"Can't say for sure," Sal said with an ominous tone. "No one who leaves ever comes back."

That wiped the smirk off my face. "Oh."

"Do you think they . . . Would they . . . ?" Reg stuttered.

"I don't think they'd hunt you down to kill you," Sal said, a kind note cutting through his gravel voice. "Most likely a mind swipe, I imagine. Maybe a hundred bucks and a hotel room."

I wasn't sure that scenario was any better.

"That's barbaric," Reg protested. "Memory fades are not meant to be punitive."

Sal busied himself at the stove, adding this and that to a giant pot.

"Not okay as a punishment but okay to use on human victims for mere convenience, eh?"

"The fade is used on newborn vampires as well, not solely humans," Reg objected. "And it's not convenience. It's necessity."

I smiled. After all his waxing poetic about humanity, it was good to hear Reg defending vampire culture and traditions.

Sal grunted a humorless laugh into his pot. "Necessary to protect your immortal arses. I'm sure you did a number on that boy you bled."

Reg stiffened. "His fade was more than we were capable of. We usually only need to take a few small memories—our faces, the feeding. It is a talent that takes years to perfect. The Elders have to assist with . . . *messier* situations. But I assure you, the process is quite humane."

I chose a chair at the end of the table and leaned back, hands behind my head. Watching Reg spar with Sal instead of kissing his ass was pure entertainment.

"That's rich!" Sal twisted around to wave a wooden spoon at Reg. "Vampires deciding what's *humane.*"

"Take a little blood, heal the wound, clear their memory. No permanent damage. It's a kindness to spare them any trauma." Reg sounded less sure of himself now.

"Oh yeah," Sal said, his attention back on the stove. "Steal someone's blood, inject them with venom so they pass out and then violate their brain. A kindness indeed. Nicest thing I ever heard."

I made eyeballs at Reg behind Sal's back. He was letting the old man win. Reg opened his mouth, but before he could speak, Sal went on.

"And what happens when it's more than a little . . . when it's a wound that won't heal? It's not just one or two memories to erase, is it?"

Sal's meaning was heavy, and we all fell silent, thinking of the boy and what the Elders had to do to make him forget. Total amnesia. Reg and I had panicked once we realized we . . . *I* . . . had taken too much. He was so close to death, and to kill a human for any reason other than self-defense was to violate one of the highest vampire laws. Thanks to the Treaty of Annis, to turn him at his age would have been even worse.

So we panicked. We dumped him outside that emergency room, even though we knew the memory work we'd attempted was useless. Vampires could manipulate the mind only when the person was under the influence of our venom—a poison that became more potent with time—and the more blood lost, the harder the memory work. It was a delicate thing to pull the threads of memory—keeping some and discarding others. Sometimes the threads got tangled into a knot that couldn't be undone. The Elders had to send in a team later to wipe the boy's mind entirely.

For a few minutes, the only sound was the scrape of Sal's spoon against the bottom of the pan and the quiet bubble of whatever was inside the pot. It smelled more amazing with every passing second, but I had lost my appetite.

Finally, Sal's shoulders sagged. "You're young. Impulsive. You weren't in control of yourselves."

I glared at the back of his head, feeling more patronized than pitied.

"Okay, yes," I said. "We made a mistake, but this punishment is still beyond. We had never left a mess that big for the Elders to clean up before."

"Well . . ." Reg squinted one eye and scratched the side of his face, where a fine stubble was sprouting from his new human skin. "There was that one time, in Burma, with the—"

"Oh, right." I'd forgotten.

"And that other time, in Helsinki—"

"And New York."

"And Peru."

"We agreed never to speak of Peru."

I frowned. Maybe we *were* just teenagers.

Sal covered the pot with a lid and joined us at the table. "Well, now that I've got you in such good moods, here's another ray of sunshine for you."

He pulled a folded envelope from the front pocket of his plaid flannel.

When this was over, if I never saw plaid or flannel again, it would be too soon.

"Two in one day," Sal said, letting the envelope fall to the table. "One guess who this is from."

But we did not have to guess, and we probably didn't even have to open it to know the contents. The front of the envelope was written in blood, the crude signature of the Blood Clan, and it was addressed, venomously:

To the Disgraced Drakes, Reginald and Charlotte

I huffed. "*We're* a disgrace? They would bleed puppies if the Elders allowed it."

Reg took the envelope between the tips of two fingers and pried it open, careful to avoid the address, but more blood was waiting inside. They had used it to script the entire letter.

"It looks like they've been playing with their food," Reg said with disdain.

I sniffed at the red scrawl, but my mortal nose could not detect whether the blood was human or animal. In either case, it was wasteful and, to my new human senses . . . kind of gross.

Most of it was hard to read, due to where the blood had run or smudged, but we got the gist. The Blood Clan leaders had not only refused our request but they had also *forbidden* anyone in the clan from sponsoring us.

"'Imagine,'" Reg read aloud from the letter, "'Bone asking Blood for favor for *free*. Centuries, Bone hoard wealth that ought be shared with Blood and other clan.'"

"Oh, this again." I rolled my eyes. "If the Bloods ever climbed out of their coffins for anything but dinner, maybe they would have a few bucks of their own."

"This grammar is atrocious," Reg said. "I've always detested the way this clan speaks. Where did they come up with this dialect, anyway? It's so primitive."

"Better primitive than pretentious." I would have laughed at my own jab if I didn't feel like crying. "What else does it say?"

Reg turned the paper over in his hands. "That's pretty much it. There's something about entitlement and superiority and . . . I think this bit is a vague threat that they might come feed on us now that we are . . ." He squinted at the page. "Tasty little humans."

Sal humphed. "Let them try."

"You going to protect us, slayer?" I asked.

"I wouldn't mind seeing a few Blood vamps decorating my fence," he growled. "Probably not the lot you want sponsoring your appeal anyway. I hear they've been giving your Elder Seat some trouble lately. Feeding without cleaning up their messes. Risking public exposure. Best not to get mixed up with them."

Reg tossed the letter aside. "Two rejections in less than twenty-four hours."

"It will be a while before you hear from the third," Sal said. He stood to stir his stovetop concoction. "Shadow Clan rarely uses a courier. They prefer to send letters the old-fashioned way."

"Aren't they in Iceland or something?" I complained. "That could take forever!"

Sal shrugged. "Who knows why the Shadows do anything? Maybe they're like the Starlights, trying to keep connected to humanity."

"Well, someone should tell them *humanity* is now using email."

"Charlie can be a little impatient," Reg said.

My stomach rumbled as a savory steam escaped Sal's pot. Apparently my appetite was returning. "Is that almost ready?"

"Case in point," Reg quipped.

I showed him my favorite finger in response.

"I'm not impatient. That smell is just too good."

"Fine, fine," Sal grumped, but I thought I saw the corner of his mouth quirk up.

He scooped heaping ladles of something into bowls that he passed around the table.

"Not yet," he warned, before I could take a bite. "It's too hot. You'll burn your mouth."

I twisted up my face into a cross between doubt and disgust. "Burn my mouth?"

"It's a human thing."

I dropped my spoon. "Oh, come on! This is torture."

Sal laughed—a hearty belly laugh. "You were trapped in a postpubescent phase of hormonal development for one hundred years, and you think *this* is torture?"

I shuddered. "Please don't ever say 'postpubescent' again."

That only made Sal roar louder, pounding the table with his fist. Reg caught his infectious laugh, and soon, even I had joined in. By the time we were done cracking up, the food was cool enough to eat. Sal declared the contents of the bowls to be chili, and Reg and I declared it to be delicious.

"Do all humans know how to cook?" Reg asked between bites. "Is this a skill we would be expected to learn if we remained mortal?"

"Nah, it's not a requirement to join the human club. I just happen to have a lot of family recipes."

I frowned down at my near-empty bowl. "Slayer soup."

"Chili," Sal corrected. "And I got the recipe from the other side of the family."

I tilted my head at his bitter tone. "Are you not proud to be a Sicarius? I mean, I get it. *I* would be *mortified*. But it seems like a slayer would be writing that name in little hearts all over their notebooks."

Sal's smile was brittle. "I was proud once."

"Until?" Reg prompted.

Sal wiped chili from his beard and let out a tired sigh. "Until I started to doubt the mission."

"Which is what? Vampire extinction?" I guessed.

"You got it. All vamps off the face of the earth. Period. No exceptions." He nodded to us. "Not even for the children."

"And slayers just go along with that, no questions asked?" Reg said.

"Most of them, yes. A slayer is a soldier. Obey the mission at all costs. Never mind if the enemy is waving a white flag or pleading for mercy or"—he glanced away, eyes closing for just a moment—"more human than any mortal you've ever met."

"Monstrous," Reg declared.

Sal agreed. "That was my conclusion too. Not that your former kind are any picnic though. Monsters on both sides, if you ask me, and I just couldn't see the point of fighting in a war that will never end."

Sal pushed his bowl to the side and folded his thick hands. "I'm surprised you're interested. But then, I reckon you've never met a slayer?"

"Never cared to," Reg said. "No offense."

"None taken."

"I've always wanted to meet one," I said. "But when I pictured it, there was a lot more chasing and biting involved—not so much with the sad stories."

Sal chuckled softly. "Well, the saddest part of all is that we spend a lifetime training to turn vamps to smoke when we are born with the power to turn them to flesh and blood." He pulled his hands apart to spread them on the table. "No stakes required."

I leaned in, watching his hands as if they might give up their secrets.

"How does it work, what you do?"

"It's as simple as touch." Sal lifted one hand, palm out, and Reg and I both leaned back, instinctively, even though there was no damage left to be done. "In the early days, we called ourselves healers, not slayers. Our kind emerged about two thousand years ago, in the time before immortals took care to conceal themselves. They lived in the open and turned people often—spreading vampires like a virus across villages. When someone was turned, families would try to contain them long enough to contact the local healer in hopes of reversing the damage. One touch was all it took back then."

"And now?" Reg asked. He sounded as breathless as I felt.

"Powers have faded over the generations. One touch only works if you can hold on for a good few minutes and stay focused. And that's if you can get your hands on 'em to begin with. It's like trying to catch a ghost. But engage one in combat, get those fine motor skills going, and now you've got a fair fight."

It was a valid point. Most vampires were invisible to humans when flat out running—barely more than a puff of air. But the finer the movement, the slower the speed. A vampire could probably set a dance floor on fire, but put a couple of knitting needles in their hands, and they'd be no faster than a human.

"Healing just took too much time," Sal said. "So slayers got lazy and settled for the stake and the smoke."

"But the fence," I said. "The healing's not just in your hands."

Sal threw his shoulders back with pride. "That's uniquely me. No one else can do it."

"Do what?"

"Transfer the power. Discovered it by accident. I was carving a fresh set of stakes and thinking about . . ." He faltered, his expression distant for a second, before continuing. "Thinking about how I wished we could heal instead of kill, and the first time I went out with those stakes—the vamps I hit did not turn to smoke."

"They turned human," I said with quiet awe.

For all the power wielded by vampires—the strength, the speed, the memory manipulation—one step through Sal's gate, and it was all undone.

"They did. Instead of smoke, they became flesh and blood, but it wasn't what I expected." He grimaced. "Turns out, when humans get staked in the chest, it's not too pretty. They . . . didn't make it."

"How sad," Reg said.

"Yuck," I added.

"So I wondered if there was a way to channel the healing into objects so that it could change immortal to mortal without physical harm. It took years, but I perfected it."

"Excuse me." I held up a disagreeing finger. "That thing

that happened to us in the front yard was *not* without physical harm."

Sal chuckled. "Fair enough. But if you ask my family, it doesn't hurt enough."

"They're not proud of what you do?" Reg asked.

"Proud?!" Sal threw his head back and laughed until he coughed. "I am a black scorch on the Sicarius name. Reforming vamps instead of smoking them? Shameful stuff."

But I could tell by the way he said it, with glee in every word, that he wasn't the least bit ashamed.

"I do miss the action though," Sal said with a wink.

"It's unfortunate it doesn't work the other direction," Reg said. "Or can you . . . ?"

Sal shook his head. "I'm no vampire," he said. "I can't make you. I can only unmake you."

For a second, he almost looked like he pitied us. "I don't recommend going back to the dark side, but if that's what the Elders agree to, I won't stop it. This is just business for me. Wait to see what the Shadows say. In the meantime, find yourself a distraction."

"Like what?" I asked.

"I don't know. Ask your new friends. Join a club or a sport or something."

I pouted. "The only sport we know is hunting."

"I hear ya," Sal said.

The kitchen fell into an awkward silence as we realized we'd once hunted each other.

111

I think I was the first to let a snicker escape, followed by a snort from the old man and an outright laugh from Reg. For the second time that evening, the kitchen was ringing with our laughter, each of us busting up until our bellies full of slayer soup ached with the effort. I never would have guessed that laughing so much it hurt . . . actually felt kind of good.

FOURTEEN

LIFE GOES ON

Once upon a time, an assassin and two former immortals lived together in a tiny cottage and managed not to kill each other.

Sal became more tolerable as the days went on, and after a week or so, I stopped minding the way he hovered at the front door, watching us come and go—or at least, I managed to ignore it. He made up for a lack of charm by sending us to school every day stuffed with eggs and sausage and pancakes and other things that were probably going to give me acne, according to Sydney and Sophia.

The twins were keeping me busy with more than just human skin-care tips. By Friday afternoon, I was already in my third Halloween Hoopla planning meeting of the week. Sydney and Sophia sat at either end of a long table in the Hope High library, with me and a dozen other students stretched between them.

"So, we are down to 'A Full Moon' and 'A Night of Immortality,'" Sophia said, consulting a clipboard.

One of the committee's responsibilities was the Hope High parade float, and the group had been debating a theme for the float all week, though I wasn't sure why we were even going through the charade of a discussion. It had become obvious to me in a matter of just days that Sydney and Sophia Carlone always got exactly what they wanted. Reg and I had clearly stumbled into the right group of friends.

The committee had already settled on an overall event motto for the 50th Annual Halloween Hoopla: *No more, no less than horrifically fun!*

But the fight over the Hope High parade float theme was dragging on. The freshman and sophomore committee members didn't seem to care much, probably because their task was just to build the thing. Juniors and seniors got to ride on it.

"I still say those are both boring," a boy across from me complained. "We need a cinematic theme, like *The Purge.*"

Sophia gave him a withering look. "Mark, we are not theming the official Hope High float after a mass murder movie."

"'A Full Moon' would be the easiest for decorating," a girl to my left suggested. "There are still a bunch of props and set pieces stashed in the theater closets from the 'Howl at the Moon' theme a few years ago."

"Exactly," *Purge* boy, Mark, said. "It's already been done."

"'A Night of Immortality,' then," Sydney said. She and Sophia wore matching expressions of irritation with the group. They had been pushing this theme all week and were clearly ready for a vote.

"What's scary about immortality?" the girl on my left asked.

She had a point there. Being mortal, with all its dreary death nonsense, was infinitely more scary than eternal life.

"Immortality doesn't have to be scary," Sophia said. "But it can be, if you want. Like, Frankenstein's monster, brought back to life."

"And cursed mummies," Sydney added. "And vampires and ghosts and zombies and just, y'know, general undead."

"Plus, if you really love the full-moon idea so much, you can still dress as a werewolf with the immortality theme," Sophia said.

"Werewolves are not immortal." The words slid out of my mouth with such ease and authority, I didn't even realize I had said them out loud until the whole table turned to look at me. "I mean, I think I saw that in a movie once."

The girl next to me nodded with an air of authority. "*Twilight*. The wolves live a long time but not forever."

Sure, what she said.

"Can we just vote on it?" Mark asked. "I don't think it's going to be unanimous."

The twins agreed and called for a show of hands. Half the table, including the *Twi*-hard girl on my left voted for "A Full Moon." The other half, including Sydney and Sophia, put their hands in the air for "A Night of Immortality." Only Mark the *Purge* boy and I abstained—him in opposition to both themes, me because I could not possibly care less.

Sophia dismissed the boy protesting the theme. "Charlie," she said, leaning forward so her straight blond locks fell into a frame around her face. "You are our tiebreaker. Full moon or immortality?"

I looked up from the fingernails I had been inspecting and saw the entire table watching me in anticipation. I honestly didn't like either theme, but I very much liked it when all the eyeballs in a room were on me, so I made a show of thinking it over—chin in one hand, the fingers of the other hand tracing an invisible pattern on the table.

After a long moment, I looked up at Sophia and said with absolute honesty, "All I have *ever* wanted is immortality."

"I knew you would be a good addition to the committee!" Sydney squealed, locking arms with me as we swept down the hallway. She blew a stray strand of pink out of her face. "But you didn't have to pick that theme just because it was my idea."

Was it? I couldn't recall who suggested it. But if it made her happy . . .

"Sure, I did," I said. "And it was the better theme anyway."

"By far," Sophia agreed, falling into step on my other side.

I noticed then that other students were stepping to the side to make way for us, and I imagined how we must look—the mysterious new girl with the dark hair and blue eyes, flanked by the popular and statuesque Carlone twins, cutting a path through the crowd. It was just like every teen movie I'd ever seen, and I couldn't keep the smile off my face.

I was born to Bee.

The boys were waiting for us at Poe's locker, which had become our gathering place before and after school. My eyes went first to Dexter, as they had done all week, but his own gaze was on his phone, thumb scrolling the screen in lazy swipes. He leaned against the wall of lockers, turned away from us enough that I could see the *O'Shea* printed on the back of his shirt, tight against the lean curves of his muscles.

I slid up beside him and pretended to read his phone. "Are you googling me again? I'm telling you, I'm not on social media."

It was only a tease, but the lightning-fast way Dexter snapped his phone off and the red that crept up his neck told me I might not have been too far off.

He recovered quickly, turning around with his signature grin splashed across his face. "You mean those naughty pictures I got weren't from you?"

"You wish."

"Maybe I do wish," he said.

I felt a tingle in my toes that was as frustrating as it was exhilarating. He'd been flirting with me like this for a week, but still he hadn't asked me out. Why did humans always act like they had all the time in the world, when they had just this one little blip?

The evidence seemed to indicate that he was playing hard to get, but if that was his game, he would lose. I had preyed on more challenging boys than Dexter O'Shea. Still, I had to grudgingly admit that his delay in asking me out had only made him all the more enticing. My mild flirtation with the tall, tan, and blond boy was growing into a more focused fascination. Clearly, I missed the hunt, and this could be the closest human equivalent.

"And Charlie saved the day by voting for immortality!"

Sydney wrapped up her account of our meeting just as Reg scooted up to the group, and her final word caused his tennis shoes to practically screech to a stop.

"What's that about immortality?"

"Parade float theme!" I spat out.

He visibly relaxed. "Oh, good. Now, if you can just come up with a new name and rebrand the entire event."

Sydney and Sophia looked surprised, but I had to side with Reg.

"He's not wrong. I mean, Halloween *Hoopla*? Really?" It was hard to keep the disdain out of my voice. "Isn't there anything a little less . . . quaint?"

"Like what?" Sophia asked.

I shrugged. "I don't know, but you really can't get much worse than *hoopla*."

Dexter considered it. "Hootenanny?"

"Hullaballoo?" Poe offered.

I cringed. "Okay, I stand corrected. Clearly, it *can* get worse."

"Well, I have news too," Reg said. "One of my less offensive instructors has suggested I join the debate team. She said my knowledge and poise would be an asset." He puffed up his chest in an exaggerated superhero pose. "At last, someone recognizes my superiority."

The twins giggled, and Poe gave Reg a high five that lingered for just a second into a loose-finger hold even after their hands lowered. I tried not to be jealous that Reg had reached the fingertip-touching stage with his conquest, when I was still playing cat and mouse with mine. I wasn't even sure who was the cat and who was the mouse.

"And the play?" Poe asked. "What did you decide?"

"I believe I can do both," Reg said.

"What play?" I asked. What had my brother been up to while I'd been tied up in boring party planning meetings?

"I'm auditioning for the school play."

"Oh yeah." I recalled our conversation from the first trip to All Hours. "Shakespeare, right?"

Reg was a massive Shakespeare fan and often talked about what a missed opportunity it was that no one had ever turned him immortal.

"*A Midsummer Night's Dream*," Poe said. "My favorite."

"And mine," Reg said. "Poe and I are both auditioning for the part of Puck."

"Let the best man win." Poe held his hand out to shake Reg's in an overly dignified way that I think was just an excuse for more touching.

Dexter teased, "I see no men here. Only boys."

I matched Dexter's smile. "Guess we'll have to keep ourselves occupied while these *boys* run off to the theater."

"And debate," Reg added.

"You don't plan to join any clubs?" Dex asked, feigning surprise. "And here I pegged you as a 4-H girl."

"I don't know what that is," I said with a flip of my hair. "But I can tell when I'm being mocked."

"You could try out for soccer," Sophia said. "We could train together."

"I don't kick things."

She laughed. "Well, Poe and I are also in student government, and I'm the president of the National Honor Society. NHS is great on college applications. If your grades are high enough, I could recommend—"

Sydney dropped her head to her sister's shoulder and pretended to snore.

Sophia responded with a playful shove. "Okay, okay. I know when I'm being too much."

"You really don't," Sydney said.

When the pair of them left for home, I turned to Dexter, my lips pulled into a side pout. Now was his chance. Maybe he just needed a little push.

"I guess I'm just interested in other kinds of *extracurricular activities*," I said.

Push.

"Speaking of extracurriculars . . ." Dex leaned in close, his voice low. "I'm late for an FFA thing. Thanks for reminding me."

Whatever face I made in response caused him to smile in that teasing way he had, then he waved goodbye to Reg and Poe and took off down the hall.

Reg caught me watching Dexter's retreat and sidled up next to me. "Ouch. Did you just get sidelined by Future Farmers of—"

"Shut up."

He grinned and slung an arm across my shoulder. "A worthy

opponent for Charlotte Drake, if ever I saw one."

I shushed him, even though he was already being quiet. "It's Charlie Smith. And no boy from Iowa is a match for me."

On the way home, I let Reg do most of the talking, and he chatted Poe and plays and clubs and classes all the way back to the cottage. I genuinely enjoyed seeing my brother happy, even if a little jealousy clung to the edges of my enthusiasm. He was clearly having more fun on his human vacation than I was.

He was wearing it better too. The dark layer of stubble that had sprouted on his face was coming together in a nice frame that showed off his jawline, while the only thing bursting from my own skin was a spray of bright red acne spots that I had to take care to cover with concealer every morning. Maybe that was why Dexter hadn't asked me out.

Zits, I decided, were definitely the worst part of being human.

FIFTEEN

FRIENDS, NOT FOOD

As if we didn't get enough torture at school during the week, it turned out we were supposed to do school on the weekends too, in the form of homework. I protested, of course. Worrying about homework was like an admission that we'd be around long enough to get a report card, and I still refused to believe that. Reg put up a fight too, saying the assignments were insultingly easy and beneath his "considerable studies."

But Sal insisted it would draw too much attention if we failed out of high school. So that's how we found ourselves at All Hours the following Saturday for a caffeine-fueled study session with our new crew. At least if we had to do homework, we didn't actually have to do it at home.

"Strict."

"Sévère"

"Polite."

"Polie."

We were gathered around our barrel table, our favorite drinks in hand, quizzing each other on vocabulary—French for me, Reg, and Poe; Spanish for Dex and the twins. For the first time in a century, I wished I'd spent a little more time on my education, or at the very least picked up a few languages. English was the primary tongue in Drake House, and it turned out we really didn't need to speak a bunch of languages to hunt all over the world.

I tried to participate as Poe read from a stack of index cards in his hands, but Reg was too busy showing off to let me get a word in, and I was distracted by the fact that Dexter was sitting just to my left smelling like something fresh and green, as if he'd been rolling around in grass.

And then I was distracted by thoughts of rolling around in the grass *with* him.

"Finally."

"Finalement."

Poe frowned and thumbed the edge of the cards. "More like, *at last!*"

"Oh," Reg said. "Enfin!"

"Perfect." Poe's eyes sparkled behind his glasses as he stared at Reg. "Parfait."

No doubt those two were headed for a roll in the grass themselves.

"That's all the cards." Poe tucked the stack away.

"Enfin!" I cried.

Dexter hefted a broad textbook from his backpack. "We still have a chem test to study for." He tapped the cover. "Periodic tables and atomic structures."

"Ugh," I groaned. "There's more?"

I silently cursed all my teen TV shows that never seemed to show students slogging through hours of schoolwork.

"There's always more," Sydney complained. "It's like the teachers are trying to give us so much work that we won't have time to get into any trouble."

"And yet, somehow, you always get into trouble anyway," Sophia needled her sister. "How do you do that?"

Sydney tipped her chin into the air. "Years of practice."

Sophia gave Sydney a playful shove, and I found myself smiling at them.

Homework was on my list of the worst things about being human, but our new mortal friends made it tolerable.

Dexter scooted close to me, spreading the chem book across both of our laps. His arm brushed mine as he reached over to turn the page, and I felt a little current of static electricity run through my skin.

"Oh, sorry," he said. "I didn't mean to zap you."

I bit my lip in a way I knew boys liked. "It's okay. That's *my* kind of chemistry."

"Actually, that's physics," Reg piped up from my other side.

I responded with a murderous glare, until Dex leaned in to whisper, "Feels like chemistry to me."

After another hour, the twins finally declared the study session done and treated everyone to another round of coffee.

Reg sipped his latte and made a face. "This tastes a little off today."

"It's the weekend barista," Sophia said. "She always uses too much syrup."

Sydney nodded. "We have a rule. No Lina, no latte."

"Noted. Avoid sugary concoctions when the proprietor is away." Reg set down his drink, so he missed the warning look I shot him about using words like "concoctions" and "proprietor."

"The only times she's not here are pretty much weekends and breakfast," Poe said.

"All the busiest times," Sophia added with a wink. "I'm pretty sure Lina doesn't actually like people that much."

"I'm kind of glad she's off," I admitted. "The last time we were here, I got this sense that she was watching me the whole time. It was kind of creepy."

"Oh, please!" Reg drawled. "Stop pretending you don't like to be looked at."

"I don't mind admirers." I tossed a wink in Dex's direction. "I just prefer them to not be middle-aged shop owners."

The group laughed, all but Dexter, who was suddenly very distracted with packing up his books. Maybe he hadn't seen my wink.

He left a little while later with a friendly, if not very flirty, goodbye, and the twins followed. When Reg and Poe and I finally got up to leave, Reg let Poe walk ahead and stopped me just outside the front door.

"Charlie, can you let Sal know I'll be home a little later?"

"What do you mean? Where are you . . . ?"

I looked over his shoulder to where Poe was waiting on the sidewalk a few yards away, fidgeting with his frames.

"Oh. Are you two . . . do you . . . ?" I lowered my voice. "Is it like a date?"

125

"Yes, I suppose it is. Do you mind?"

I *did* mind. It was Saturday night and Reg had a date, while all I had was a backpack full of still-unfinished homework. But I didn't want him to think I was jealous, so I plastered on a smile.

"Of course not. Obviously, you will share *all* the juicy details later."

"Obviously."

He turned to join Poe, and I crossed the street in the opposite direction, passing the boarded windows of the old cinema and recalling the story about the fire that had gutted it. Where were Reg and Poe supposed to go on a "date" anyway, if this town couldn't even keep a movie theater open?

My phone rang, and Sydney's pink hair and blue eyes filled the screen. She and Sophia invited me over for a movie and makeovers, and I hung up feeling grateful. Slumber party was a little lower on my human bucket list than dating, but anything was better than spending Saturday alone in the slayer's den.

I spun around to holler at Reg that I had plans too, but he was already at the end of the street, lost in conversation with Poe. A small thread of worry tugged at my insides. There was nothing wrong with dating—I had every intention of trying it myself if Dexter ever got around to asking me out—but it was just a diversion while we waited for our sentence to be reversed.

I watched Reg slip his hand into Poe's just before they rounded a corner and disappeared from sight. I hoped my brother still felt the same way.

SIXTEEN

FADE INTO FALL

Sal was right. Time flies when you're fitting in. The first month of school passed in a blur of pop quizzes, party planning, and surprisingly interesting new friends. I finally made it to a mall, where I was able to find casual clothes that were neither plaid nor flannel, and I started combining Prada with my new pedestrian pieces in a look Sydney coined "fashion fusion." Too soon, it was the end of September, on the cusp of October.

When the first crisp afternoon hit, the twins and I were at our usual table at All Hours, fighting off the chill of fall with hot lattes. I'd learned to order mine without sweetener to keep the taste as close to coffee as possible. We were waiting for the boys to join us, but even so, I barely recognized Reg when he burst through the bright yellow door.

His soft stubble had grown into such a full beard, I might have mistaken him for a werewolf if the face behind the beard wasn't still so pretty.

"What is this?" I yanked on his whiskers as he sat down, and he swatted my hand away.

"I'm growing it out. Haven't you noticed?"

Noticed? I'd hardly even seen him in the last few weeks. When he wasn't with Poe, he was tied up with debate practice and play rehearsals. He'd fallen understudy to Poe's Puck, but you'd think he won the lead the way he crowed about it. He was keeping busy enough that he even forgot to torment the teachers—or perhaps that was Poe's influence, as he seemed to be the favorite of everyone on staff at Hope High.

"You look like an animal." I caught his eye and gave him a look to let him know exactly which animal I meant, but he just smiled.

"Well, I think it's distinguished."

I opened my mouth to mock him again, but as I watched him stroke his beard, it struck me how old he looked. He could almost pass for an adult, and the sight of it caught my chest in a vise. We were already aging. The proof of it was there on Reg's face. In a minute, we would be adults, and a minute after that we would be old and wrinkly.

My hands went to my own face, as if I could feel lines sprouting from my skin as easily as facial hair sprouted from Reg's. My fingers found only soft skin and the occasional pimple, reminding me that I was still, mercifully, teen. But the tight feeling in my chest remained and began to pulse in time with my heart, like a clock counting out every passing second.

We'd been mortal nearly a month already and still no word from the Shadow Clan. How many more months would pass before we could file our appeal with the Elders? How many years? It was shocking how fast time moved when you had limited quantities of it.

Reg must have seen something in my face, because he closed a hand over mine. "It's just a beard."

His tone was brighter as he said to Sydney and Sophia, "Charlie has a hard time with change."

"Tell me about it," Sydney said, popping a fresh stick of gum in her mouth and working it down to a ball. "It took us weeks to convince her to buy a pair of flats. I thought we were going to have to teach her to walk in them!"

I tried to mimic Reg's breezy air. "I accept change just fine, if the color and fabric are decent." I propped my pink ballet-slippered feet up on the barrel table as evidence and stuck my tongue out at everyone.

"Where are Dex and Poe?" Sophia asked.

"Poe is still at rehearsal," Reg said. "Not sure about Dex. Maybe he decided not to come."

I took a sip of my latte to help swallow my disappointment.

While Reg and Poe had spent the last few weeks joined at the lips, I hadn't seen Dexter much at all. Our paths only crossed at Poe's locker and the occasional co-ed outing at All Hours, where I struggled to get him in a private conversation. Our exchanges were still flirty, but we never seemed to be alone. It could be the only explanation for why he hadn't asked me out.

Sophia gave me pathetic pity eyes, and I scowled in response. I'd made the mistake of asking one too many questions about Dexter, and the twins had picked up on the fact that I had a "crush." Their words, not mine. Crush implied some kind of defeat, and I was merely delayed, not defeated.

"His loss," I said, with a flip of my hair.

But a second later, Reg's phone lit up with a text message, and I was quick to ask, "Is it Dex?"

Reg smirked. "It's Sal."

"He texts? Who knew?"

I didn't add that as recently as last month, Reg wasn't much of a texter either.

Reg's face changed as he read the message, then he quietly passed me his phone with a warning look—the one he used when he wanted me to stop making a scene. I rolled my eyes. As if Sal could possibly text something scene-worthy. And anyway, when is the last time I made a—

"What?!"

As soon as I read the text, I stood up so abruptly that my drink spilled all over the floor, soaking my pretty pink shoes.

"We have to go," I said.

I scrabbled for napkins and tossed them in the general direction of the spreading coffee.

"Right now."

A little splash under my slipper told me I may have stomped my foot for emphasis.

Unflappable Reg raised one eyebrow.

Scene, his eyebrow said.

I know, my pout replied.

"Is something wrong?" Sydney asked.

"Is your uncle okay?" Sophia added.

"It's a—a—" I stammered, at a rare loss for words.

Reg glided smoothly to my rescue. "It's just something from our parents' life insurance company. A letter."

His eyes met mine, and beneath the stone set of his features, under the still current of his voice, I sensed emotions churning.

I let out a shaky breath. "The letter we've been waiting for."

"Where is it?!" I burst into the cottage, letting the heavy wooden door crunch against the inner stone wall.

"And hello to you," Sal said.

I stepped up to where he was seated at the kitchen table— he'd stopped lurking in doorways waiting for us—and stretched out my palm.

"Hand it over."

I added, with effort, "Please."

Sal patted his shirt and pants pockets, feeling all over. "There was something, now that you mention it, but . . . hmm. I seem to have misplaced it."

My palm remained up, hovering near his face, so that I would only have to thrust my arm forward to land a fingernail in his eye. Not that I really wanted to poke Sal's eyes out anymore, but fantasies of slaying a slayer are a hard habit to shake.

"I don't have time for your games, old-timer."

He started to respond with a quip of his own when he caught sight of Reg over my shoulder and pulled back in surprise.

"Holy beard, Batman! There's a whole forest on your face, boy." He stood for a closer inspection, taking Reg's cheeks and chin in his hand and turning them left and right. Then he said the thing I had feared when I first caught sight of Reg at All Hours. "I wonder if I misjudged your age."

"It's really come in, just in the last week," Reg said, pawing at his beard again.

"It's a nice one, but it won't do for high school. Guess I'll be teaching you how to shave then. I assume you don't know how?"

Reg confirmed with a shake of his head.

"Come on upstairs, I have a spare kit—"

"Excuse me!" I burst out. "As much as I'd like to attack you *both* with razor blades right now, could we please save the shave for after we read our letter?"

Sal raised his hands in apology, and Reg shoved his in his pockets, looking appropriately ashamed to have so quickly forgotten why we'd rushed home.

"It's in your room, on your bed," Sal said.

I lay in the center of the bed, on top of the covers, with the envelope clutched to my chest—the answer we had been waiting weeks for, our last hope, already rumpled from each time I had opened it to read the reply once more.

Through the open bedroom door, in a bathroom down the hall, I could hear Reg and Sal admiring their work.

"I bet you used a straight edge back in your day," Sal said. "Classier, but not as clean as an electric shave."

Reg sighed. "I'm sad to see it go, but Poe will probably like this better."

132

They were only a few yards away, but they sounded like they were in another time and place entirely.

I sat up, my hands making fists around the envelope, and I tried to connect the message inside to the voices down the hall. How could they read it and just go on acting as if nothing had happened, when everything had happened?

I flattened the envelope in my lap—pitch-black paper addressed with beautiful white script, from the Clan of Shadow to Charlotte and Reginald. Pulling the equally black fold of paper from inside the envelope, I spread the page open and read it one more time—in the same lovely white script, a single word in the center of the page.

No.

I crushed the paper between my hands and folded my body over it, collapsing forward onto the bed, where I cried until I soaked the comforter and fell asleep in a puddle of mortal tears.

SEVENTEEN

DOES THIS DRESS MAKE ME LOOK MORTAL?

"It's never been done, Charlie."

"That doesn't mean it *can't* be done."

"It means it's highly unlikely and ill-advised," Reg said.

"You are *ill-advised* to keep disagreeing with me." I kicked at the dirt road, spraying rocks and dust at Reg to drive my threat home.

We were on the now-familiar path to school, but today the walk felt somehow like a death march, and the school more of a prison. Every clan had turned their back on us: Blood, Bone, Starlight, and Shadow. Without a clan representative to sponsor our appeal, we could be trapped in these mortal bodies forever, and Reg was just kind of *meh* about the whole thing, which was really pissing me off.

"You're overreacting," he said now, stepping neatly around the little tornado of dirt I'd created. "There's no need to take drastic measures. We can always write to the Elder Seat, request an appeal without a sponsor. It doesn't hurt to try. But to subvert the council entirely . . ."

I threw up my hands. "I'm just saying we could speed up this process by going directly to the Ancients. They outrank the Elders, right?"

"In a manner of speaking," Reg said. "But there are reasons vampires are governed by our Elders instead of the very oldest among us. The Ancients are . . . unpredictable."

Which was Reg's polite way of saying the Ancients were dangerous and, in some cases, downright crazy. Something happened to immortals who lived thousands of years. Many began to lose control of their powers or, worse, lose touch with reality. When they wrote the Treaty of Annis, the Elders argued that the most unstable Ancients were the smallest children. And no matter what age they had been turned, after a millennium of immortality, a vampire was bestowed the rank of Ancient and "retired" from responsibilities like serving on the Elder Seat. It kept the governing body young, with Elders ranging from five hundred to one thousand years old, but they continued to consult with Ancients who were still of sound mind.

The truth was, even if Reg had agreed with me, neither of us had the first clue about how to get in touch with an Ancient. It was probably some kind of crime to even try, since only the Elders were in contact with them, as a general rule. The Elder Seat occasionally referenced consultation with the Ancients in the drafting of new laws, but most of us had no idea how the Elder-Ancient relationship worked. Did the Ancients—the lucid ones, anyway—still exert any influence, or were they just figureheads, like family patriarchs withering away in some vampire nursing home?

"Fine, we'll start with a request to the Elder Seat," I said. "We'll ask for an appeal without a sponsor . . . even though it's probably a massive waste of time."

"Perhaps we reached out to the clans too early," Reg said. "A few weeks is hardly enough time to show penance."

"*Perhaps* it is too soon, or *perhaps* you just want to spend a little more time with your human boy toy."

"Hmm." Reg frowned the tiniest bit. "You may be right."

"About Poe or about the Ancients?"

"About the word *perhaps*. It does sound a little archaic. Perhaps I'll . . . *maybe* I'll try to make a few adjustments."

I shook my head, feeling that familiar mix of frustration and amusement reserved solely for Reg.

"Just don't get too comfortable," I warned him.

This time, when I kicked dirt his way, he anticipated it and was already halfway across the road laughing before my foot hit the ground.

"Sexy nurse, sexy firefighter, sexy CEO, no sexy mummy."

Sydney thumbed through costumes on a rack, cataloging the series of short, tight skirts and equally skimpy tops.

"We could just wrap her up in ACE bandages," Sophia offered. "What else do you really need to be a mummy?"

We were at the Halloween pop-up store in the closest mall, an hour away from Nowhere, prowling for costumes. Sydney and Sophia had explained that the best strategy was to choose any costume that fit the immortality theme, then give it a slutty spin. When I came up empty, they'd decided for me—an Egyptian queen, mummified but immortal. The only part that sounded remotely appealing was the "queen" bit, but other than that, I couldn't figure out what was so sexy about a corpse.

"I'm really not feeling the mummy thing," I said.

"What about ghost?" Sydney suggested.

I yawned.

"It doesn't have to be boring. You can basically dress up as any famous dead person and say you're their ghost."

"I know!" Sophia snatched a plastic gavel off a shelf cluttered with props. "You could be the ghost of Ruth Bader Ginsburg, back to haunt the patriarchy."

"Respect to RBG," Sydney said, fist over her heart, "but that is not a sexy costume."

Sophia jabbed her twin with the gavel. "Not everyone wants to be half naked on Halloween, Syd. Charlie, what about a grim reaper? You could do a black hood attached to a long dress with a high slit . . ."

"No." Sydney blew a bubble as pink as her hair. "Long black dress? She'll just look like a vampire."

Oh please.

Such a stereotype, assuming vampires only wore black. I looked good in all kinds of colors. A memory flashed through my mind—the mound of dark clothes piled on the bed in the cottage, Reg criticizing my all-black wardrobe.

"I want something more colorful," I declared out loud.

"Something bright and just . . . pretty."

"Fairies are pretty!" Sydney said.

Sophia added, "And according to Celtic myth, they are immortal."

We found the fairy aisle, exploding with pinks and pastels and shimmer and glitter. It felt utterly un-me, and wasn't that the whole point of Halloween?

"Yes." I smiled. "This is perfect."

Sydney inspected a lock of her pink hair. "Maybe I should be a fairy too."

"No!" Sophia cried. "You promised to do angel and demon with me!" She gave me a sheepish look. "It's a twin thing. But you will make an awesome fairy."

I plucked a rainbow-colored crown off a shelf, settled it into my brown waves.

"Fairy *queen*," I corrected.

"Nice crown."

I turned to seen Dexter ambling down the aisle.

Sophia tugged her sister's arm. "Hey, Syd, let's check out the angel section again. I'm thinking of getting a different halo."

"I thought I was the angel," Sydney protested.

The twins said hello to Dexter as they elbowed around him in the narrow space, then Sydney winked at me over his shoulder before Sophia yanked her out of sight.

Subtle.

"Sooo . . ." Dexter shoved his hands in his pockets. "Shopping again?"

138

"Again? You keeping track of my whereabouts, O'Shea?"

He matched my flirtatious tone. "I just noticed that the twin's wardrobe has changed recently. I figured that was your influence. You all seem to spend a lot of time at the mall."

"Not changed," I corrected. "Improved."

Dexter's smile faltered. "It's sometimes hard to tell when you're joking."

I wasn't joking, but it was clear I'd said the wrong thing, so I scrambled for something else to say, something witty and charming and flirty and—

"Halloween costumes!" I blurted. "We're here for Halloween costumes."

Something other than that.

"Uh, yeah," he said, the corner of his mouth tipped up. "Kind of figured you weren't here to get groceries."

I pulled a dress at random from the rack. "I'm going as a fairy," I said. "Sydney claims they're immortal."

Dexter nodded appreciatively. "Cool."

"A *sexy* fairy," I added.

"Is there any other kind?"

"What are you wearing?" I asked.

"Not sure yet. Costumes aren't really my thing."

"Oh no," I said, stepping closer and putting on my prettiest pout. I knew it was pretty. I'd been practicing it in the mirror on my new lips, fuller than before. "But you can't get into the after-party dance without a costume. And what about that nice girl you planned to dance with?"

He played along, his big smile beaming down at me. "Are you the nice girl?"

"Me?" I let out a breathy laugh. "God, no. Nice girls are so boring."

Dexter's mouth twitched, as if he wanted to say something.

Or maybe he wants to kiss me.

I started to close my eyes, but instead of a kiss, Dexter backed away, opening up the distance I had closed between us.

Where was he going? He couldn't possibly be leaving without asking me out. Again!

The anticipation was maddening, and I couldn't wait one second longer.

"Are we ever going on a date?" I blurted.

His eyes widened, but I rushed on before he could respond. "I don't typically ask guys out, but it seemed like maybe you weren't going to—"

"I wasn't."

His words were a slap. "What?"

"I mean, I was," he said. "I was actually going to ask you to be my Halloween date, and then . . . I like you, Charlie, but . . ."

But? BUT?!

How could there possibly be a *but*?

As much as I was dying to know the answer to that question, I wouldn't give him the satisfaction of explaining. This moment was humiliating enough without watching him bumble through some *let's be friends* apology speech.

"Relax, O'Shea. I thought maybe we could hang out, but it's

fine." I forced a smile that hurt my cheeks. "And obviously, I already have a date to the dance."

He looked confused by my lie, and maybe even a little disappointed, but he recovered quickly.

"Of course you do," he said, with his usual confidence and a cool smile. "I'm not surprised. Cute new girl from the big city . . . I bet you got a hundred offers."

"Well, not a hundred."

Not even one.

Dexter moved slowly backward down the aisle, still smiling. "And I have a date too."

What?

"So we both have dates. Good. That's good." He reached the end of the aisle, and his expression finally faltered. He caught my eye and held it. "Then, I guess . . . maybe next year."

"Right, next year," I echoed.

"See ya, Charlie."

And he was gone.

Next year? I closed a fist around the sparkly purple dress in my hand. *Next year, I will be immortal again and will have forgotten all about you, Dexter O'Shea.*

My heart skipped, and I felt that weight of mortality that seemed to come in waves.

I hope.

A hand touched my shoulder, startling me into dropping the dress.

"It's his loss," Sydney said.

I busied myself with picking up the dress and shoving it back onto the rack so that the twins would not see me flustered. Unlike the pout, *flustered* was not a look I had practiced.

"You may be more woman than Dex can handle," Sydney said.

"He's definitely intimidated," Sophia agreed.

Dexter didn't seem the least bit intimidated by me, but girls lying to their friends to make them feel better was one human custom I could get on board with. I let them sling their identical arms around my sagging shoulders and leaned into the support.

An awful, ugly doubt was creeping around the edges of my confidence. Was it possible my power over boys was an immortal charm that had been ripped away when we stepped through Sal's gate?

My lips met in a grim line. "Boys like that are the worst part of being . . . um . . . in Iowa."

"And girls like us are the best part," Sydney said, giving me a squeeze.

I returned her one-arm hug. I could not agree more.

As much as I appreciated the sisterhood of solidarity, I didn't want Sydney and Sophia to see how truly mortified I was. There was only one person I could trust with that, and when I got back to the village, I went looking for him in the hills behind the cottage.

The landscape had changed in recent weeks from vibrant

green to warmer golden hues. Here and there, a bright red tree screamed for attention, and the fields in the distance were flat and brown, dotted with pale yellow rolls of hay. I found Reg sprawled out on a blanket at the crest of a hill, reading a book and waiting for the sun to set. I flopped down beside him in a dramatic swoon.

"If humiliation is on our human agenda, you can check it off my list. I've just had the most embarrassing moment of my entire life."

Reg didn't look up from his book. "Your mortal life or your immortal life?"

I reached up and snatched the paperback out of his hands. "It was embarrassing enough for *all* the lives."

"Do tell."

I proceeded to recount the costume-shop encounter in detail.

"And after I said I had a date, *he* said he had a date, so he will definitely be there, which means now I actually have to *find* a date, or he'll know I lied!"

Reg's face was folded into a mask of concentration. "So let me make sure I get this straight. Sydney and Sophia think fairies are immortal? That's utterly ridiculous. Fairies have the life span of a—"

"Reg, pay attention!"

"Look, Charlie, if you want a date to this *hoopla*, I'm sure you can take your pick of any boy at school. But if you don't want to go with anyone else, don't. I see no need to scramble to find a date."

He picked up his book and flipped through the pages to find where he'd left off.

"And if Dex sees I'm alone?"

"Say you got stood up."

I huffed. "I do *not* get stood up."

"It's an imaginary date."

"I don't get stood up on any kind of date!"

Reg laughed and gave up trying to find his spot, tossing his book to the side in favor of his phone. He bent his head over the screen, texting as he talked. "Has it occurred to you that he doesn't have a date either?"

I perked up at that idea. "No. Do you think so?"

Reg shrugged, eyes still on his screen.

"Why would he lie?" I asked. "That's ridiculous."

"I concur." Reg shot me a pointed sideways glance before returning to his phone. He was grinning to himself as his thumbs flew over the screen.

"Really embracing technology now, aren't you?"

"It's Poe's preferred method of communication."

"Communication or flirtation?"

"One and the same."

"Just don't send any dirty pics."

Reg looked up finally. "Dirty pics?"

I pointed below the waistline, and Reg tutted.

"Oh, Charlie. How crass."

But when he went back to texting, his private smile returned, and this time it looked a little mischievous.

I leaned back on my elbows, face tipped up to the sky. My own chance at mischief seemed to have disappeared, and with it, my primary distraction. The flirtation with Dex was one of the things that had kept me busy as summer faded to fall, but I swore I would be immortal again before this scenery change to winter white. If not, I might just lie down right there on the hill until the snow buried me for good.

EIGHTEEN

A PRISON & A PARADE

When the bell rang to end final period Monday, I was counting all the ways I could drain Madame Bissett's blood and make it look like an accident once I was vampire again. What kind of teacher gave two days' notice for an exam? I had way too much going on this week to cram a bunch of conjugations into my head, only to forget them all the next day anyway.

I gave her my most evil glare on the way out the door and didn't break eye contact until I ran smack into Poe.

"Graceful," he said.

Then he smiled over my shoulder. "Bon après-midi, Madame Bissett!"

"Bonjour, Monsieur Dupont!" she called back.

"How do you say 'kiss ass'?" I snarled under my breath.

Poe laughed and looped my arm through his, pulling me down the hall. "Lèche-cul, and guilty as charged. I have a message for you from the sisters Carlone. They wish for you to join them on the fifty-yard line for an impromptu committee meeting."

"The fifty-yard line?"

"The football field. I'm here to escort you, as it is surprisingly tricky to find for such a giant plot of land."

And it was soon obvious why. Poe dragged me past the east gym, where junior girls were subjected to the torture of physical education twice a week, and led me right through the mega gym on the school's west end—a cavernous space with glossy floors unmarred by scuffs or scratches. This gym, it seemed, was too fancy for PE, though inexplicably, it was fine for us to allow girls in spike heels and all manner of costume glitter and glue for the dance portion of the Halloween Hoopla.

Large double doors leading out to the school's front lawn sat open, but Poe steered me in the opposite direction, to a small side door practically hidden under the gym's collapsible bleachers. The door was unmarked but lit from above by a simple red exit sign. It looked like the kind of door you weren't supposed to touch because it would probably set off an alarm.

Poe pushed it open, and my eyes soared upward, taking in the sight beyond the threshold. We stepped onto a wide swath of grass between two long, high brick walls on either side, stretching at least two stories up to open blue sky and extending out from the school, like a tunnel with the top down. The walls were the same brick red as the school and seemed to go on forever, the football field only just visible at the end.

Poe must have seen the wonder on my face as I took it all in, because he launched into his tour guide mode, detailing how the fortresslike walls came to be. He explained that when the

147

new school was built, the state-of-the-art football field was surrounded by a common chain-link fence, but that wasn't enough to keep the riffraff out.

"People kept using it to picnic and party and, well . . . you know."

"Know what?" I asked.

"Let's just say, don't walk on that fifty-yard line with bare feet. It might be . . . sticky."

"Ew."

We made our way down the high-walled tunnel, and when the field was in full view, I could see the soaring walls surrounded the entire arena. I'd noticed the walls on the school welcome folder but hadn't realized how tall they were. It was a far more imposing sight in person. Poe pointed across the length of the field, to a high brick arch and a giant iron gate, nearly as wide as a two-lane highway.

"That's the only way in for the public, and this"—he lifted his hands to the brick walls around us—"this is the only way in from the school."

A stray thought crossed my mind that Hope High would make an excellent lair for the Drakes or another vampire house. We were always looking for places with strong defenses.

I spotted the planning committee gathered in the stands and waved. Sydney popped up from her seat and jogged across a corner of the field to meet us at the tunnel entrance.

"Special delivery," Poe said, with a flourish of his hands in my direction.

"Took long enough," Sydney said.

"I was giving her a tour of the fortress."

"It's all a little prisonlike, if you ask me," she said. "But hey, it keeps the neighbors off the grass, right?"

Poe checked his watch. "I have to get to rehearsal."

"Tell my brother hello," I said. "You see him more than I do."

Above his glasses, Poe's eyebrows wagged suggestively. "I'll send your love."

"Gross. Just stay off the fifty-yard line, okay?"

"I make no promises."

Up in the bleachers, the freshman and sophomore committee members were giving an update on float building progress. As Sydney and I joined the group, one girl was nursing the pads of her fingers and complaining of permanent glue damage from the thousands of pomps needed to build the float.

"Pomps?" I asked.

"Tissue paper," Sophia said, scooting over for me to sit.

"Tiny, tissuey, torture devices," the girl spat.

Sophia made a check mark in a notebook perched on her knees. "Okay, in addition to the Hope High float, we've sold entries for most of the usual suspects: 4-H club, Village Veterinary Clinic, the dentist—"

"*The* dentist?" I asked.

"We just have the one," Sydney confirmed.

Sophia continued, "American Legion, Future Farmers, the *Nowhere Gazette*—"

"What's that?" someone asked. It was Mark, the boy who'd lobbied for a *Purge*-themed parade float.

"The newspaper."

"What newspaper?" Sydney asked.

"We have a newspaper?" another girl added.

There was a pause as the group exchanged shrugs, then Sophia zipped through the rest of the names and moved on to the list of bands scheduled to play during the street party. A jazz group was nixed for being too tame, and Mark shot down a rock-and-roll group made up of freshmen who couldn't actually play their instruments.

"And inside the gym, the AV club will play DJ for the after-party and also take care of the sound system for announcements both inside and outside," Sophia said, making another check on her sheet.

"We've got you covered," Mark said. "The audiovisual crew is renting some killer speakers. This party's going to be the loudest thing in Iowa—maybe even the loudest thing you've ever heard."

I had seen the Beatles at the Hollywood Bowl, circa 1964, along with a few thousand other screaming teenage girls, so I highly doubted that.

I tuned out as Sophia made her way methodically through her checklist, detailing duties from designing flyers to directing traffic. My eyes drifted out over the field, wondering why we couldn't just have the party here, though I supposed it would be impossible to stage floats in the arena without trashing the turf. It was a shame, though, because the field was by far the nicest, newest thing I had seen in all of Nowhere.

"Can you do that, Charlie?"

The sound of my name brought me back to the conversation. "Sorry, what?"

"Can you ask Lina about the coffee cart?" Sophia said. She sounded impatient, so I didn't want to admit that I had no idea what she was talking about.

Fortunately, Sydney came to my rescue. "We're going through the list of food trucks and vendors for the street party. We're wondering if Lina will run a coffee cart, but she always says no. Says Halloween is not her thing."

"And you think she'll listen to me?"

"We think you won't take no for an answer," Sydney said.

Well, that was true.

"Plus, you're so mature," Sophia added. "You've got that whole big-city vibe, so she might take the request more seriously coming from you."

I pursed my lips to the side, eyeing the twins. "Are you trying to flatter me into this chore?"

"Is it working?" Sydney asked.

"Sure, fine," I said, unable to suppress a smile. "I'll ask her."

I didn't know why Sydney and Sophia thought I would have any more luck with Lina than they did. If the coffee shop owner said no to the girls she already knew and liked, why would she say yes to a stranger?

I recalled, with a shiver, the way Lina had watched me so intently during my first visit to All Hours. Maybe to someone that strange, everyone was a stranger.

NINETEEN

BLOOD & BONE, STARLIGHT & SHADOW

Poe Dupont was barely five-four in heels, but he was a giant onstage. I sat in the back of the Hope High auditorium after school the next day, waiting for Reg and Poe to finish rehearsals so we could walk to All Hours together. I had planned to use the time to prepare for tomorrow's French exam, but the study guide sat forgotten on the seat next to me as Poe pulled me in with a presence that filled the auditorium.

Most of the cast had quit for the day, and just Poe remained onstage, delivering *A Midsummer Night's Dream*'s famous final monologue to an audience of three: Reg, the director, and me.

He had to get through it only once clean before we could leave, but he kept starting and stopping.

"It just doesn't feel like the rest of the script," he called from the stage. "It's not coming out the same."

The director—I was pretty sure he was the drama coach, choir teacher, and maybe even the bandleader—stood to reply. "It's meant to feel different. Remember, in this moment, you are not Puck, the mischievous fairy, but Poe, the humble player."

I could hear Poe's smirk, even if I couldn't see it from my

seat in the back. "Well, therein lies the problem, sir. I've been accused of being both mischievous and a fairy, but never humble."

The director laughed in response, then gestured at Reg, who hopped up to join Poe onstage.

"Perhaps a duet, just for rehearsal," the director said.

There was a soft moment, where Poe and Reg turned to each other, lost to the audience, to all but each other, and I felt a painful twinge. I wanted Reg to be happy, and if I could have picked the thing to make him happy, I would have picked him a Poe . . . but at what cost?

Fortunately, we had just written our appeal to the Elder Seat that morning, otherwise I might've been worried about him changing his mind, wishing to stay a little longer, maybe even forever. Reg had tried to convince me to wait, that it was too soon for a direct appeal, but watching him now onstage, so comfortable in his human skin, I was glad I'd insisted. Our message was already on its way to the council. It had no clan sponsor to carry it, but I hoped we'd struck just the right tone of reverence and desperation. At the very least, they might give us an audience just for the fun of watching us squirm in person.

There was a quiet pause onstage, broken by the opening line of Poe's monologue, and any tension I was feeling released, unwinding with the soft power of his voice.

"'If we shadows have offended, think but this, and all is mended, that you have but slumbered here while these visions did appear.'"

Reg took the next line, his own performance not holding the weight of Poe's, but carrying that same softness, meant not for the audience, but the boy next to him.

"'And this weak and idle theme, no more yielding but a dream, Gentles, do not reprehend. If you pardon, we will mend.'"

"'And, as I am an honest Puck—'" Poe broke away from my brother's gaze, to wave the script at the director. "See, I'm still Puck, not a player. It feels like the delivery should be . . ."

I tuned out while Poe and the director debated, my coffee craving now top of mind. The human need for coffee was not unlike the vampire need for blood. Going too long without either made me weak, tired, and cranky. Strange that a thing that defined us as vampire was not so inhuman after all.

A short while later, I was curled up in my favorite chair at All Hours, a cup of hot coffee cradled between my hands and Dexter present to keep Reg and Poe from excessive PDA. Of course, I wouldn't have minded a little public display of affection from Dexter to me, but after the Halloween-store incident, I was actively fighting the urge to flirt. It didn't matter how green his eyes were, how defined his muscles, how natural his charm— if he wasn't interested enough to ask me out, there was clearly something wrong with him.

I tossed my hair and humphed a little.

"Problem?" Poe asked, catching my pout.

All three boys looked up at me, and I felt my face flush. Avoiding eye contact with Dexter, I stammered, "It's just too quiet in here today. Isn't it? Quieter than usual. Super quiet. Yeah. Huh."

Reg and Poe exchanged looks, and Reg said, "It *was* quiet, anyway."

Dexter sipped his latte, his face unreadable.

"Well, you're right that it's quiet here without Syd and Soph," Poe said.

The twins had missed school to attend the funeral of an aunt who'd passed away a few days before. They kept saying it had been coming for some time but was still sudden, and everyone else nodded as if this made sense. Reg and I had asked Sal about it, but he couldn't manage to effectively explain how death could be simultaneously expected and unexpected.

I actually had zero interest in learning the nuance of death and every intention of reclaiming my immortality as soon as possible. Still, I didn't want to seem like an insensitive monster to my new friends, so I had googled something appropriate to say to Sydney and Sophia, and it seemed to work, since they hugged me and cried on my shoulder.

My words may have come from the internet, but the hug I'd given them in return was all mine. I wished I could save them from the tragedy and suffering of mortality. During my quietest moments, in that waking dream space just before sleep, I imagined returning for them once I was vampire again, to offer them the gift that had been given to me so many years ago. But they were too young, of course. It was a total violation of the Treaty of Annis, and with my luck, I'd just get caught and shoved right back through Sal's stupid, magical, human-making fence.

Something of my thoughts must have shown on my face, because Dexter asked if I was okay.

"I'm fine," I snapped. How annoying of him to notice me now when I was probably making some sad-girl face. Sad girl was not a good look for me.

He didn't flinch from my sharp reply. "I just meant your parents."

Oh, right. Maybe sad girl was the appropriate look after all.

"Of course!" Poe said, gripping Reg's hand.

I barely had time to be annoyed with this PDA, because he quickly leaned forward and wrapped his other hand around mine. His grip was tight and sincere, and it brought a prickle of tears to my eyes. Why Poe's sympathy over the death of my imaginary parents would make my eyes want to leak was inexplicable. Tears remained an utter mystery to me.

Poe said, "This must be bringing up terrible memories for you both. It's okay if you don't want to talk about it."

"Talk about what?" Lina was looming over us, a serving tray tucked under her arm and her wild blond hair escaping from the haphazard bun on the back of her head.

"Charlie and Reginald lost their parents recently," Poe said. "It's unimaginable."

"So much for not talking about it," Dexter muttered, shooting me an apologetic look.

"Lost your parents, huh?" Lina asked. She didn't sound

remotely sympathetic. In fact, she could have been talking about the weather.

I knew she was eccentric, but that was just downright rude.

Poe managed to hold both pity and curiosity in his eyes, while Reg's gaze communicated an intense warning to be careful how I responded.

I sniffed at Lina. "We don't like to talk about it. It's very painful, as you can imagine."

Lina stared at me inscrutably, holding my gaze so that it felt impossible to look away.

"Terrible thing to lose a parent. Almost seems like it would be better to have the mind erased to forget the person, rather than feel the ache of losing them."

I didn't have to look at Reg to know his face was probably a startled mirror of my own.

"That would be awful," Dexter said to Lina. "I would be so sad to forget someone I lost."

"But you wouldn't be sad," Lina argued. "You wouldn't remember."

Poe shook his head. "I'm with Dex. 'Better to have loved and lost,' as Tennyson said, 'than to have never loved at all.'"

"Depends how you see it. Could be a kindness." She patted Poe on the shoulder and wandered back behind the coffee counter. Reg and I locked eyes behind her back and held one of our silent conversations.

You hear that stuff about memory?

I'm sitting right here.

157

It's like she knows about vampires.

Or she's just crazy.

Oh, she's definitely crazy.

Maybe it took a crazy person to think it was a kindness to erase someone you'd loved and lost from your memory. And maybe my dream of turning Sydney and Sophia immortal was selfish, even cruel. To make them forget their family, their friends . . .

My breath caught as I wondered if I'd had friends like this before—friends I had forgotten, wiped from my mind like cobwebs to be simply swept away.

The idea that Sydney and Sophia and Poe and even Dexter could be so easily erased made me uncomfortable. But at least I would always have Reg. Though, as I watched my brother leaning into Poe, hands still linked, faces close, the doubt I'd felt in the theater crept back in. Would Reg be as willing to sever these mortal ties?

I asked him as much on the way home, and he brushed me off with a nonanswer.

"We have time enough to worry about that."

"But that's the whole point, Reg! Time is running out."

We stepped to the side of the road to make way for a passing car, a small cloud of exhaust creating a hazy view of a "No More, No Less" bumper sticker on the car's rear end.

"Every day, every *minute* we are mortal, we are losing time," I said. "Time is the entire curse of mortality. Time killed Sydney and Sophia's aunt."

"We are far from death."

"We're closer than we were a month ago."

We reached the cottage mid-argument, dropping our bags on the kitchen floor and slinging our jackets over chairs. Sal grunted a greeting and gestured for us to clean up our mess.

"I'll concede that point," Reg said, moving his coat and bag to their proper, tidy spot. "But worrying over something you can't control will only hurry those human wrinkles."

My hands went instinctively to my face, and he grinned, casually amused in that infuriating way only Reg could be. But just behind that grin I saw a small flicker of doubt, a crack in my brother's cool facade. It was there and gone in an instant, and when he spoke, there was no trace of it, his tone as self-assured as ever.

"Whatever happens, at least we'll face it together."

"What if *nothing* happens? What if they turn us down? What if—"

"Be patient, Charlie. Everything's going to work out."

"Well, I guess you'll know soon enough," Sal said, tossing something on the kitchen table. "That came for you today."

The envelope was abnormally long and slim, the paper a shimmery white that gave off flashes of light with every tiny movement. It was addressed, insultingly, not to Charlotte and Reginald Drake of the Bone Clan but to simply "the Smiths."

The taunting address should have been the first clue to what was inside, but I tore it open with wasted hope in my heart anyway. The inner paper had none of the sparkle of the envelope, and it was emblazoned with the Elder Seat motto in stark black ink:

By Blood and Bone, By Starlight and Shadow

Below the motto, a simple message read:

Dearest Charlotte and Reginald Smith,

Your request has been carefully considered, but as you may know, custom—if not law—dictates that any appeal of judgment must be sponsored by a representative of a recognized vampire clan. As such, it is the council's decision to decline to hear your appeal.

Best wishes to you both in your new life.

Most sincerely,

The Representatives of the Elder Seat

"Oh sure," I sneered. "They considered it *carefully*. So carefully I bet they gave themselves a paper cut with how fast they threw our letter in the trash."

Reg tilted his head to one side. "Vampires don't get paper cuts—"

"THAT'S NOT THE POINT!"

"Charlie, calm down." Reg held his hands up and backed away as if I were a bomb about to go off.

Because I was.

"How can you take this so—so—*casually*. Like you're not insulted or furious or—or like you don't even care at all!"

"It's not that I don't care, Charlie. It's that I am unsurprised. And neither should you be. Sal warned us we were unlikely to get an appeal without a sponsor."

"So, what then?" I asked, my shouting taking on a desperate edge. "What do we do now?"

Reg turned his hands from their defensive position to a palms-up, helpless gesture.

I could not look at it, could not bear the fact that while his hands looked helpless, his face looked indifferent. I wheeled around to Sal, instead.

"Well?" I demanded. "What's next?"

Sal stroked his beard, a look of actual pity in his eyes. "You know how I feel about your quest to get back to that . . . *life*. But still, I'm sorry this didn't work out the way you hoped."

"Don't you pity me!"

"Charlie!" Reg admonished. "There's no need to be rude."

I spun back to Reg. "It's him, isn't it? He's the reason you don't care."

"Who? Sal?"

"Poe." I was breathing heavy now. An annoying but well-timed reminder of my incessant mortality. "You don't really want to be vampire again. Because of him!"

"Charlie, that's ridiculous. Of course I want—"

"I don't believe you!"

Reg paused, a hurt look on his face. When he finally spoke, his voice was quiet. "And since when do we not trust each other?"

"Since I can see with my own eyes how much you're enjoying the humans."

"Not all the humans," he argued. "I'm not too fond of some of the teachers."

"But you're plenty fond of Poe."

"As are you," Reg said. "And of Dexter and Sydney and Sophia."

He was dodging the question, and we both knew it.

Tears threatened to flow, but I held them back, forcing them to retreat to whatever endless pool they came from. I would not cry again.

"You've been with me a century," I growled at Reg. "You've been with him five minutes."

With those words, the tears trying to escape my eyes miraculously dried up, and I celebrated a brief, silent victory over this one, insidious, human condition. Then I dropped the Elder letter to the floor and raced out into the comfort of night.

TWENTY

DARKNESS, MY OLD FRIEND

I hit the road running, gravel grinding under my shoes and spitting out behind me like tiny bullets. I turned right, away from the village, away from Reg and Sal, away from all the crumpled letters of rejection, away from the hilly landscape where the sun rose every morning, counting off one more day in the march toward certain death. I ran as fast as my human legs could move, until blood pounded in my ears and my heart hammered at such a pace, I couldn't tell one beat from the next.

I slowed to a walk, panting and cursing at the cornfields about betrayal and injustice until eventually my breath came normally, and the only sound in my ears was the crispy rustle of the cornstalks in the night breeze. The fields had turned from lush green to brown and brittle in the six short weeks since we'd arrived in Iowa. Just another living thing doomed on a relentless path that humans called the "circle of life."

More like a straight line with a dead end.

The narrow lane between towers of corn crops opened eventually into a yawning abyss. The light from a low-hanging, nearly full moon showed an endless stretch of field in either direction, where the crop had already been harvested. My feet wandered off the road and into the field, the darkness wrapping around me like a favorite old blanket. Except unlike a blanket, I felt a chill out here in the open, without the cornstalks to hold back the cool fall air. I felt exposed, vulnerable.

My feet stopped, and my mind caught up a split second later. Vulnerable like a human. Like vampire prey.

I searched the dark all around me, half hoping to see my immortal kin emerging from the shadows, but none came. Still, it wasn't such a wild hope, was it? There had to be one or two vampires around here. I would not have said that a month ago, but if I'd learned one thing, between a retired slayer's cabin for wayward souls and oddball coffee shop owners who seemed to know more than they should, Nowhere, Iowa, wasn't such a normal place after all.

If the Elders would not reverse our punishment, perhaps it was time to seek immortality the old-fashioned way. I pushed up the sleeves of my sweater and pulled the scarf from my neck, exposing my strongest pulse points to any vampire within hearing distance. A young woman alone in the dark with a bare neck was almost irresistible.

And young men, too. My mind reached back to the boy whose blood had been too sweet to stop, who we'd nearly drained, who'd been administered a memory fade so thorough he couldn't remember his own friends and family. Except when I pictured his face now, I saw Dexter; I saw Poe. A tiny pinch of guilt squeezed at my heart, gave it a little twist. Guilt was a mortal condition, rarely inflicting vampires, and it had to be the worst thing about being human. I would be happy to be rid of it. I just needed one thirsty friend. . . .

The seconds ticked by, and the only movement was the occasional scurry of a field mouse or a curious rabbit poking its head out from its hole. The rest of the night remained devastatingly still.

"COME ON!" I let loose a wild, guttural cry. "WHAT ARE YOU WAITING FOR?!"

My chest heaved in and out, and my body shook, every muscle taut. "I'M RIGHT HERE!"

But of course, they weren't coming. Even if there were immortals within earshot, they wouldn't dare violate the treaty and turn a teenager. Any greedy vamp who did find me would be more likely to drain me than change me. Defeated, I knotted my scarf and wrapped my arms around my body, partly to protect against cold and partly as a reflex, as I imagined what it might feel like to be drained of my blood. It was an immortal power I'd thought little of, until I found myself potentially on the receiving end.

A snapping sound in the corn rows to my left caused my heart to race—but not in the way I expected. It pounded not with excitement but with sudden fear.

What if it hurts?

Another snap . . . and an unnatural shift in the stalks . . . something moving.

What about Reg?

I was about to run for the road when a figure glided out of the corn and into the field, between me and the pavement.

Stupid, stupid!

I was trapped, outmatched. I wondered if I would have time to speak, to explain who I was and make my case before it was over, before all my human blood was gone, before—

"Who's there?"

My fear evaporated with that familiar voice, even as the figure took form and stepped into the moonlight, revealing the sharp angles of Dexter's face.

"Oh, it's you," I said.

"You were expecting someone else? In a cornfield, in the middle of the night?"

"Says the guy hanging out in a cornfield, in the middle of the night."

Dexter's face cracked into a smile that looked a little like it had snuck past his lips, even as he tried to hold it back. He dragged a long strand of wheat or grass through his hand, for once looking more like a boy from Iowa than California. Maybe it was because he appeared a little less golden in the moonlight.

But no less hot, I noted. The thought felt like Dexter's smile— escaping against my will.

"So, really," he said. "Why are you out here? Everything okay?"

"I got in a fight with Reg. Needed some air."

Sometimes the truth was the easiest lie.

"And you?" I asked.

Dexter stepped closer so that I could make out his features now with or without the moonlight. He was quiet when he spoke, but his voice carried out into the field around us.

"This was our farm—my family's farm. We sold it last year."

"Right," I said, remembering. "Your parents wanted you to be closer to friends, less isolated."

He shrugged. "That's the party line, anyway."

"It's not the truth?"

"Not the whole truth."

I waited.

He tossed his fidget grass to the side and shoved his hands in his pockets instead.

"The truth is my parents sold out. It's tough to keep a family farm afloat, and a corporation finally made an offer they couldn't refuse."

That didn't sound entirely right. An offer you couldn't refuse was the kind I had been seeking just minutes ago. But I didn't correct Dexter.

"How much is unrefusable?" I asked.

"I'm not sure 'unrefusable' is a word."

"Thanks, Poe."

Dexter laughed.

"Enough for my dad to retire. Enough to pay for all four years of college."

"That's not so bad."

"I guess. But it was still a shock when they sold. One day, my dad said he'd give up the farm over his dead body and they'd have to plow right over him. The next day, we were moving to town and building a big new house." Dexter paced the ground, stepping from row to row with a sure foot, even in the dark. "He doesn't like to talk about it. Whenever I bring it up, he gets really annoyed and just keeps repeating 'It's all for the best, and we should be grateful' over and over like a broken record. I think he feels guilty, so I try not to give him a hard time about it. . . ."

"But . . ." I turned in a slow circle to follow the path he was cutting around me.

"But I miss it. I miss the wide-open space, I miss the smells—"

"Of manure? Agree to disagree."

We laughed, and it seemed neither of us was trying to hold it back now.

"I come at night when no one can see me, since it's technically trespassing, but it doesn't feel like that. It just feels like . . ."

"Home," I finished.

He stopped circling and looked me in the eye. "Yeah."

I fidgeted with my scarf, tying and untying the knot at my neck. "I know something about being ripped out of your home, not welcome to return."

"New York."

Close enough.

"So, you know how it feels," he said.

"Kind of like all these cornstalks after the harvest." I gestured to the nothingness around us. "Cut down and disposed of, like so much garbage."

"Actually, most farmers till the fields, using the remains of the crop to prepare the land for next year's harvest."

"Whatever," I said. "It was a metaphor."

"In some places, they burn the—"

"*Okay,* future farmer of America." I laughed. "You got me. I don't know what happens to corn after it . . ."

I started to say *dies,* but the word stuck in my throat.

Dexter mistook my shiver for a chill.

"It's getting cold," he said.

"Is this the part where you offer me your jacket?"

"Nah, this is the part where I suggest we go somewhere to warm up."

"What's even open this late?" I asked.

He spread his hands. "All Hours, of course."

TWENTY-ONE

AWAKE AT ALL HOURS

I paused outside All Hours, its lacquered door a sunny yellow, even in the dark. "This is a little embarrassing. We were just here a few hours ago."

"Yeah, it's almost like there's nowhere else to go around here." Dexter winked and opened the door, stepping aside to let me through first. So, he hadn't offered me his coat, but apparently chivalry wasn't entirely dead.

"It's not the first time I've hit up All Hours twice in one day," he said. "And Lina likes the company. She doesn't get many nighttime guests."

As if on cue, Lina came out from the kitchen, throwing a towel over her shoulder. She waved at Dexter, but when she noticed me, her hand faltered in the air, and her eyes darted quickly back and forth between the two of us.

"Oh, great." Dexter leaned close to whisper in my ear, the way he had on my first visit to the coffeehouse, and I felt the same delicious tingle I'd felt that day—incomparable to anything in the immortal world. "She's going to tease us. Brace yourself."

But the laser focus of Lina's gaze betrayed more than a passing interest in the mating habits of teenagers. She was looking at me in that curious way she had the first day we met, like she was trying to figure out what I was doing here.

You and me, both, lady.

"Well, don't just stand there lurking in the doorway," she scolded. "You're blocking all the other customers."

Lina burst out laughing at her own joke, the sound echoing through the empty coffee shop. She was an oddball, but that laugh was pretty contagious, and even I had to crack a smile.

Lina turned up the music on the coffee shop's speakers, to give us a little ambiance. Then she wiped down our usual table, but Dexter led me instead to a smaller table for two, positioned in front of a large window, framed in white lights. The setup was so small that our knees touched under the table, but neither of us turned to the side to make room for the other.

I studied Dexter's face as he ordered us drinks. He had a few blemishes in his golden skin, and his hair was a little too long to be trendy, but damn, the boy had a jawline like a Hollywood movie star and an air of confidence that was just short of cocky.

I didn't drop my eyes when he caught me staring. I was confident too, and I was done playing games.

If my gaze made him uncomfortable, he didn't show it. He leaned forward, elbows on the table, and asked, "Do you really have a date for Halloween?"

"Do you?"

"I asked you first."

"No."

He grinned. "I guess we're both liars, then."

It seemed like Dex was done playing games too.

"So, the fight with Reg," he said. "Everything okay?"

"It will be," I said. "Do you have siblings?"

"Nope. Only child."

"Lucky."

"Lonely."

"I guess I wouldn't know. I've always had a brother."

Well, maybe not always, but for as long as I can remember.

"I don't want to get in your business," Dexter said, "but you and Reg seem really tight, so I hope you work it out."

"It's not just Reg," I said. I took a breath, and when I let it out, I exhaled a whole bunch of truth. "It's Iowa and school and everything new. It's being cooped up in a cottage that feels like a prison, and even when I step outside, each way I walk out our front door just takes me to another cornfield. It's Sydney and Sophia at a funeral. It's Reg onstage, doing better here than I am. It's Sal telling us what to do and when to be home. It's starting a new life when I never asked to stop my old one."

Dexter let out a low whistle and leaned back in his chair. "Well, I don't think I can sell a city girl on Iowa, and I definitely won't say the right thing about funerals and death to someone who has lost her parents, but I can tell you this much: your brother is a cool dude, but he is not 'doing better' than you are just because he joined a few more extracurricular activities. And Sal—he's your uncle, right?"

I nodded.

"He was a bachelor with his own pad," Dexter said. "Now he's got two teenagers to look after. That's got to be tough. So, if he gives you a few rules to follow . . ."

"It's more than a few."

Lina appeared at our table with two steaming mugs of coffee.

Dexter took his and rolled it between his hands. "I'm just saying, maybe cut your uncle some slack."

"Uncle?" Lina said, setting my coffee on the table. "Sal?"

I started in surprise. "You know Sal?"

"I do." She was smiling, but her eyes were guarded.

"Everyone around here knows each other," Dexter said. "And knows each other's business. It's kind of annoying."

"I can see that," I said.

"Welcome to life on the prairie," Dexter joked. Then he said to Lina, "If you know Charlie's uncle, maybe you've seen this cottage she claims to live in? It sounds pretty cool."

"Define 'cool,'" I deadpanned.

Dexter laughed, but Lina frowned.

"I know the place," she said.

"Have you been there?"

It wasn't quite the right question. Or maybe it was just the tip of a growing iceberg of questions about how she knew Sal, why she'd been to his cottage, what she knew about him and what else she might know . . . none of which I could ask in front of Dexter.

"It's been a long time . . ." She was quiet, almost wistful, but then she hardened. "Not since he put up that awful fence."

All my questions were instantly flushed away by a new load of questions, but I was keenly aware of Dexter watching us. Apparently, Lina was aware of it too, because she put on a smile and waved her serving tray with a casual air.

"White picket fences are just not my style," she said. Then she squeezed my shoulder and disappeared into the shop's back rooms.

I resisted the temptation to follow her and tried to focus on Dexter, who was telling me something about wanting to get out of Iowa after graduation.

"But what about farming?" I managed to ask.

"There are farms in other states, city girl."

I sipped my coffee while Dexter shared his dream of opening a farm-to-table restaurant someday, maybe in New England, where he would grow all the food himself and hire a gourmet chef to run the restaurant, all on one property. As he spoke, I listened, amazed at the human ability to dream of the future, to be excited for it, even though it meant they'd be closer to the end.

"And what's your dream?" Dexter asked. "Besides getting out of Iowa."

I set down my coffee, thinking. It felt good to be honest with Dexter, and I didn't want to stop.

"I just want to live forever," I said.

"So . . . you want to be famous?"

"Not necessarily. Immortality isn't just for celebrities."

"Yeah, I see what you mean," Dexter said, though he couldn't possibly. "Invent something that changes the world, maybe, or write a bestselling novel?"

"Or a farm-to-table cookbook," I mused.

"Hey, eyes on your own paper!"

The laugh we shared was quiet, close, and totally out of my comfort zone. Even in the shadows, I had lived my life fast and loud. Quiet was for the hunt, and close was something I simply didn't do. But this . . . Dexter leaning forward on the table, his fingers brushing mine where they wrapped around my mug . . . this wasn't so uncomfortable.

"Charlie, would you want to maybe go out sometime?" His green eyes looked up at me through long lashes.

I seriously don't know how I went a century without knowing they grew them like this in Iowa.

"Aren't we out right now?"

"Yeah, but I mean—on a date."

"This isn't a date?"

"You're messing with me."

"A little."

His smile revealed that he didn't mind.

"What took you so long?" I asked.

"Honest answer?"

"No, lie to me. Of *course* honest answer. I've been trying to read you for weeks."

"I've been trying to read you too," he said. "You are so pretty . . ."

I tucked my smile into my shoulder with a surprising shyness.

"But you're also pretty full of yourself."

My smile dropped like a rock, and I looked at him with lips pursed and arms crossed.

"Don't get me wrong," he rushed to explain. "Confidence looks good on you . . . *real* good."

My arms uncrossed.

"And clearly you have a lot to be confident about."

My lips un-pursed.

"But you kind of take it too far sometimes. At first, you acted like—like you thought you were better than us."

I did.

"I don't. I'm not. I'm . . . sorry?"

"Always with the question mark," he teased.

My hands slid back around my coffee mug, close to his.

"Well, what changed your mind?"

Dex gave the question some thought, then said, "Look, it's fun to flirt. And you are really good at it."

"I try."

"But that's just surface stuff. Tonight, on the farm—that was a real conversation."

"So, you're saying this whole time I could have just screamed at some corn, and that would have won you over?"

He stretched his fingers out to hook over mine and gave me another lopsided smile.

"Let's just say that pretty and strange are a winning combo."

"I'm going to take that as a compliment," I said. "But watch it."

We talked until our coffee turned cold, and when the clock wound round to a number I thought would worry Reg and piss off Sal, I told Dexter we had to call it a night. He agreed and excused himself to use the restroom first.

I paced the shop alone while I waited for him, taking in the photos from every inch of the world. Here was Lina on a boat, sea-foam churning in an impossibly aqua sea; there she was on the Spanish Steps, drenched in sunlight; here she stood atop a snow-covered mountain; there she sat surrounded by children in a remote island village.

How did the woman travel so much and still manage a business? It was more places than anyone could visit in a lifetime.

I froze.

It was more places than anyone could visit in a lifetime.

My eyes raked over the photos again. The locations, timeless. The fashion? Not so much. Lina's face was virtually unchanged from image to image, but the threads she wore spanned decades. Most of her outfits were classic, almost deliberately basic, so you had to really know something about clothing to see it, but once I noticed, it was as clear as a moonlit night. Nobody's closet had that much vintage—not even mine.

Lina *had* been to all these places in a single lifetime. Just not a human one.

"See any place you want to go, princess?"

I jumped at the sound of her voice, knocking clumsily into a nearby chair.

The kitchen door she'd come through was still swinging

closed, and she was already beside me. I didn't have to ask how she'd appeared so quickly. I'd done it myself a million times over the years. But I had other questions—so many I didn't know which to ask first, but before I could get even one out, Dexter was emerging from the bathroom, drying his hands on his jeans.

"Hey, Lina, you're out of towels in the men's room."

Ugh. He was cute, but we'd have to work on that timing.

"When *you're* in there, it's a boys' room, not a men's room," Lina teased. "Charlie and I were just chatting about my travel shots."

Dexter craned his neck to take in the many frames. "So many destinations, so little time."

"Some of us have more time than others," I said.

Lina smiled. "We sure do."

I took in her messy blond hair, her dark eyes—dark, but not black. She looked every inch a human, but I knew, beyond a shadow of a doubt, that she was immortal—that she was vampire.

But how? To look like this, to *live* like this, among humans, in the light, it was impossible.

Unless . . .

"It's getting late," Dexter said. "I guess we should head out. Coffee's on me, okay?"

He pulled a wallet from his back pocket and met Lina at the cash register to take care of the bill. She made a show out of refusing his money but dropping heavy hints that he should leave a tip worth far more than the coffee. Which, of course, he did.

I tried to make up an excuse to stay behind, claiming I didn't want to see Reg and Sal, but Dexter insisted on walking me home.

"I just asked you on a real date. That means I need your uncle and your brother to like me. No way will that happen if I leave you alone in the middle of the night."

I shot a meaningful look at Lina. She knew exactly why I wanted to stay, and from the look in her eyes, it almost seemed as if she'd been waiting for it. But she didn't come to my rescue. Instead, she sided with Dexter.

"Let the boy walk you home. It's dark."

"I'm not afraid of the dark."

"You should be. Nowhere's not as safe as you think."

Dexter held the door for me again on the way out, and just before I passed through it, my eyes fell on the picture by the front door, the one that had caught my eye on my first visit to All Hours, of Lina in the arms of a man in front of a pyramid. Lina looked ever the same as her other photos, but this time it was the man who caught my attention. He was clean-shaven, about twenty years younger, hair black instead of gray, but the strong build and the keen eyes were the same.

The man holding Lina was unmistakably Sal.

TWENTY-TWO

HE SAID

"WHAT IS SHE?!"

The question flew from my mouth before I'd even crossed the cottage threshold, and it was punctuated by the front door slamming against the wall as I threw it open.

At the kitchen table, Sal looked up from the coffee mug he was rolling between his hands and took a deliberately slow sip, his eyes on me the whole time. It did not occur to me until much later to wonder why he was up so late, drinking coffee alone in the kitchen, to puzzle over the strange combination of worry and anger on his face. In the moment, I was too focused on another mystery.

I dropped into a chair across from Sal. "Well? What is she?"

The answer was already there, churning in my gut, but it couldn't be true. I had never met one, in more than a century, and I just stumbled across one here? I needed Sal to confirm that what seems like an impossibility was the *only* possibility.

Sal set his cup down and folded his hands. "It's difficult to tell you *what* she is when I don't know *who* she is. So, who might we be talking about?"

"Don't play dumb, old man. Who else could I have been with this late at night?"

Sal's face clouded over. "Been asking myself that for the past two hours."

"I was at All Hours," I said. "With Lina."

Sal took another sip of his coffee.

"I think you might know her," I pressed. "Blond hair, little off her nut, likes to *travel*?"

"I'm familiar," he said.

"Very familiar, according to the pictures on her walls."

He looked up sharply and growled, "She has pictures of me on her walls? The walls of that shop?"

I shrank a little. "Well, just one picture. One wall."

"*Hmph.*"

"You've really never been there? It's the only coffee shop in town."

"I have all the coffee I need right here, thanks." Sal lifted his mug as evidence but set it down again when he saw the dissatisfaction on my face. "I don't go there. She doesn't come here. And we try not to meet anywhere in the middle."

"So, you are in some kind of tiff with the village vampire. Why?"

"She told you she's vampire?"

"She didn't have to. And I'm asking the questions."

He raised his mug to take another sip, and it was all I could do not to climb across the kitchen table and smack it out of his hand.

"She's more than just a vampire, isn't she?" I pressed. "She's . . . she's . . ."

I closed my eyes and saw the coffee shop photos, dozens of them, spanning decades but featuring the same ageless woman, basking in the sunlight. *The sunlight!*

"She's an Ancient." I said it with a quiet reverence.

Every immortal knew of the Ancients, vampires who had lived for thousands of years, but for young turns like me and Reg, they existed as fairy-tale creatures—the tales about them almost too unbelievable to be true. It was said that Ancients could alter their appearance at will, walk in the sunlight, even go years without feeding.

Other stories told of Ancients reverting to human behaviors, like eating (which sounded so totally gross before my new human senses discovered Lina's coffee and Sal's cooking). Some Ancients claimed to have memories of their past human lives or premonitions of the future; some lived so long they simply got bored of life, lay down in a coffin, and never came out; but most just went mad. Which was why the Elders governed.

If you asked me, a ban from politics and a tiny bit of crazy was a small price to pay to shed all vampire limitations, while strength and speed only increased, and immortality endured.

"Why would she be here? In this tiny town? She could go anywhere, do anything! She could—"

"She is not a god," Sal snapped. "It is not a divine achievement to simply pass the years without growing old."

"I'm just saying, she has options."

"Many immortals live among humans," Sal said. "Not all believe humanity is the hell you make it out to be."

"If Lina loves humans so much, why not take a stroll through your gate and become one herself?" I asked.

Sal's knuckles turned white where they wrapped around his coffee mug, and I wondered for a second if the ceramic might shatter in his strong slayer hands.

"I told you. Some vamps won't give up immortality for anything."

"You were talking about *her*?" My eyes opened wide, as the possibilities exploded. There was more between Sal and Lina than a turf war over some scrap of dirt called Nowhere, Iowa. The photo of them all tangled up in each other was proof of that, wasn't it? The stormy look in Sal's eyes would have been enough to confirm my suspicions, even if he hadn't opened his mouth and spilled his heart out on the table.

"So, now that you know *what* she is," he said. "You might as well know *who* she is."

I leaned forward, hands pressed against the polished wood of the table, afraid to speak in case my words made him think twice about his own.

"She calls herself Lina now, but before that, she was Adelina la Prima."

"La Prima," a voice echoed from the dark hallway beyond the kitchen. Reg emerged from the shadows. "The First."

Sal didn't ask how long he'd been standing there. He only kicked out a chair, a rough invitation for Reg to sit, which he did.

183

"It's a name she gave herself, because she has probably long since forgotten whatever moniker was assigned to her at birth." Sal's mouth slipped out of its grim line for a moment to reveal the slightest lift at the corner. "She's never been one to let others tell her who she is, but it takes some real moxie to name yourself *the first*."

"Could she actually be one of the first?" I asked.

No one seemed to know the true origin of vampires, thanks to the "welcome to the team" mind swipe and the addled brains of the oldest Ancients.

"Charlie, really?" Reg chided.

"What?"

"The first vampires were much shorter in stature than Lina, from a time before humans evolved to modern heights."

"And I'm supposed to know that?"

"How could you possibly *not* know that?"

"Well, I can't exactly google it, can I?"

That earned a smile from Reg. "Crack a book for once."

"Vampire books are dusty and boring," I said. "Just like the Elders."

"And yet you are so interested in someone even older than they are."

I turned my attention back to Sal. "How much older is she?"

"Adelina walked this earth long before clans were formed," Sal said. "And like a lot of vamps of a certain age, she had little use for the new vampire politics and structures. Every clan wanted her as a founder. Every clan was declined."

I tried to imagine which clan would have been a good fit for Lina. She clearly wasn't thirsty enough for the Blood Clan, and she was much too social for the Shadows. She was a business owner and still sharp, despite her immortal age. With that intelligence and ambition, she would have been a nice fit for Bone Clan.

"She hated killing," Sal said. "So, even though she never made it official, she spent a fair amount of time among the Starlight."

I frowned. I supposed human-hugging hippie sounded like Lina too.

"In fact, if she liked killing a little more, we probably never would have met, and I wouldn't be sitting here now." He drained the last of his coffee and slid the mug to the side. "Back when I was still . . . active, I liked to hunt down the traveling groups— the ones that roamed the world, feeding and turning as they went. I tracked one group up to Canada, cornered them on an island in the middle of a great lake. I could have taken them all out that night, but they refused to fight—kind of took the fun out of it."

"And you just let them go?" I couldn't keep the skepticism out of my voice. No slayer would be so benevolent.

"I would have set the whole island on fire," Sal growled. "But Adelina . . . She appeared like an apparition, right at the edge of the island, where the rocky shore met the water. I was standing on the end of a dock, my pockets full of dynamite and my hands wrapped around two stakes."

Sal opened and closed his hands, as if feeling the cursed wood in his palms still.

"Adelina stood in front of the whole group like a shield, all that blond hair glowing white in the moonlight, looking so *human*. And then—" Sal shook his head.

I was breathless. "And then what?"

He ran a hand over his face—a gesture that was becoming familiar and distinctly Sal.

"And then she walked right off the island. All the way to me."

I didn't see the big deal. "She walked down the dock? I mean, I guess it's brave to approach a slayer, but—"

"No, Charlie." Sal said. "She didn't walk down the dock. She walked on the damn water."

Reg gasped, and my jaw dropped open. Now, that was a new one.

"And for the next ten years, as far as I was concerned, she never stopped walking on water." Amusement and disdain were at war on Sal's face.

"Ten years?!" I cried. "You were—were—*together*? For a decade?"

Ten years wasn't exactly epic in the scope of an immortal life, but it was ten years longer than I'd ever heard of any other vampire-slayer friendship. And the story Sal was telling was clearly one of more than friendship.

"How long ago?" I demanded to know.

"We met . . . wow, some twenty-five years ago now. I couldn't have been older than thirty-five."

Sal saw me doing the math in my head.

"Yeah, she was robbing the cradle a bit," he joked. "Hard to believe, but I looked quite a bit younger than her at the time. It took those ten years for me to catch up to the age where she was frozen in time."

"And then what happened?" Reg asked.

"I realized that in another ten years, we'd be back where we started, but in reverse. And ten years after that, I'd be old enough to be her father, then her grandfather."

"Ew," I said.

Sal agreed. "Ew, indeed."

"So why didn't she just change you?" I asked.

"Now, why is that always the question? Why is it always me who has to change in this story?"

I wondered how many times he'd told this tale—how many poor souls had passed through Sal's cottage had heard his sad love story.

"She offered, of course," Sal said.

"You refused?" Reg asked.

"I made the same offer in return."

"And she refused too," I said.

"Not quite." Sal frowned down at his hands, and it almost looked for a moment like he was angry at them—at what they could do. "She wasn't as resistant to change as I was. But she wanted more time. She refused to become mortal until she had walked every inch of the earth."

He went quiet then, and both Reg and I leaned forward, waiting.

After a moment, I said, "And?"

"And well, you saw the pictures!" Sal exploded. "She did it! She . . . *we* walked every inch of the earth. Everywhere she hadn't already been—twice! And she still chose immortality over me. Over *us*!"

Reg reached a hand forward, as if to comfort Sal, but then pulled it back again awkwardly. "I'm sorry," was all he said.

"It's not that she didn't love me. Oh, she did."

I squirmed, trying not to picture whatever Sal was picturing as he reminisced.

"Maybe she still does," he said. "But she loves life even more. And she just can't give up the opportunity to keep living it."

And she shouldn't, I thought. I didn't want to kick Sal while he was down, but wasn't this the twenty-first century, and hadn't we females been told for decades now to not give up our lives for a man? It wasn't cool, even metaphorically, but Sal *literally* asked Lina to die for him. I wondered if he couldn't see that because he was a slayer . . . or because he was a dude.

Reg waited a tactful moment before asking Sal a question that would have sounded insensitive from anyone but my brother. "But your touch—the power to turn immortals mortal—is it something you can turn off and on?"

I recoiled. "Reg, are you asking how they—"

Sal cleared his throat, and I saw a blush blooming over his mustache. "There are ways to be . . . careful," he said.

Please no details. Please no details. Please no—

"If I concentrate, I have a degree of control over it." His expression darkened once again. "But after a time, I pushed hard enough that she began to distrust me. She worried I would turn her against her will."

"Would you?" I asked.

The darkness in his face blurred to something more like shame. "She was right to fear me."

"Wow," I said. "That is so wrong."

I wanted to feel for Sal, but I was fully on team Lina.

"She thought so too. So, she moved out of the cottage—"

"Wait, Lina lived *here*?"

"Fifteen years ago. When we first came to Nowhere."

"Here in this cottage?"

"We split not long after."

"I just can't picture her in this—"

"But she couldn't leave me in peace! She opened that damn coffee shop right in the village, just minutes away. I gave up slaying for her—became a traitor to my own kind to better serve *her* kind, and she couldn't just let me be. She stuck around just to torture me."

"Damn," I said, impressed.

"Can't really say I blame her," Reg said. "Woman scorned and all that."

"Well, I wasn't about to turn tail and run," Sal said. "So I built my fence to make sure she could never come back."

"You built it for her?" I marveled. No wonder the pickets looked more like stakes.

Reg let out a low whistle.

"Fat lot of good it'd do me anyway," Sal said. "If the woman can walk on water, she can probably walk through my damn fence."

He looked toward the window, glowering at the fence outside. "She just doesn't want to."

I wondered if an Ancient really would be invincible to slayer powers. It was beginning to seem as though there was nothing an Ancient could not do—except sit on the Elder Seat, but even in that case, the Elders still consulted with Ancients, still afforded them certain privileges, still . . .

"Of course."

It came out as a whisper, my lips forming around the words, but with barely enough breath to make a sound.

"She can sponsor us."

I looked at Reg as I said it, hope blooming in my chest. But the light that had just turned on for me seemed dimmer in him. He blinked, as if to hide it from me, and bobbed his head in an overenthusiastic way that was just so not Reg.

"Yeah. Yes! Sure, she can. Great. Great thinking, Charlie." His words were right, and he even *sounded* right, but . . .

I pictured the way Reg lit up when he texted Poe or took the stage at school or enjoyed a sunset on the hills behind the cottage. He had none of that glow now, and I felt a pinch of guilt. Maybe it was selfish of me to hurry us home. But the further we got from our vampire lives, the less likely it seemed that we would ever reclaim them, so I hoped he would forgive me if I cut his human vacation a little short.

It was unlike me to spend so much time worrying about

someone else's feelings—even my brother's. I never used to care what was good for anyone but myself. I didn't know if that was an immortal thing or just a Charlie thing, and with an inner squirm, I realized that I wasn't sure which "me" I liked better.

But there was no version of me that could leave Reg behind. Mortal or immortal, Smith or Drake, Reg and I were nothing without each other. For a century, we'd been two halves of a whole, and everyone else was just extra. On that much, we agreed . . . at least for now. But if we were stuck here much longer, I worried Reg might just leave me in the dark and stay in the sunlight forever. And not in a cool way like Lina.

Adelina la Prima. An Ancient. Our ticket back to immortality.

Reg cleared his throat. "So, naturally, we'll take this slowly—feel her out, earn her trust. Then, when the time is right, we'll go to her—"

"I'll go now." I jumped up from the table and grabbed my jacket from where it was slung on the back of the chair. "I can't sleep anyway, and she works the night shift."

TWENTY-THREE

SHE SAID

A tiny bell jingled as I pushed open the door to All Hours, and a flush filled my cheeks as I traded the night chill for the cozy warmth of the coffee shop.

"This is your third visit today. You may have a caffeine problem, princess."

Lina was perched on the counter, legs crossed under her, using a rag to polish an antique-looking copper kettle.

"Why do you bother with heat?" I asked, pulling my scarf away from my neck.

"Customers tend to enjoy temperate climates." She didn't look up from her polishing, and I found myself irritated that she was doing it so slowly. Still pretending.

The door closed behind me, jangling the bell once more before it sealed shut. I frowned up at it.

"And the bell? You can hear people walk through this door from a block away."

"Superpowered hearing but no power to outshine this spot." Lina sighed, holding up the kettle in the dim shop light.

"So you admit it," I said. Not that I needed her confirmation at this point. "You're vampire."

She met my eye finally. "Took you long enough."

"If you were expecting this, why not just tell us sooner?"

"I try to mind my own business . . . and stay out of Sal's. I figured it was best to let you come to it on your own. To be frank, I expected you back here ages ago. But I suppose you're not as quick as you used to be."

Was she talking about my physical speed, or was that a crack at my intelligence?

The smirk she gave me as she hopped off the counter told me it was probably both.

She was lucky I needed something from her, or I would show her just how quick-witted I could be.

Lina gestured to a table, and we sat in opposite chairs. She leaned forward, eyes alight with both curiosity and invitation. I sensed in that moment that I could ask her anything, but a million questions were competing to get out, causing a bottleneck in my throat so that not one could squeak through.

"Coffee?" Lina asked, and no sooner had she said the word than she was behind the counter, her hands already working the brewer. Once the coffee was poured, I blinked, and two steaming mugs were on the table between us, not a drop spilled. I wondered if I'd have been able to see her move even with my old immortal eyes.

But then she lifted her coffee to her lips, and I could see only a human, because what vamp would drink anything other than blood?

The thought that I might lose my taste for coffee when I

returned to immortality gave me a fleeting moment of sadness.

"How do you do that?" I asked, nodding at her cup. "Doesn't everything just taste like ashes?"

"A little. But after a time, you can sort of taste *through* that. Same with smells."

"And do you still drink—?"

"No."

"But how . . ."

"It's no longer necessary."

"And sunlight?"

"Glorious."

"Stakes?"

"Those still sting."

I grinned. "As if any mortal could get close enough to try, at your speed."

"You underestimate humans," she said. "Even now."

"I don't hold them in any estimation at all," I said, doing my best to channel Reg and sound a little more formal. I needed Lina to think we were mature enough for immortality.

"Doesn't look that way from where I'm sitting," Lina said with a deliberate glance to my crew's usual table.

My crew.

My new clan.

I shook off the thought. Mortal friends were not forever. That was the whole big thing about mortality . . . the *un*-foreverness of it.

"So, you and Sal," I said, changing the subject.

Lina sniffed, frowning for the first time. "What about me and Sal?"

"He told us about your history . . . together."

"He told you *his* version of history. I'm sure it was spotty. Age addles the brain, you know. The mortal brain, anyway."

"Now who's underestimating humans?"

"Touché." Her smile returned.

"Did you love him?" I blurted out the question, partly out of curiosity and partly to buy time while I worked up the courage to ask the question I'd really come here to ask.

Lina took another slow sip of her coffee. "I'll never love anything more than I love . . . loved . . . that man. Undeserving of my affection though he may be."

"I didn't know we could do that," I said.

"What?"

"Love."

Her smile was warm. "Sure we can. It's like all things with vampires—there, but quiet, buried under the deeper desire—under the thirst."

"Like coffee." I held up my mug in a salute. "My one true love, uncovered after a century."

Lina clinked her cup against mine. "You and me both. But you are not new to love. You have a brother."

She was sort of right. I cared for Reg, of course, but that wasn't the kind of love I meant. I had found many . . . *many* boys attractive over the years—even smooched a few before feeding. But real love . . . Lina was right, the need for blood overpowered all, and I couldn't say I even knew what love was.

"That's different," I said of Reg. "He's my kin. It's . . . loyalty."

"It's love, I assure you. Just not the sexy, passionate kind."

I wrinkled my nose. I was warming up to Lina, but grown-ups—even the vampire kind—should never say things like "sexy" or "passionate." *Blech.*

She smiled. "You will get more in tune with the many different ways we can love. It's just harder when you've buried those feelings for so long."

"But you're still immortal. How do you do it? How do you love?"

She shrugged. "How do I drink coffee? How do I walk in the sunlight? I suppose it's like anything else: the hunger fades, other things we've lost come back."

Lost love.

Who might I have loved before, when I was human the first time? What love had I lost, and was it a cruelty or a kindness for my maker to erase the memory of that love from my mind? I pictured the matching pain in Sal's and Lina's eyes when they talked about each other.

A kindness, I decided.

"Well, I'm on your side when it comes to Sal," I said. "If you love someone, why ask them to grow old and die when you can live and love forever? The choice is totally obvious."

I hesitated, and Lina took note.

"But?" she prompted.

I bit my lip. "But you could have gone anywhere. Did you . . .

you didn't really open this shop just to torture him, right?"

"Is that what he said?!" Lina's coffee mug smashed against the table, breaking in two, as her careful control wavered and she set the cup down a touch too hard. She didn't flinch at the hot liquid that coated her hand. "That stubborn self-centered, piece of . . . I've half a mind to go over there and—"

"No, I'm sorry!" I waved my hands in placation. "I may have misunderstood."

It was so not my goal to get her angry before popping the big question.

"Torture him, indeed!" Lina snorted, indignant. "I opened this shop to be near him. Even if he never changed his mind, I could at least look after him."

"Out of love," I said.

"Out of obligation. It's partly my fault the old coot went soft on vampires, and a soft slayer is an easy target. I thought he might need my protection. But clearly, I was wrong. He got right to business with his little halfway house for transitioning immortals."

She sneered as she said the last part, and I felt a touch defensive. Sure, I was on the side of immortality, all the way, but there had to be *somewhere* to go when mortality was unfairly flung upon a person. Where would Reg and I have been without Sal and his cottage?

"Are there many?" I asked. "Many like me and Reg?"

Lina seemed to finally notice the broken cup floating in a lake of coffee, and she pulled out a rag to mop up the mess.

"Many like you and many not like you. Immortals of all stripes come and go through the revolving door of Salvador Sicarius."

"Why him?" I asked. "Why here? In the middle of, literally, Nowhere."

The rag that had been in Lina's hand was suddenly on the counter far behind her, the table between us spotless. Even the fastest vampires I knew would have created a blur while wiping down the table, a glimpse of something in the corner of the eye. But with Lina—there was nothing at all. The ability to manage fine-motor skills at top speed had to be a gift bestowed only on the Ancients. It was disorienting, and a part of me wished she'd go back to being slow and careful.

"Why him?" she said. "Because there aren't many in the business of rehabilitating the formerly immortal. And why here? Well, that's a longer tale, but there's history here for both vampires and slayers."

"Here?" I raised a doubtful eyebrow. "In Iowa?"

"Both our kind and theirs settled in the area when America was still young, back in the 1800s. But even before that, around the age of—"

"Fascinating," I interrupted. "But I'm getting all the history lessons I can handle in third period Monday through Friday. Can you skip to the present?"

"Let's just say, it's neutral territory. And it has been for quite a long time. Sal's had that cottage fifteen years, but it was home to generations of slayers before him, and you and your brother are far from the first immortals to pass through Nowhere.

People here have grown accustomed to strangers and strange events. Even the humans who live here are a little abnormal, if you ask me."

"Truth," I said, and we both laughed.

A quiet moment followed, and in that quiet, I summoned up the courage to make my case.

"Reg and I didn't ask to be mortal," I said. "We're being punished for a mistake."

"A mistake," Lina repeated.

"Overfeeding, by accident." That was as much as I cared to elaborate, so I rushed on. "And not making excuses, because what we did was super uncool, but honestly, I've seen other vampires get away with much worse, so I think this whole thing is just a big smoke screen for the truth, which is that the Elders are trying to weed out all the underage immortals. It's been total discrimination town ever since—"

Lina held up a hand to silence my blabbering. "The Treaty of Annis."

"Yes," I said. "They think we're too young to know who we are and what we want, but I don't care that my brain got stuck at age sixteen or seventeen or whatever. I've been around for a century, and I know *exactly* what I want."

"And you've appealed?" Lina asked.

"We can't get a sponsor. We asked every clan, and they all turned us down. But you . . ." I took a deep breath—such a human thing and so natural now, it scared me. "If you sponsor us, the Elders will be forced to hear our appeal."

"And what does the slayer say?"

"Sal? What do you expect? He thinks we should be throwing him a parade for making us human."

Though it looked like she was fighting it, the corner of her mouth turned up. "Yes, that sounds like him."

"So?"

She sat back in her chair and folded her hands on the table. "It's true I can get you an audience with the Elder Seat, but I hesitate to cross Sal. You are his responsibility."

I opened my mouth to argue, but she was already moving on.

"On the other hand, I also believe we all have the right to choose our destinies for ourselves . . . for better or worse. For ages, I argued that we should not turn humans immortal against their will, and the same goes for turning them human again. It's not right either way. And that goes double for kids. You ought to have a choice."

"So . . . you'll do it?"

"I'll do it."

Speechless, I yelped with delight instead.

"You'll have to make your own case, mind you," Lina cautioned. "I've only known you for a minute, and it's not for me to testify about what's best for you."

I leaned forward, nodding so hard, I thought my head might wobble right off my neck. "Yes, yes, we'll speak for ourselves. We just need to get in the door. I can convince them."

Lina reached across the table to squeeze my hand, deliberately gentle so as not to crush my delicate human bones. "I have no doubt about that."

"You know, we could skip all this messy council business, and you could just . . ." I lowered my voice to a conspiratorial hush. "Change us yourself."

Lina's laugh was barking loud after my whisper. "I rather like my *own* freedom, thank you very much. I am not above the law and am not keen on breaking the treaty myself. I supported the laws against turning children. I just think it should go both ways."

"Well, as far as I'm concerned, the Elders can take the Treaty of Annis and shove it up their own an—"

Lina stopped me with a disapproving look, but I could tell she was hiding a smile.

I put my hands up. "Okay, okay. I'm just surprised that an Ancient would be such a rule follower. You're stronger, faster, and, let's be honest, way more popular than the council."

"Nobody loves a politician," Lina conceded. "And I'm no fan of the current Elder Seat representatives or their actions, but I do respect the structure."

She smiled at my questioning look. "You don't know the chaos before the council. Why do you think humans have vampire lore? Before the Elder Seat was created, before we organized into clans and houses to help keep order, our kind were far too exposed, drunk on our own power. But even an immortal can't survive a mob with torches and pitchforks."

"It depends," I argued, pretending to seriously consider it. "Are the pitchforks made of wood?"

"Joke while you can," Lina said. "You may be back to avoiding wooden stakes soon enough."

"Thanks to you," I said in earnest.

"Dexter will be disappointed, you know. And your friends too."

At the mention of my friends, I slapped my palm against my forehead. "I keep forgetting to ask you—will you run the coffee cart after the parade? I know it's lame, but I promised the Halloween hillbilly committee I would ask."

"Oh, so you need another favor now?"

I held up two pinched fingers in front of my sheepish expression. "Just a teeny one. Pretty please."

Lina's expression was a cross between an eye roll and a helpless grin. "This town and its silly traditions, I swear."

"That's a yes?"

"That's a maybe. Let's get you past the Elders in one piece, and then we'll worry about a party, deal?"

I raised my now-empty mug. "Deal."

TWENTY-FOUR

SAMPLE, DON'T INDULGE

The next week had me tied up in knots, between waiting for word from the council and anticipating my first official date with Dex. Both were things I had wanted for so long, and both were making me a little nauseous. I should have wondered how I could feel excitement and dread at the same time, but I was starting to get used to all my conflicting human emotions.

Reg, meanwhile, apparently had no feelings about the appeal at all. When I'd told him Lina agreed to be our sponsor, he'd responded with casual surprise and a vague "How kind of her."

Still, I'd take my brother's casual indifference over Sal's utter fury. The slayer had slammed around the cottage for hours, barking about Lina interfering in his business. Or, as he put it, "sticking her big vampire nose in it."

Neither one of them was interested in my constant jabbering about the appeal, so I tried to put a lid on it, but by Tuesday morning I was about to burst.

"What do you think is taking so long?" I complained.

"It's early," Reg said. "They'll be here soon."

"No, not our friends. The Elders."

We were lounging around Poe's locker waiting for everyone else to arrive. Reg had insisted we get to school early so he could explain to his world history teacher why his grasp of anti-communism in the postwar era was stronger than hers. I had talked him out of it, worried he might tell her he *lived* through that era, if it meant she'd turn his B to an A. Now, I figured I could at least distract him with something more important than history—like, our entire future.

Reg gave a casual wave of his hand. "It's only been a few days. Really, Charlie, you have alarmingly little patience for someone who desires all eternity."

"It's not the wait so much as the not knowing," I said. At this point, I wouldn't mind waiting months for my chance to get in front of the council, as long as I knew that chance was coming.

"Waste time worrying about it if you want," Reg said. "But don't say I didn't warn you about the wrinkles."

He squinted at my forehead, then pulled back in mock alarm, as if the creases were sinking into my skin right then, and I pushed him into the wall of lockers.

"Are you going to miss Poe?" I asked after a beat.

The question caused Reg's face to falter, but only for an instant. "I may not even remember him, if we are given the memory fade."

My breath caught. "They would do that again?"

"I have no idea," Reg said. "It may not be necessary. But even if our memories remain intact, when our thirst returns, we are unlikely to feel things like loss—at least not to the degree we feel it as humans."

"You didn't really answer the question," I observed. "What exactly is the deal with you and Poe? Is it . . . serious?"

Reg smiled and struck a pose. "I am far too pretty to be tied down, mortal or immortal. But that's no reason not to sample the local flavors."

"Sample or indulge?" I asked.

"A gentleman doesn't kiss and tell." His smile turned to a devilish grin. "So, it's a good thing I'm no gentleman."

I laughed, but deep down, I recognized Reg's response for what it was—a half-truth. I'd seen him with Poe, and it wasn't just a fling. I had an uncomfortable feeling that Reg was telling me what I wanted to hear, instead of the truth. Didn't he know that after a century, I could see right through his casual disguise? Nonchalance was one of my brother's hallmarks. Keeping secrets was not.

I decided to ask him, point-blank, if he still wanted our immortal lives back, but just as I opened my mouth to speak, I felt a hand on the small of my back.

Dex.

I turned toward him, careful to keep in contact with his hand. Our date was still a few days away, but the confident, familiar way he touched made it feel like we were already a couple. If Reg had even a fraction of the same chemistry with Poe, I wouldn't blame him for wanting to stay. A part of me wondered if I should cut things off with Dex now, before I found myself in the same tricky situation. But it was drowned out by the other part of me, that was focused on how Dex's one hand could make my whole body tingle.

"Hi," I said, voice so low it was almost a whisper.

Dex's smile was just for me. "Hi."

Reg leaned into our private space, arms wrapped around us both and face just inches from ours, his own grin stretched from ear to ear. "Hi."

I will murder you, my eyes said.

It will be worth it, his wagging eyebrows replied.

Out loud, he said, "Sample. Don't indulge."

"Oh my God, get out of here, right now. I hate you."

"What was that about?" Dex asked when Reg was gone.

"Sibling stuff." I remembered Dex was an only child. "Be glad you don't have a brother."

Dex leaned against the lockers. "He's more than your brother though. He's your best friend."

It was so simple the way Dex said it, and yet, it hit me like a truck. I had never thought of it that way. Reg was my family, someone you are stuck with by definition, but a best friend . . . that's someone you choose. And when it came down to it, that's all I really wanted from Reg—not for him to choose immortality but to choose me.

I nearly fell back down the well of worry over our appeal, but Dexter's hand touched mine just in time, bringing me back to the Hope High hallway. This farm boy was proving to be an excellent distraction.

TWENTY-FIVE

SAVE THE DATE

Dexter was just one member of Team Distraction. Sydney and Sophia helped me pass the week with endless chatter about my upcoming date and final hoopla details, which included constant reminders by Sophia that we were falling short of our fundraising goals and counter reminders from Sydney that what really mattered was that we throw the "best party ever."

It was almost enough to make me forget about the council meeting.

Almost.

Every afternoon at All Hours, I looked at Lina with the question in my eyes, and every afternoon she responded with a small shake of her head. Some days, when the twins were being extra entertaining, it was almost a relief that we hadn't heard from the council yet. I did have a party to attend, after all.

I wondered, if the Elder Seat ruled in our favor, if we would return to immortality right away or if we would have time to tie up our human affairs. I tried to imagine the Elders' faces if I asked for an extension in purgatory in order to attend the annual Halloween Hoopla. They would probably deny my appeal on the spot just for asking.

The parade and party were only two weeks away. Maybe it wouldn't be the worst thing ever if we didn't get a hearing until after the festivities were over. Our human adventure deserved a finale.

By Saturday night, I had something new to focus on. My date with Dex was less than an hour away, and Sydney and Sophia sat on my bed, picking through a pile of designer clothes.

"I can't believe all the labels you have," Sophia said, sighing over a deep gray Chanel sweater. "I think I've died and gone to fashion week."

I smiled. "You can keep that one."

"OMG, really?!" she squealed.

"No way!" Sydney sat up from where she'd been lounging against my pillows and pawed at all the fabric. "What do I get?"

I tossed her a pink sequined dress I'd just pulled from a hanger. "This. To go with your hair."

She caught it with one hand. "I knew you owned something that wasn't black!" She checked the label. "Just my size."

Sophia looked guilty, as if they were stealing. "Charlie, are you sure?"

"She's sure." Sydney shushed her sister. She stretched her arms out and bowed in my direction. "We humbly accept these gifts from the queen of all fashion."

See, now this was exactly what I expected out of high school. Finally.

"Just like you've always wanted," Reg said, appearing in the doorway.

"No boys allowed." Sophia tossed a spiky heeled shoe in his direction.

He dodged it, and it smacked into Poe, who was waiting behind him in the hall.

Poe fell to the ground, feigning serious injury. "Dear Sophia, why hast though forsaken me?"

"Rehearsing, I see?" She giggled.

He answered with an expertly voiced death rattle, then collapsed.

"Debate practice, actually," Reg said. "Poe is helping me prep for next week's tournament."

Poe popped up from the floor, bouncing a little on his feet. "It turns out, I'm very argumentative."

"I could have told you that," Sydney said.

"Maybe I'll go out for debate team next year too," Poe said.

A small shadow flickered across Reg's face—too subtle for anyone else to notice and too quick for me to interpret. As much as he protested being tied down, I could only assume he was reluctant to say goodbye to Poe—to all of them—or at least felt guilty about pretending we would still be here next year.

I was feeling a little guilty about that myself, if I was being honest, and something more too—like a hollow spot was being carved out inside my chest, right where my human heart did all its thumping. I touched my hand to the spot for just an instant, then made an effort to shake it off.

"Well, I'm prepping for a date." I waved a hand from head to toe. "And all of this takes time. So get out of here already!"

We closed the door on the boys, and I turned to the full-length mirror on the back of the door, inspecting my little black dress from every angle.

"You look awesome," Sydney said.

Less than two months ago, I would have answered "I know" without a second thought, but now I only smiled.

My brief time as a human had taught me that mortals drew a thin line between confidence and arrogance, and teenage girls had an unfortunate habit of declining compliments and pointing out their flaws instead. Maybe I could break Syd and Soph of that pattern before my mortal adventure was over.

Insecurity might be the worst part of being human. Fortunately, I was mostly unafflicted.

There was a knock at the cottage door.

Dexter.

I tossed my hair, posing for Sydney and Sophia.

"Fabulous?" I asked.

"Fabulous," they agreed.

Dexter picked me up in a car—or something resembling a car.

"Is this beast yours?" I asked, giving the side-eye to the battered Jeep parked just beyond the picket fence.

Dexter held open the gate for me to pass through, and as I did, I got a whiff of a clean-smelling cologne that made me want to bury my face in his shirt. Maybe later, he would let me.

"It's on loan," he said.

I pointed to my stilettos. "And how am I supposed to get in it?"

"With a little help from your date." He grinned, enjoying my discomfort, and I wondered if he deliberately brought this off-road ride because he knew I'd be in heels. I started to argue, but then his big hands were around my waist, lifting me into the passenger seat.

"Oh," I said, a warmth creeping into my cheeks. "Okay, then."

He jogged around to the driver's side and climbed in.

"I guess I should have asked what we're doing before I picked an outfit," I said.

"Nah, it wouldn't matter. Whatever I planned, I knew you'd be dressed to kill."

"Actually, it's better to wear snug-fitting pants and shoes with decent traction while hunting."

Dex gave me that one-sided smile I'd come to recognize as his *Charlie's an oddball* look.

"Yeah," he said. "I was just kidding."

"Um . . . me too."

We laughed the awkward laugh of two friends on a first date wondering if this was the beginning or the end.

It turned out my heels weren't the only thing that didn't pair well with a Jeep—especially one with the top removed so that it was little more than seats in a frame with no roof or doors. As Dexter rocketed down the gravel roads, a tornado of wind whipped my hair into a wild mess. After only a few minutes, I gave up trying to hold it down and let it fly. It reminded me of how it felt to run when I could move at the speed of a vampire— the power, the freedom of it. I unclipped my seat belt and stood up to clear the windshield and let the wind hit me full in the face.

"Whoa, careful," Dex said, but the smile he gave me was big and genuine.

And it lasted a touch too long.

"Eyes on the road, farm boy," I said.

He grinned and slowed the Jeep to a safer speed.

I stayed on my feet, and from up here, the smell of Dexter's cologne was drowned out by something sweeter.

I sniffed the air. "That's amazing. What is it?"

"Don't you recognize the smell of apples, city girl?"

"I've never smelled an apple like that."

Dex pointed to a copse of trees in the distance. "There's an orchard right on the other side of those woods. Morgana Farms. Best Honeycrisp apples around. No more, no less."

"That phrase." I looked down at him. "It's everywhere here. What does it even mean?"

"It's just an expression, like . . . that's how it is. No exaggeration or undercut—just the truth."

I inhaled, getting another taste of the sweetness in the air. "Apples, huh?"

"They also make fresh cider and have hayrides and a haunted house. It's my favorite time of year."

I dropped back into my seat. Haunted houses were offensive, the way they depicted vampires as evil and, worse, hideously dressed in cheap fabrics. But I forgave Dex for not knowing that, and the rest of it sounded—and *smelled*—pretty okay.

"I think maybe it's my favorite time of year too," I said.

He reached over to grab my hand.

And he didn't let go.

Not for the whole drive and not even at dinner, where he managed to down a whole burger, one-handed, without dropping a single pickle. I didn't need any hands at all to eat, because I was afraid to add food to the strange fluttering in my stomach. Also, the gross way my hand was sweating was enough to kill my appetite. Why did human bodies produce disgusting fluids in response to romance?

He was still holding my hand when we wound up back at All Hours, which Dex called "our place."

The coffee shop was crowded, but we found a tiny table tucked up against an inside wall, under a photo of Lina perched on the edge of a boat floating in impossibly clear water. She was decked out in a wet suit and surrounded by oxygen tanks she didn't need.

Dexter caught me staring at the photo. "That's going to be us, next year."

"What do you mean?"

"Grad trip, senior year. Every Hope High senior class takes a big organized trip right after graduation, and Sydney and Sophia have decided we should go to a beach in Mexico, spring break–style."

"Sounds a little cliché," I said. Like a cautionary episode of every teen TV show I'd ever watched.

"Agreed, but when Syd and Soph want something . . . well, you know."

I smiled. "I do know."

"Crazy that graduation is less than two years away," he said with wonder. "Sometimes I feel like we're all still just kids."

He took a sip of his drink. "Except for Poe, I guess. He's an old soul."

Old soul.

Could a soul age, even if the body and mind remained frozen in time? Was I really a hundred years older than Dexter? And if so, did that make me some kind of pervert?

A guy with a guitar hopped up on a stool near the shop's front window and started an acoustic set that made it a little harder to talk, so Dex and I mostly held hands and listened to the music.

Lina was hustling around, tending to customers, and she caught my eye only a few times. I was grateful to her for giving us some space, though at one point, I did catch her watching us with a sadness in her eyes. I wondered if she saw herself and Sal in me and Dexter.

We stayed until the music wound down, and the shop cleared out. Dex suggested we get our last coffees to go, and he switched to decaf.

Amateur.

Lina brought the drinks to our table and flopped into a chair with perfectly faked exhaustion. "I'm beat."

"Busy night," Dex commented. "Someone should bring *you* a coffee."

A mischievous twinkle lit up her eyes. "That's an excellent idea, O'Shea. Why don't you hop behind that coffee bar and pour me one?"

Dexter looked taken aback for a moment, but then his face broke open with a smile like a kid whose just been given the keys to a candy factory. "Can I steam some milk and do the foam thing?"

"Sure, but you break it, you buy it."

He raced behind the counter and started pulling levers on the giant espresso machines.

I laughed. "Oh my God, he is so excited. Look at him just—"

"Listen," Lina interrupted, leaning in close over the table and whispering. "The hearing is set."

"Oh . . ."

"It's next Sunday at midnight, at the—"

"Sunday? That's a week from tomorrow."

Lina blinked. "I thought you'd be happy."

"I just . . ." I glanced over at Dexter, at his giant, gorgeous smile as he mixed up something probably disgusting for Lina to drink. I cleared my throat. "I need time to prepare is all."

"Uh-huh."

"And Reg has rehearsals every day after school, and I'm so busy with the hoopla coming up—I'm on the planning committee, you know . . ."

Lina placed a hand over mine, and her whisper coated over with honey. "Charlie," she said. "It's okay to change your mind."

"I don't. I haven't." I pulled my hand from under hers and tucked it in my lap. "I'm surprised is all. After weeks and weeks of no, I didn't think the yes would come so quickly."

Lina sighed. "Then this is your chance. The Elder Seat never meets in the same place, and they won't be back in the US for more than a year. You got lucky that we caught them in time and that they're meeting so close. I'm actually surprised they're not overseas with the Blood Clan."

"Sal mentioned the Bloods have been causing trouble," I said. "But what else is new?"

"As I understand it, they're getting careless about exposure laws. The council's been very preoccupied with it. The fact that they're meeting here and not there is almost"—she chewed the inside of her cheek, thinking—"almost too convenient to be a coincidence."

"What do you mean?"

"It just makes me wonder if they have other business here."

I found that hard to believe. "What business could the Elders possibly have in Nowhere, other than to deliver more vampires to Sal's doorstep?"

"You might be surprised to—"

"Oh no, that's it, isn't it? We're getting roommates."

"I don't know if—"

"Well, that cottage is too small already. I'm not sharing a room."

Lina threw up her hands in surrender. "I'm sure you won't have to worry about that."

"Not for very long anyway," I said. "So, where exactly is this meeting?"

"Minneapolis."

Cold and dark. Sounds about right.

"How do we get there?"

"I'll drive."

"You drive?"

"I'm literally older than cars."

I smiled. "And buggies."

"Watch it."

Dexter returned to the table to present Lina with the most poorly made latte ever to come out of a coffee shop.

"Ugh!" She spat the drink back into the mug. "O'Shea, this is all foam."

"There's some coffee in there," he protested. "At the bottom."

Lina pretended to kick Dexter out of the shop, and he made a show of acting wounded as he left. I waited at the front door for him to pull up the Jeep, and Lina hovered at my shoulder.

"You sure?" she asked.

"I'm sure."

And I was.

So why did I feel sick to my stomach?

TWENTY-SIX

HAYRIDES & HISTORY

Reg was asleep when I got home, so I had to wait until the next morning to unload all the details of my date. He was still bleary-eyed and snuggling under his blankets when I got to the part where Dex walked me to the front door.

"So, he just kept standing there on the porch, saying good night but not leaving, and it was so obvious that he wanted to kiss me, but when he finally leaned in to do it, Sal turned on the porch light! On purpose!" I stood to demonstrate the next part. "So Dex, like, dodged left and gave me this half-hug, half-ear-kiss thing that was honestly just kind of gross, and I swear when I'm vampire again, I am coming back to drain that old guy. If I don't murder him with my own human hands first."

Reg finally sat up, propping himself against a pile of pillows. "That was . . . utterly exhausting."

I collapsed back onto Reg's bed in a fit of laughter. I was annoyed with Sal (but also kind of impressed by his timing) and mostly just giddy from a great date. So giddy, in fact, that I realized with a start that I'd forgotten to tell Reg the most important part of the night.

As I shared with him that our appeal would be heard, and the hearing was only a week away, I got that same sick sensation I'd experienced at All Hours.

"It's a good thing," I said, as much to Reg as to myself. "It's just so soon."

Reg seemed surprised but otherwise unflustered by the speed of the hearing. He said he was "far more distressed" about the outcome of his debate tournament the day before, which he proceeded to tell me about in great detail. And even though debating was way less interesting than dating, I listened to Reg for nearly as long as he'd listened to me.

"The judges don't know an argument from their armpits," he complained. "They're so plebeian."

"They probably just don't understand old-timey terms like 'plebeian,'" I said.

I expected a laugh, but Reg only grumbled, "Poe made a similar observation. Right after he told me to stop torturing the teachers."

"Uh-oh. Trouble in Poe-radise?"

He cringed. "Must you mutilate the English language?"

"I must."

"Well, it's fine. It's fun. Poe's great . . ."

"But?"

"But is someone still great if they *know* they're so great?"

"You're kind of asking the wrong girl," I said, finally drawing a smile from my brother.

"I suppose in the end, he is still only human. And a pretty decent one, at that."

"One of the best," I agreed. "After Dex."

"Yeah," Reg muttered. "I just don't see why he has to be the best at *everything.*"

A sudden thought churned my stomach. "It will be weird, won't it? If they go back to . . . *when* they go back to being our food?"

Reg pretended to think it over, a teasing smile on his face. "I don't know. They're pretty tasty right now."

"Agreed."

"Downright delicious."

"Okay, don't make it weird."

We joked and jabbered about boys and school and dates and debates for another hour. But we didn't talk much about the hearing, and every time I brought it up, Reg did a neat little verbal side step, asking me about Dex or hoopla planning, even though I'd already spilled every detail of my date and he could not actually care less how many floats were in the parade.

Reg and I could always talk about everything, but now, no matter how much we talked, I couldn't shake the feeling that there were some things still left unsaid.

I have been to hundreds of places on this planet, including the most glamorous cities and the most extravagant palaces. But there may be no better place on earth than tucked under a warm flannel blanket, bumping along a dirt road in the back of a flatbed truck, curled up next to Dexter O'Shea. I didn't even mind the sharp needles of straw poking me in the rear from the hay bale I was sharing with Dex.

For our second date, he'd brought me to his favorite orchard, where we'd already tried hot cider and bobbed for apples. (Well, Dex had bobbed. My makeup was on point and not waterproof, so I passed.) Now, we were wrapping up a long hayride that I didn't want to end, but Dex insisted that apple picking was the last, best part. I was just grateful we were there on a weekday, after school, otherwise he might have dragged me through the haunted house the farm ran on the weekends.

The truck trundled to a stop, and Dex hopped off first, holding out his hand to help me down. I landed on the dirt next to him, and he pointed to a large sign on the side of a nearby barn.

MORGANA FARMS

"Same company that bought our farm. They own a lot of land around here."

"I thought you were angry about that," I puzzled. "But you don't mind coming here?"

"I wouldn't say angry. More like disappointed. Like Dad says, 'It's all for the best, and we should be grateful.' At least here, the original owners stayed on to run the farm. It's corporate owned but locally operated, so they can still do all this fun fall stuff."

"Your family didn't want to do the same?"

"We could have, but my folks wanted me in town to be close to school. Also, I think my dad is too proud. Farming is a lot of backbreaking work just to line someone else's pockets."

I smiled. "I like the way your dad thinks."

Dex plucked two large, sturdy baskets from a mound of baskets and barrels piled against the barn wall. He passed one to me. "You ready, city girl?"

"Lead the way, farm boy."

We filled our baskets with a variety of apples, chatting and snacking along the way. Dex was right that Honeycrisp was the best, and I think I had eaten more than I'd gathered when he pulled me behind a tree, out of sight of other apple pickers, and surprised me with a small kiss. The tingle I always got at his touch shot through my whole body, and my lips smiled under his.

Finally! We should have been kissing for weeks.

I stood on my tiptoes as if it were possible to bring our mouths even closer together. It wasn't exactly a make-out session, but it was sweet, and I noted that apple tasted even better on Dexter's lips than off the tree.

When we pulled apart, faces flushed, he peered into my basket and tutted. "You're falling behind. That's not even enough apples for half a pie."

"I don't bake."

"I'm not surprised." He smiled. "But my mom does, so load up, and I'll make sure to save you a slice."

We split up to finish filling our baskets, and I wandered far enough that I reached the edge of the orchard, where the neat rows of apple trees gave way to more natural forest of tall, knotty trees with fat leaves and soft green undergrowth. A century of hunting had made me a half-decent navigator, and I knew if I kept walking straight through these woods, I would cross flat brown fields and trek over a series of rolling hills before finding myself back at the cottage.

There were no walking paths in this wild little forest, but I noticed a break in the trees to my left that caught my attention, and when I looked a little closer, I could see a line that seemed to cut through the underbrush where a path may once have been. I set down my basket and followed the line to a small clearing, overgrown with ferns and wildflowers and poison ivy.

The plants were so dense, I almost didn't see the giant stone at the center of the clearing. It was dark, a black granite of some kind, and flat on one side, almost like a gravestone. It definitely wasn't natural to these woods, and I found myself drawn to it, folding away the ferns to see the flat side clearly. I gasped. It *was* a gravestone!

Well . . . maybe.

I cocked my head, trying to read the words roughly carved into the side of the boulder. Moss had seeped into the cuts and cracks over the years, running the letters together. I was pretty sure the language was Latin, but I only recognized one word.

Primus.

The first . . . something.

I had no idea what the next word meant, but I knew who would. I pulled out my phone to take a picture of the full text, then I circled to the other side. It was rougher, and the flat plane on this side seemed to have been hacked away with a manual tool. There was more writing in a totally unrecognizable language. I'd seen enough dusty old texts and learned enough history over the decades to know the language was far older than the town of Nowhere—older than Iowa or America itself. I snapped another photo, then hurried back to the orchard to find Dex. Maybe it was nothing. Maybe some farmer dropped the boulder to mark his land as the first farm in Iowa, for all I knew. But my gut told me it was more than that, and that this place was keeping secrets.

"So, what do you think? It's Latin, right?"

Reg hunched over the kitchen table, squinting at my phone screen. "Yes, but it's hard to read. Primus . . . primus . . ."

"It's the moss," I said. I reached over to zoom in to the words. *Primus interitus.*

Reg sat up and blinked. "The first death."

I shivered. "Really?"

"Or first destruction? First decay? What an interesting little mystery."

I didn't know if Reg was really that fascinated by my find or if he was just glad I was talking to him about anything besides my date. He hadn't said much about Poe since our last conversation, and I got the feeling he wasn't up for my gushing.

"Where did you say you came across this marker?" he asked.

"In this overgrown stretch of woods by the apple orchard. It looks like nobody's been back there in a hundred years."

I took my phone from Reg and read the words again.

"Primus interitus. The first death."

"Close," Sal said, rumbling into the room and banging through the cabinets to start dinner.

"You speak Latin?" Reg asked with a note of doubt in his voice.

"I speak uppity vampire, and I know how they interpret that rock."

Reg and I were mirror images of raised eyebrows and dropped jaws.

Sal set some water to boil on the stove, then joined us at the table.

"The first *undoing*."

Reg frowned. "I supposed that interpretation works too. . . ."

"Undoing?" I asked. "Undoing what?"

"Immortality."

"I don't understand. . . ."

But slowly, I did.

"What you do." I nodded to Sal's hands. "It's *undoing*."

"I've never heard the term," Reg said.

"Probably not a popular topic of conversation where you're from," Sal said. "But it's what the Elders call it."

I swiped to the next photo and held up my phone for Sal to see. "Do you know this language?"

He stood up again, not even looking at the picture. "I do. It's the tongue of the people who walked this land before it was colonized."

"And? What does it say?"

225

Sal's rough hands gripped the back of his chair.

"Birth of the Assassin."

Sal's brand of torture was making us wait until dinner was on the table to elaborate, but I could hardly eat a bite anyway. Reg, on the other hand, was stuffing his face with pasta as if it was the last time he'd ever taste it. And maybe it was.

"There's more writing on the Latin side of the stone," I said, producing the picture again, even though it was obvious Sal had already seen the marker himself, possibly many times. "Circa AD C. That's a date, right?"

"AD 100," Reg confirmed around a mouthful of spaghetti.

"The year one hundred," Sal said, "marks the birth of the slayer. Though, I'm half tempted to take a knife to that old rock myself and mark it the birth of the healer."

"But why is the marker here? Why—" I paused, then answered my own question. "The first undoing. It happened here? In Nowhere?"

Sal shrugged. "Sort of. There was no village then, of course. It really was *nowhere*, at least to the civilized world at that time, still undiscovered by European settlers. But vampires, with their speed, could travel the world, and they especially loved remote corners of the earth.

"Among slayers, the legend goes that a small vampire pack was hunting in the area and came across a young woman, indigenous to this area. She was alone and probably pretty far from her home, but she was fearless. Untrained and outnumbered, she fought back anyway but was quickly bested by the pack. One of the vamps went in for the kill, and she wrapped her arms around him, ready to meet death, but instead, when her hands touched his skin, she drained his immortality, just like a vampire draining blood."

Reg's fork froze, halfway to his mouth, the noodles wrapped around it forgotten. My own plate was pushed aside and my hands plastered to my cheeks, as we listened, spellbound, to Sal's story.

"The rest of the pack beat it and lived to tell the tale. It was the first documented case of vampire returning to mortality."

"The first undoing," I said.

"And the birth of the slayer, so far as we know. Slayers—healers, back then—started popping up all over the world after that. Hard to say if the powers were always there, or if it was some kind of global awakening, but suddenly, we were everywhere."

"Fascinating," Reg breathed. "And it all started here, in this sleepy place."

"Sleepy by design," Sal said.

"What do you mean?"

"This place became sacred to both vampires and slayers. For more than a thousand years, it remained remote and mostly uninhabited, occasionally visited by healers and killers alike, who made the pilgrimage."

"And then America was colonized," Reg filled in. "I believe the French first settled in this area in the 1700s."

I nodded along, pretending that I, too, remembered that

from our history books, though in truth, I'd never found history older than my own very interesting.

Sal finished eating and sat back in his chair, hands folded over his stomach.

"Vamps worried that sacred ground would be desecrated by development, so they laid claim to a bunch of land, thanks mainly to your Bone Clan's wealth."

The Bone Clan invested in all kinds of property—penthouses, estates, villas, even a few private islands—so I guess I shouldn't have been surprised to learn they owned some fields in Iowa too.

I flashed on an image from earlier in the day: a sign, mounted on the side of a barn.

"Morgana Farms," I said. "They own the orchard. And Dex's old farm too."

"That's the one," Sal said. "Morgana. Vampire shell corp. No business except buying up land around town. And sometimes *in* town too. Keeping Nowhere small. Back when the land grab started, my kind didn't have the same loot, so all they could do was claim one of the small patches of land that vamps hadn't already peed all over to mark their territory. They built this cottage and vowed that it would always be home to a slayer."

Looking around the stone walls of the kitchen, I saw them now in a different light—built by hands made for healing, to keep an eye on creatures made for killing.

"Neither side wanted to draw too much attention to this place," Sal went on. "So this became neutral ground. No hunting from either side."

"It's impossible that we've never heard of this," Reg said.

Sal lifted one side of his mouth in a half smile. "Not everyone understands neutral ground. This history, this *place*, is kept quiet on both sides, to prevent all-out war."

It seemed unfair to keep such a special place a secret, but I couldn't disagree that a place that drew both vampire and slayer would inevitably become a battleground.

"There are a few who know," Sal said. "The members of the Elder Seat, though sworn to secrecy, and a good deal of slayers who identify as healers, like myself."

"There are more like you?" I asked. "And more places like this?"

"I don't think there's anywhere quite like Nowhere, but there are a fair number of slayers who have turned in their stakes."

"Is that how you came to be in your current line of work?" Reg asked.

"This work existed long before me. It's amazing what can happen when we stop trying to kill each other and find time to talk to each other. Vampires were just getting organized back then, developing the council and clans and houses. They were interested in more civilized solutions than smoking bad vamps. It became practice to pay slayers handsomely for carrying out this mortal punishment. Some families—like the Sicarius line— saw it as a disgrace."

"And what about *Salvador* Sicarius?" I asked, pointing to the old guy. "What did he think?"

"Who, Sal?" he played along. "He was one of the ones in the dark. His family never told him any of this, but he would have agreed it was a disgrace."

"What changed?"

"Oh, you know the story. Boy meets girl. Girl turns out to be a vampire. Boy changes his entire worldview. Girl dumps him anyway. Etcetera."

I thought of my own boy, of the way he'd tasted like apple when he kissed me, and I wondered if, given a little more time, he would change my entire worldview too. Would I end up like Lina, still stuck in Nowhere, watching over her human love? I shivered, suddenly grateful our hearing was just a few nights away.

TWENTY-SEVEN
SILENT NIGHT

The night of the hearing seemed to rush up on us. One week, we were anathema to all vampire-kind, and the next week, we had a priority appeal before the Elder Seat, with the backing of an Ancient. I should have been preparing a statement along the lines of *In your face, old folks!* But as I sat at the carved kitchen table, in the dim light of the slayer's cottage, I found myself at a rare loss for words. The three of us sat in virtual silence, waiting for Lina to arrive. The fact that she was picking us up had Sal all twitchy, which, it turned out, was an even worse state than grumpy.

"She's late," he said, checking his phone against a clock on the wall. It was exactly thirty seconds past 10:00 p.m.

I rolled my eyes. "She's barely late. And we have tons of time."

Our hearing was set for midnight, and Nowhere was in northern Iowa, just south of the Minnesota state line. It wouldn't take us long to reach Minneapolis.

"Late is late." Sal scratched at his beard, then ran a smoothing hand over it. "Just shows her lack of consideration. Not that I'm surprised."

Reg frowned, which had been his general expression all week, since his tiff with Poe, but I was vaguely surprised to see him directing his scowl toward Sal. "If you dislike Lina so much, why maintain this retirement? You gave up slaying for her. You could just as easily take up the stake again."

Sal thought a moment, then said, "It wasn't only for her. She was the . . . catalyst. Once I knew her, I knew vampires had souls, and that's the sort of thing you can't unknow. Takes the fun out of the hunt, knowing your prey has a heart that feels, even if it doesn't beat."

We all fell silent at that, but the quiet didn't last long, as a car horn blared through the night.

Reg and I both started at the sound, and Sal jumped all the way to his feet, bellowing, "Hearts and souls, but NO MANNERS!"

He threw open the front door, glaring at the black car with tinted windows idling on the road alongside the white picket fence.

I pushed past him, yanking a black beanie over my hair and bracing against the cold. "What's she supposed to do? Come to the door? You know she can't walk through the gate."

The car window slid down, and Lina's voice sliced out. "I wouldn't darken that doorstep again even if he tore down the whole damn fence!"

"I'll never take it down!" he shouted back, unnecessarily. Lina could have heard him at a whisper, and he knew it. I think it just felt good to shout.

Reg followed me onto the porch, wrapping something

around the collar of his shirt as he walked. When he pulled his hands away, I saw it was a bow tie.

"Oh my God, what are you wearing? You're so embarrassing."

"I'm much more concerned about the words that will come out of your mouth than the ornament around my neck," he said, gliding out to the car.

I looked once more at Sal. A part of me wanted to ask the old guy if he was okay, but I knew Lina would hear, and it felt like some kind of betrayal to womankind.

"Last chance to stay out of the wolves' den," he said.

"Gross," I scoffed. "I wouldn't be caught dead in the lair of a wolf. Filthy beasts."

One side of Sal's mouth ticked up. "They're not so bad after a bath."

"I do *not* want to know how you know that."

I started down the steps, but Sal called me back.

"Charlie."

I turned, waiting.

"Be careful tonight."

I feigned annoyance. "Don't talk like you're the grown-up and I'm the kid. Your gray hair doesn't actually make you older."

"Only wiser."

I started to retort, but I could see his half smile was strained and his eyes downcast. I decided to let him have the last word for once and simply gave him a goodbye salute before jogging out to the waiting car.

"They're meeting here?" I asked with disdain.

When Lina had told us the location was a theater, I'd pictured a grand space and a dramatically lit stage. Instead, we were standing in the basement of the building, surrounded by mildewing concrete walls with the steady, echoing *drip drip* of water.

Reg was at my elbow, wearing a similar sneer of disapproval. "It's not at all befitting of the governing body of the most advanced species on the planet, is it?"

"The Elder Seat never meets in the same place twice," Lina said.

She guided us to a door at the far end of the basement. "After a few millennia, that gets pretty difficult."

She threw the door open without waiting for a response and ushered us into a very different environment.

It was still the basement, but the concrete was bathed in the glow of a hundred candles, perched on pipes and tucked into wall nooks, filling every available space. Either this place had no power, or someone went to a lot of trouble to set a mood. The *drip drip* was still audible, but it seemed in harmony with the soft hum of voices on this side of the door. The murmuring only grew when Lina stepped into the room, and one by one, the Elders backed away to clear a space for the Ancient in their midst.

My chest puffed up a little. They thought they'd had us beat, forcing all the clans to turn us away, but they hadn't counted on us playing this card.

As the crowd parted for Lina, it became clear that there was a hierarchy in the room. A few dozen Elders lined the space, a representative for every house in every clan. They milled around on foot, while five stood together on a small platform at one end of the room, slightly elevated above the rest. I recognized Elder Adante among them and felt a small current of shock to realize he was among the council's highest-ranking members.

"Adelina," Elder Adante's voice floated out over the room. "Always a pleasure to be in your presence. Ladies and gentlemen, please welcome our honored guest, Adelina la Prima."

The whispers in the room rose to applause, and Lina nodded politely in response.

Adante's gaze slid from Lina to me and Reg, hovering by the door. "And, of course, our *human* guests."

I gritted my teeth at the way he emphasized "human," followed by a little cluck of his tongue, taunting us with his mock pity for our sad circumstances. Or maybe he did it to scare us, to remind us we were prey for the rest of the room. A quick ripple of fear threatened to wash over me, but I steeled myself against it. I would not give them the satisfaction.

The door slammed shut behind us, causing the hundreds of candle flames to flicker in a wave around the room. Not so long ago, a rolling fire in a room full of Elders clad in black robes would have been exactly my kind of drama. But something had shifted in me in the last couple of months, and after letting a little color into my life, this scene now seemed more drab than dramatic.

In fact, as I looked around the room at all of the bloodless skin, faded like river rocks worn down by an endless flow of water, and all topped by the same dark eyes and shiny black hair, it struck me how one-note and boring it all seemed. The guests were as much of a letdown as the venue. Lina shone like a diamond in a bowl of ashes, and I half wondered if the Elders were keeping their distance from her out of reverence or out of fear they would catch her blondness.

If you asked me, this crew could benefit from a few high-lights.

"Thank you for the kind introductions," Lina said, warm but formal. "If only we could stay until dawn, catching up, but we have a journey home to make yet tonight, at mortal speed, so the sooner we get started, the better."

"Yes, of course," Adante said. "Let us begin."

TWENTY-EIGHT

A BUNCH OF OLD FOLKS . . . REALLY, REALLY OLD

"By Blood and Bone, by Starlight and Shadow, I call this conclave to order."

The voice that spoke the pronouncement was clear and melodic, and belonged to an Elder girl who looked barely older than us in human years. She, Adante, and the other ranking elders had formed a line on their makeshift dais, while Reg and I stood before them in the center of the room, Elders circled around us.

I narrowed my eyes at the Elder girl. With her doe eyes and slick black ponytail, she could practically pass as a teenager. I wondered if she had voted against us when the Elder Seat decided to cast us back to mortality.

Hypocrite.

"Well?" she asked.

It took a beat for me to realize that they were waiting on us to speak.

"Oh," I said. "Was that it?"

The Elder girl looked offended.

"I just meant . . . it was so . . ."

"So efficient," Reg supplied. "How refreshing to be back among kindred who waste no time getting right to business."

"Kind of you to say," the Elder girl answered. "But, of course, we are no longer kindred."

Reg did not miss a beat. "A matter we hope to rectify here this evening."

He had the charm on full volume.

"As you can imagine," he went on, "humans take a painfully long time to do anything. It's almost as if they don't realize their time is limited."

A twitter of appreciation went around the room, and I'm almost certain I saw Reg wink.

There was no sign of the Reg who had warmed up to humans and even had a mortal boyfriend. He just seemed his old self. He really was a talented actor.

Elder Adante stepped to the edge of the platform, looking down at us. "Well then, since your limited human hours are so precious, I suggest you not waste time with any further comedy."

I don't know if it was his condescending tone or the way he stood deliberately towering over us . . . or if it was simply that seeing his face again took me back to that night outside Sal's fence, but something in me snapped.

"You're right that this is no comedy," I seethed. "It's a tragedy. And the time that's been wasted is ours. All the hours we spent drafting letters to the clans, seeking a sponsor for an appeal, only to discover we'd been . . . *blackballed*. It should not have taken an Ancient for us to earn our place before this council."

"Charlie."

I heard Reg's words, felt his hand on my shoulder, but both seemed very far away. Out of the corner of my eye, I spotted two Elder women whispering to each other and giggling. At me. At us. We were a joke to them. I knew now, with certainty, what I'd felt the moment we'd stepped into the chamber—that this whole thing was a farce. Lina could get us in the door, but she couldn't give us our immortality. She had said as much, hadn't she? I should have listened.

Well, if I wasn't going to get my life back, at least I would say my piece.

"What a sham," I whispered. Then, raising my voice: "It's so clear to me that this isn't about what we did to that boy."

The words came out in a shuddered breath. It felt so good to release them, to speak that truth, but it also coated me with dread, because now that they were out, I couldn't take them back. I could only charge forward.

"You've all done as much or worse." I shot my accusation around the room, and where Reg had earned laughter, I got only bared fangs. "This is about the treaty."

Adante feigned ignorance. "Which treaty is that? There are so many."

"The Treaty of Annis. You are just waiting for young vampires to make mistakes so you can cast them out, whether they . . . whether *we* deserve it or not!"

The doe-eyed Elder glided forward to stand next to Adante.

"Were that true, I would be there beside you."

Her voice had the rhythm of youth, but the way she carried herself was far more mature. Annoyingly so. I briefly, begrudgingly wondered if maybe they were only chasing out the immortals who *acted* like teenagers.

Adante tilted his head in a patronizing way. "While it is true that we are wary of the actions of immortals turned before they achieve emotional maturity, it is also true that we fiercely guard our own. Your penalty had everything to do with your actions and nothing at all to do with your age."

"Bullsh—"

"Charlie!"

This time Reg's hand was not on my shoulder but slapped over my mouth, protecting me from making a fatal mistake, even if that mistake meant he could spend more time with Poe, with the humans. I still suspected that's what he wanted, deep down. But he was my brother, and he took my side even when it meant not taking his own. Lina was right. We were family, and human or vampire, we loved each other.

So, because—and *only* because—I loved my brother, I managed to shut my trap.

"We understand the treaty to be only another layer that protects vampires from exposure," Reg said, his hands now pressed together instead of covering my mouth. "But I beseech the Elder Seat to consider whether it is possible that these new age limits have biased you unfairly against the actions of young immortals?"

"On the contrary. Age limits are for the benefit of the young, to protect children," the Elder girl said.

"Protect," Lina blurted out with a snort. She was scowling at the edge of the open circle, the nearest Elders still providing her an invisible buffer. "More like control."

"Something to add, Adelina?" Adante asked.

He gestured to the platform, offering Lina a stage, but she held her ground. She did not need to look down on others to command their attention.

"Only that the Elder Seat has not changed. As always, you take the law and manipulate it to your advantage. The treaty protects mortal children from being turned before they are of age, but where is the law to protect the *immortal* children? Your alleged passion for the rights of children only extends to humans, while you turn your own kind mortal without a second thought."

"They violated the treaty," Adante demurred. "Surely you don't suggest we allow young vampires to disregard our laws. If children were immune from repercussions, chaos would reign."

"I'm suggesting only that the punishment does not fit the crime. What these two did was an accident. What was done to them in return was more than an injustice. It was a cruelty."

My heart swelled with gratitude and— *Damn it, here come the tears.*

I quickly swiped at my eyes, nodding once at Lina in thanks before facing forward again.

Adante bowed to Lina in a bored way. "Thank you,

Adelina, for your wisdom. May we always seek the counsel of our Ancients."

The other four Elder leaders also bowed.

"However," Adante said as he straightened. "While Ancients may counsel, it is the Elders who govern. And so, our decision has already been made."

I knew it.

"That's not fair," I said, though it hardly mattered.

"No, it is likely not," he said. "And I see now that it would have been better to wait to hear all you had to say tonight."

Was that sarcasm? I felt my cheeks pink, knowing I had not impressed. Even if they had heard us out before making a decision, I was sure I had done very little to help our case.

Adante considered us a moment, thinking to himself, then said, "Yes, perhaps had we waited . . . Nevertheless, it's done, and the answer is yes."

"Wait!" I cried. "You can't just—"

Just . . .

"Did you say . . . ?"

Yes?

"Yes?" Reg finished.

"Against our better judgment," Adante said.

Yes!

"But we have a need," he added.

"What need?" Reg asked.

I had the same question but was too breathless to speak.

"Tell them about the conditions," the Elder girl said.

My shock, poised to spill over into excitement, now stuck in my throat like tar. I forced it down with a swallow. "Conditions?"

"A formality, really," Adante said, straightening the sleeves of his robe. "We simply need your help procuring something."

Well, that didn't sound too bad. Reg and I could still be pretty stealthy, even without our immortal powers. As long as they didn't want us to rob a bank or something, in which case . . . whatever, I would still figure it out. We were going home!

I flashed a smile at Reg, but his eyes were hooded. Of course he wasn't happy. He wasn't quite ready to return to our true lives, but it was now or never. He had to see that!

"What we need," Adante went on, "is something you are uniquely positioned to help us acquire."

"Anything," I promised.

Adante actually smiled, the tips of his fangs just visible. "Lovely. Perhaps this will not be a mistake after all. Simply deliver the village of Nowhere, and you'll once again be one of us."

"Deliver the—"

"Nowhere?"

Reg and I talked on top of one another.

"The whole town?"

"How do you deliver a—"

"Exactly what would that entail—"

"The *whole town*?!"

Adante closed his eyes and touched a hand to his ear. "One at a time, please."

"So noisy," the Elder girl said. She looked at us as if observing animals in a zoo. "Were they also loud vampires, or is it a human-acquired condition?"

"You can study them later," Lina snarled from behind us. "I want to hear the rest of this proposal."

I felt her presence as she positioned herself at our shoulders, sensed a kind of angry heat radiating off her.

Adante said, "As you know, the Blood Clan has been having . . . *difficulty* maintaining a home base. Always so ostentatious, so loose with our laws." He smiled around the room. "Present company excluded, of course. But on the whole, from Vlad Dracula on, our Blood brethren have been practically screaming for attention."

A grumble of assent went around the room, and I had to concur.

Dracula. So embarrassing.

Not only did he have some pretty disgusting feeding habits, but also, he was a total nutjob—known for staking humans to prove they were as vulnerable to a spear of wood through the heart as we were—and much more susceptible to pain. Just, all around, not the best spokesperson for immortality.

Adante continued. "For centuries, we've been moving the clan from one continent to another, always seeking more remote locations. But this world is getting smaller, and there are fewer places for the Blood to dwell in anonymity."

"I hear Antarctica is nice this time of year," Lina drawled.

The Elder girl hissed at Lina, her fangs bared.

So, she was a Blood. I knew I didn't like her.

"Unfortunately, the food in the Antarctic is in short supply," Adante quipped. "And keeping the clan remote has made them difficult to police. It is time to settle the Blood Clan in a place where we can keep them under a watchful eye, and where better than a community where we already have such deep ties?"

I assumed by deep ties, he meant the old rock in the woods and the history lesson Sal had given us. Or maybe there was more. Maybe Madame Bissett was a fairy, and the guy who ran the barbershop a werewolf. At this point, very little would surprise me about Nowhere.

The Elder girl regained her composure but continued to shoot eye daggers at Lina. With effort, she added, "I must agree my brethren could benefit from close monitoring."

Her Blood dialect was nearly undetectable. I wondered if she spent more time with the other Elders than with her own kin.

"But it is not our sole purpose," she said. "The time comes to take what is ours."

A flicker of candlelight shone in her black eyes, and in that gleam, I saw the black rock of the stone marker. The two sides carved with an equal claim.

"Primus interitus," I breathed.

"It is a sacred place," Adante confirmed, with a hand over his unbeating heart.

"Sacred," the doe-eyed girl said. "But also completely boring and invisible."

Lina bristled at the insult, and I was surprised to find Reg and myself prickling alongside her. It was one thing for *me* to insult Nowhere. It was another thing entirely for this baby-faced Elder to take potshots.

Adante placed a warning hand on the girl's arm.

"The village has always belonged to us. It was only a matter of time before we had need for it," he said. "It is an appropriate choice to make a home for our kind, to reduce their risk of exposure."

"How exactly are they safe from exposure there?" I asked. "I mean, yeah, it's a tiny town—village, whatever—but it's still town*ish*. There are hundreds of people—"

"The people will be dispatched," Adante said.

I gasped, and, next to me, Reg made a strangled sound.

"You're going to kill them?" I managed to choke out.

"Certainly not! Messy business, killing, and against our law." He looked me directly in the eye. "As you well know."

Oh, that was totally uncalled for.

"We didn't kill . . ." I growled, but Lina gave me a warning poke in the back.

"The village of Nowhere has nearly one thousand souls," she said to Adante. "Surely this isn't necessary."

"The infrastructure provides an immediate home for all clan members," he said.

"But perhaps another village—"

246

"It is ours!" Adante burst out.

He closed his eyes a moment and fussed with his sleeves. Then he repeated with calm, "It is ours."

"Why now?" I asked. "You already own most of the land. Not that I understand why you're so interested. It's basically a graveyard for the first . . . *undoing*." I managed to say the last word without air quotes. "But what about neutral ground? Wasn't that the deal?"

Adante gave me an appraising look. "I see you've learned something of our history. Well, be assured, the promise of neutral ground remains. Our agreement was with slayers, and our interests protect the history of both our kind and theirs. It is the humans we are tired of working around. *They* have invaded *our* land. It's time to take it back."

Reg said, "So you intend to steal their homes and . . . what? Wipe their minds?"

"The memory fade will be part of it," Adante answered.

"A migration," Lina said at my shoulder, her words coming through gritted teeth.

"What's a migration?" Reg and I asked in unison.

"It's when entire mortal communities are displaced," Lina said. "Over the course of our history, it has, in rare cases, been necessary to relocate mortals for our protection or for their own. But it has not been done in the modern age." She addressed Adante. "It could be extremely difficult."

He shrugged off her concern. "Protocols will be followed. We'll subdue the population for easy transport, secure their memories, and deposit the humans a safe distance away."

Translation: they'll feed on everyone until they pass out, do a brain swipe, and then dump them all in a field somewhere.

A wave of nausea rolled over me.

"I don't understand," Reg said, sounding genuinely confused. "If your goal is to remain inconspicuous, is this not counterintuitive? Hundreds of people waking up with mass amnesia is sure to draw attention."

"We have procedures in place for such things," Adante said. "The population will be taken care of. Bank accounts full. They'll be a little foggy, but they will all share a memory of the tragedy that forced them out of their village . . . a fire, perhaps. Or a flood. Yes, a flood, I think. Less drama. And, of course, they will have no desire to return or to even discuss it."

"Won't they wonder why this 'flood' didn't make the news or show up in their social media feeds?" I challenged.

Adante smiled. "Would that we could erase the whole internet. But not to worry. We have a cadre in place for the rare occasion when a memory fade must be handled en masse. They've never done a migration—mostly cleanup for incidents at nightclubs or small sporting events—but I'm certain they are up to the task. They plant newspaper articles, forge photos, perform memory work on reporters, and, yes, even handle the dreaded social media."

I blinked. "Sorry, are you saying you have a supersized memory-wipe street team?"

"More like a PR firm," the doe-eyed Elder said. "For damage control."

"So you admit you're doing damage," Lina said.

Bile rose into my throat as I imagined my friends knocked out by vampire venom, bites on their necks, and a pack of Elders, kneeling one by one alongside them, whispering in their ears, telling them what to remember and what to forget, inserting tragic memories of nightmares that never even happened.

My friends. They would lose their homes, their histories.

But they would keep their lives.

I couldn't say the same for me and Reg. If we refused to help, we were falling on our own stakes, doomed to mortality and certain death.

Adante spread his arms. "You needn't worry about these trivial details. You need only to help us gather them up, and this human detour will be but a memory."

"Gather them up?" I didn't understand.

The Elder girl folded her hands in front of her, her pose all schoolteacher, even though her face was all student.

"The process is more manageable when prey"—she cleared her throat—"*people* are all together. When they scatter, the hunt takes longer. More go astray. A gathering is more efficient."

"What kind of gathering?" Reg asked.

"How about a blood drive?" I deadpanned.

The room tittered at that, but Adante missed the joke. "The temptation would be too great," he said. "The feeding might get out of control."

"Then what did you have in mind?" Lina asked.

"A carnival, a festival, a fair—American humans love a fair." Adante pulled something from the pocket of his robe, a single sheet of paper that I recognized, with a sudden falling sensation, the instant he unfolded it. He raised the flyer with a flourish and a fanged grin.

"Or how about a hoopla?"

TWENTY-NINE

THE LESSER OF TWO EVILS

The ride home was quiet.

The darkness outside the car was broken only by the occasional streak of moonlight cutting through a break in the trees, as Lina sliced and swerved through a forested stretch of road. Her driving was expert, her every motion on the wheel and the gear shift utterly controlled. But her face was a storm of emotions, wild and enraged. She spoke aloud, though not to us and not in complete sentences.

"Should have known . . . conclave this close to Iowa . . . too convenient . . . planned this all along . . . Blood monsters . . ."

In contrast, Reg sat still and silent in the shadowy back seat, his steady breathing the only proof he was even alive. It wasn't long before I went crazy in the space between and blurted out, "Well? Let's have it, then!"

Lina frowned. "Have what?"

"You're both mad at me, right? But what was I supposed to do? They're taking the town, with or without us. At least this way, we get what we want too."

"You're being shrill" was Reg's calm response.

"And selfish?" I asked.

"He didn't say that," Lina said.

"He thought it."

"It sounds like maybe *you* thought it."

I huffed and stared out the window to avoid her gaze. Wisdom came with age and all that, but I was quickly learning that Ancients could be know-it-alls.

It was me who responded when Adante presented his plan, me who spoke first when Reg and Lina fell silent, and me who filled in the gaps the Elders needed to stake their claim on Nowhere. It had to be me. My name was on the flyer.

I'd known the second I'd seen the paper in Adante's hand that it was the reason we'd been given a second chance. They saw my name in the list of committee contacts—an insider who could ensure their plan succeeded. The Halloween Hoopla flyer promised a party where everyone is invited, but the Elders wanted to know if everyone actually attended. I confirmed for them that it was a whole-town shindig, which they called an ideal scenario for a migration event.

I shivered in the passenger seat of Lina's car, remembering how the ranking council members casually discussed plans to dispatch teams to deal with the old and infirm, or any other outliers who may not attend.

Lina had not hid her opposition, practically spitting as she argued. "This won't work. The event ends when night falls."

"I can push the awards until after dark," I'd said.

"Charlie!"

I did not—*could* not—look at Lina, so I'd kept my eyes on the council. "The whole thing ends with awards for best costumes and best parade floats. The committee says people always stay for that part, because you have to be present to claim your prize."

I had gone on to declare that I could not only extend the event into the night but also get most of the crowd inside the school, where they'd be more easily surrounded. With every promise, I'd assured myself that I was saving lives, not the least of all, our own. It came down to our mortality versus their town, and it was no contest. Wasn't Nowhere the kind of place everyone was trying to escape anyway?

If that was selfish, I could live with that. And if all went according to plan, I *would* live with it . . . for a very long time.

"And how, precisely, do you plan to do all that?" Reg had asked nervously at my side.

"I'll figure it out."

"See that you do," Adante had said.

Then he'd read from the flyer. "'October 31, from sunup to sundown.'" He'd smiled as he folded the paper and pocketed it once more. "Sundown, indeed."

Lina's voice pulled me from the candlelit basement back to the dim interior of her car.

"I agree you had little choice," she said. "They are the Elder Seat. You are a human trying to reclaim your place among them. They know full well the position you are in. It's a weakness, and they exploited it."

"What about you though?" I asked. "You have no weaknesses."

She laughed, but there was no humor in it. "Oh, I absolutely do. A weakness for humans, for one thing. Certain humans in particular..."

"But I saw the way they all respect you."

"They *fear* me."

"Same thing."

She shook her head. "Not remotely. They fear the mental instability of some Ancients far more than they fear our strength and speed. There is a reason Elders are the governing body and not Ancients. Vampire minds grow tired, if not old. Some lose their grip on reality altogether. We must follow the law to keep the system from collapsing, and the Elder Seat is best suited to make and enforce those laws... even if I don't always agree with them."

I hesitated. "And you don't agree this time?"

"I agree that you should have the chance to reclaim your lives. I just wish our friends and neighbors didn't have to pay the price."

"Do you think we should have refused?" Reg's question floated up from the back seat, and I heard in his question the same needling doubt I was feeling.

When I had pictured our appeal, I hadn't imagined that victory would come with such a catch. Immortality was within reach, but at what cost to our friends? To Sal? To everyone in Nowhere? It was a new and uncomfortable feeling, considering the needs of others in addition to my own. I hoped it would go away when I was vampire again.

"Charlie's probably right that this is happening whether you help or not," Lina said. "By agreeing, you save your immortal lives. If you had refused, the only thing you would have saved is your conscience."

Lina had a way of not answering questions that left me wondering if she was reassuring us or scolding us.

"The migration sounds awful," I said. "I wish there was another way."

Lina looked through the windshield, but she was gazing at something much farther off than the road, a thousand miles away and a thousand years ago. "I remember a time when vampires had no rules. I can still see it when I close my eyes . . . entire villages coated in blood, painted red with the feed."

The visual made me queasy, and it was almost impossible to believe that only recently, the same scene might have made me thirsty. It scared me how much I had changed in such a short amount of time—how much of myself I'd already lost.

"All of this just to babysit the Blood Clan," I complained.

"Not really," Reg said. "It's clearly about the town."

Lina agreed. "The Elder Seat has wanted it for a long time."

"I understand why they keep the location secret, to prevent war over the land," I said. "But why wouldn't they pass down the story of the slayer origin? It could actually save vampire lives. Until I met Sal, I didn't even know slayer power was in their skin, not their stakes."

"I knew," Reg said. "It's not exactly a secret. It's there in our history books, if you look for it."

"But the *undoing* . . ." This time I did use my air quotes. "If it's such a sacred moment for immortals, you'd think they'd tell us all about it."

"Do you want to see it?" Lina asked quietly.

Reg and I both leaned toward her. "What do you mean?" I asked.

Lina did not answer, but instantly, a scene filled my vision, and I could tell by the way Reg slammed back in his seat that he was seeing it too.

"How are you doing this?" I cried in wonder. "Without venom?"

"Some Ancients can touch minds without using venom." She then assured us, "I cannot take your memories. I can only share my own."

In front of me, I saw both the dark road through the windshield and also a different night, a different landscape—one of barren, rocky hills and a star-filled sky. Switching between the two visions was like shifting focus from something close to something far.

"This memory is not mine," Lina said. "It is one that has been passed to me by others, to ensure it was not lost when the Elder Seat decided to bury the story."

She went quiet then, and the volume in her memory seemed to turn up. I heard wind sweeping over the hills and a scrape of loose rock as feet climbed the hill. A woman came into view, her hair long and black, her body wrapped in furs. She carried a wooden spear in one hand and a bag fashioned out of some kind of animal pelt in the other. One moment she was alone, and the next, she was surrounded.

Six vampires circled, not attacking right away but toying with her, terrifying her.

"What poor form," Reg criticized from the back seat.

Finally, one of the vampires lunged, his movements almost too quick to see, and a second later, he was gone, the end of the woman's spear and a circle of smoke where his chest had been. The woman's face lit up in alarm, but she did not stop moving, driving her spear through another vampire, then another, turning them each to smoke.

Exhausted by her efforts, she dropped her spear and collapsed to her knees, ready to succumb to the remaining three vampires. When the first vampire approached, she actually hugged him—just as Sal had described. But as her arms folded around him, he collapsed, his strength and speed gone. He rolled to the side, clutching his chest, and I knew exactly what he was feeling, that first pounding of a newly beating heart. Color appeared in his cheeks, and he breathed heavily in and out. The last two vampires watched in horror as their companion turned human, and the woman stared at her hands, knowing she had done it without knowing how.

The awe in her expression shifted quickly to a ferocious determination, and she stood, all exhaustion seemingly gone. She had only to reach for the two remaining vampires, and

257

they were running away in fear.

The image faded, but the memory stayed, now belonging to me and Reg, just as it belonged to Lina, even though none of us had seen it with our own eyes.

"It was self-defense," I observed. "That's how her slayer powers emerged."

Lina's smile was grim. "Imagine if immortals knew the true origin of slayers. It makes them look like victims-turned-heroes, instead of the villainous vampire killers our kind make them out to be."

"True," I said. "But covering it up seems like a lot of trouble to go to just to keep vampires from going soft on slayers."

"It's politics," Reg said, and Lina nodded.

"The Elder Seat has worked hard to send the message to vampire-kind that we are not monsters but merely a superior species, top of the food chain. The truth I've just shown you complicates that narrative."

"You would almost think the Elders themselves would want to forget," Reg said. "Let the town grow and develop, bury this moment forever."

"It's a reminder that we are not invincible and that there is a punishment worse than true death," Lina said. "But I think your point is well made, Reg. It's not exactly a proud moment for immortals, which is why I believe vampires don't personally inhabit the area."

"Present company excluded," Reg said.

Lina conceded that with a smile.

"The Elders built a few homesteads to lend legitimacy to

their land claims in the early days," she said. "When they started using slayers for mortal punishments, the homesteads became a convenient location for new humans to adjust. Eventually, it turned into a little village, and the Elders named it Nowhere. They thought the place was so insignificant it was almost invisible, so I guess they thought the name was funny."

"Well, joke's on them," I pointed out. "It may be small by today's standards, but it's not invisible."

"And that is precisely the problem. They worry it's already too large, so they're looking to take it back. They'll forge whatever documents and perform any memory fades needed to take ownership of all the land in and around the town, so there won't be any place left for humans."

I groaned. "And then they're just going to hand it to the Bloods. What a waste."

"The Blood Clan is coming," Lina said. "You can help with the migration and let the Elders clear the village before they get here, or you can refuse and watch what happens when the Bloods arrive. I promise you, this way is more humane."

"The Elders promised no lives would be taken," Reg said. "You don't trust them?"

"I trust the council to do as they promise on Halloween. I don't trust what comes after—that they can control a village full of Blood vampires."

"The Bloods," I grumbled. "Can't we just run them all through Sal's fence and see how *they* like being human?"

Lina laughed. "Now *that* is something I would like to see!"

* * *

Two hours later, with a thin dawn light creeping over the fields, Lina's car rolled to a stop outside that very fence. The soft pop of gravel under her tires and Reg's soft snore were the only sounds left of the endless night.

"What will you tell Sal?" Lina said.

I sighed. "As little as possible."

The tricky part wouldn't be keeping a secret from the slayer but figuring out how to get him to play his part. It was the final promise we'd made to the Elders—to keep the slayer home on Halloween.

That particular deception turned my stomach in knots, but, of course, it was the only option. He may have been a loner, but this was still his home, and he'd die before seeing it overrun with vampires, especially the Blood Clan.

"Sal would do anything to protect Nowhere," I said.

"He'd do anything to protect *you*."

"From what? Eternal life?"

"He doesn't see it that way."

Lina's head dropped back in the seat, her face turned toward the cottage with a faraway expression.

"You still love him," I said.

"Worse. I miss him." She pointed to the cottage. "He's *right there*, and I *miss* him."

"You can see him anytime you want. He says the fence probably won't even work on you. Or I could bring him to All Hours . . ."

"No!" She snapped. She took a steadying breath, just like a human would, and it looked so natural I almost believed she needed the oxygen. "It's hard to see him. Watching him age is painful. Every day, every year, closer to an end—a real end."

"He's a stubborn ass for not letting you turn him," I said.

"I'll give you stubborn ass, but you have to understand that he made me an offer too. We both refused."

"But his offer isn't fair," I protested. "Turning mortal on purpose is like . . . like committing suicide!"

"Some days I want to take him up on the offer," Lina confided. "At least then we would pass the days and years together. The more he ages, the further away from me he gets, and one day, it will be too late."

I tried to imagine Dexter growing older without me, becoming an adult, a husband, a dad and, eventually, an old man like Sal.

My voice came out in a hush. "And when that day comes, the day when it's too late to change your mind . . . what then?"

Lina cast one more wistful gaze at the cottage, as if she could see right through the walls to the man sleeping inside.

"It took three thousand years to find him. It will take an eternity to forget him."

The way she said it, like she would spend that eternity drowning in sadness, almost made immortality sound unpleasant.

I unbuckled my seat belt, reaching around to shake Reg awake. A thin line of drool had escaped his mouth, and I added drooling while sleeping to my growing list of the worst things about being human. It was certainly one of the grossest bits.

We said good night to Lina and stepped out into the cool gray light of morning. She kept the car idling to make sure we got safely inside, putting it in gear only when the front door opened to reveal Sal on the threshold. I stood on the front porch, watching Sal watching Lina, until the sun broke fully over the cornfields, flooding the whole sad scene in a blaze of light.

And so the night ended as it had begun, with the slayer refusing to come out and the vampire refusing to come in. I supposed this was how it had always been and how it would always be—two worlds, sun and shadow, destined to stand on opposite ends of an eternal battlefield, lined with wooden stakes.

And in the middle were me and Reg, mere mortals tasked with gathering up humans for slaughter. To be fair, it was the nondeadly kind, but it still felt like a slaughter. Something would definitely die in the days to come, and it would be at least partially our fault. But as long as human lives were spared, then wasn't the death of a place called Nowhere a fair price to pay for immortality?

Gravel crunched under the tires as Lina's car finally pulled away, steering into the sunrise. I watched it go until it was swallowed up in a cloud of dust.

We couldn't stop what was coming. All we could do was pick a side, and with no good options, the best side to pick was our own. In the fight between immortal and mortal, eternal life versus inescapable death . . . I chose life.

I chose vampire.

THIRTY
THE TWILIGHT BETWEEN

The decision seemed easy there on the cottage porch, at the end of the night I'd been awaiting for months—ever since we'd been stranded in Nowhere, Iowa. But the next day, surrounded by humans in the bright hallways of Hope High, what had been so clear was suddenly a little cloudy. I was deliberately late to school Monday morning, to avoid our daily gathering at Poe's locker; I feigned illness to get out of gym class with the twins; I silenced my phone so I wouldn't see Dex's texts; and I squirmed all through French as I tried to picture Madame Bissett in some other classroom, some other school, some other town.

I had to remind myself over and over that we didn't have a choice in what happened to Nowhere; our only choice was whether we played a part. The futures of Dex and Syd and Soph and Poe, of all our teachers and classmates, were inevitable. Our own destinies, though, still hung in the balance. Our actions might not make a difference for Nowhere, but they would mean life or death for me and Reg.

Still, I managed to avoid eye contact with anyone at all for the entire day.

But after school came the moment I could not avoid. Halloween was less than a week away, and I needed to move fast to make good on our promise to the Elders. All I had to do was push the party past dark and get as much of the crowd inside as possible. I had one meeting to convince the committee to make a few small changes.

"I know it's last-minute, but I just think a Halloween party that ends when it gets dark is kind of lame," I said. "I'm only suggesting an extra hour or two."

"You couldn't have thought of this *before* we printed the flyers?" Mark muttered.

The committee was spread out across an empty classroom, some perched on desks and others slumped into chairs. Sydney had propped herself up on a windowsill, the sunlight behind her turning her hair an electric shade of pink, her jaw working on a wad of gum, as always.

"It does seem more Halloween-y," she said.

"But what about families?" Sophia countered from across the room, clipboard in hand. "Kids will want to get home for trick-or-treating."

"I hadn't thought about that," I admitted.

Mark scoffed. "Of course not."

I ignored him and paced the room, tracing a line between Sydney and Sophia, the only two votes on the committee that really mattered. "But I'm only talking about an extra hour. Plenty of time left for trick-or-treating. And I was also thinking we should move the awards at the end of the night into the gym."

"What about the after-party dance?!" cried a red-haired girl whose name I'd never bothered to learn.

"We can still do that," I said. "After the announcements. But everyone will be able to see and hear better in the gym, and we can make a big deal about the winners, let them walk up the risers to get their prizes, maybe drop some balloons or shoot some confetti. . . ."

"So now we have to buy confetti?" Mark complained.

I made a mental note to push him in front of the first Elder I saw on Halloween. They wanted Nowhere? They could start with Mark.

"That could get pretty tight," Sophia pointed out, ever practical. "The gym is big, but it will be packed with the whole town in there."

"Exactly," I said. "It will look so much bigger inside!"

Sydney popped her gum. "I see what you mean."

She did?

"It's the fiftieth anniversary, and we're just doing the same old thing."

I seized on that. "Right! We need to make a splash. If we're running the show, it needs to be the biggest one this town has ever seen. It's all about the body count . . . I mean . . ." I cast around for a different phrase. "I'm just saying, bigger is better."

"Longer hours could help raise a little more money," Sophia relented. "Extra time for raffle-ticket sales and other fundraising booths. But only if people are willing to stay."

"They'll definitely stay if we keep the prizes until the end,"

Sydney said. "Everyone's always dying to see who wins."

Her words sent a tiny chill down my body. *No one would be dying*, I reminded myself.

Sophia tapped a pen against her clipboard. "What if one more hour puts us over the top?" she mused. "Record-breaking fundraiser for charity would look pretty good on a college application."

Always with the college dreaming. See? In Nowhere, everyone was trying to get *somewhere*. I was just the pied piper helping them along.

"Okay, fine," the redhead said. "But only if we agree that after the awards, we kick out the senior citizen set and still have an after-party."

Everyone voiced their agreement while I chewed on a nail and pretended to notice something interesting on the floor. They would all have plenty of school dances in their future . . . somewhere else.

Sophia called for a vote, and then the committee got to work creating social media posts and updating the flyer. It had all been so much easier than I'd expected, with everyone just falling in line. That was the power of a queen bee. Too bad all my bees would soon forget I existed.

Reg reacted to my success with worse than his usual indifference. When I filled him in on the committee meeting, he grunted, "Great. Guess that's that, then," with a giant scowl. I didn't get a chance to ask what was eating him before Sal interrupted and put us to work helping with dinner.

Later, we sat at the kitchen table, enjoying Sal's famous chili for possibly the last time, and I waited to poke Reg until Sal took one of his "constitutionals" (a colorful term he used for taking a little too long in the bathroom that did nothing to tame the visual).

"You know we don't have a choice," I reminded Reg. I kept my voice to a whisper, even though Sal could never hear us over the bathroom fan.

"I know."

"And you know our friends will be taken care of."

"I know."

"Including Poe."

"Whatever."

"Okay, what's the problem?"

It wasn't like Reg to be this surly, and I worried he wasn't fully on board with our Halloween plan. Admittedly, I wasn't fully on board with it myself, but it was us or everyone else. I hoped Reg could see we didn't have any other options.

Sal returned then, and I jerked a thumb in his direction as he sat back down to his bowl of chili. "You're as grouchy as this guy."

"Hey!" Sal feigned offense, grasping his chest as if he'd been wounded. Then he dropped the show and nodded at Reg. "She's got a point though. Something's been eatin' you since Minnesota."

All Sal knew about our trip was that we had gained approval

to return to immortality but not the when or the how, and he definitely didn't know the price to be paid. He didn't ask a lot of questions, but he made it clear that he blamed Lina for the whole thing. He seemed to think she had pulled some strings on our behalf.

Reg pushed his bowl away. "I apologize for my foul mood. I'm brooding over some recent disappointments."

"Such as?" Sal asked.

I shot Reg a look. He'd better not reveal more than we discussed with Sal.

"Such as acquiring only an understudy role in Mr. Shakespeare's comedy. Such as failing to bring home a trophy for the debate team." He sighed. "I've always wanted a trophy."

I stared at him, thunderstruck. *That* was what was bugging him? His failure to achieve human high school glory?

"Tough breaks," Sal said. "But character building."

Reg rolled his neck, shook out his limbs, and flopped back in his chair. It was the most *teen* he'd ever looked. "I know, you're right. And Poe was right too. He probably would be better at debate than me."

"Better than *I*," I said, smirking at Reg as he looked up. But even a grammar joke couldn't get him to crack a smile, so I added gently, "To be fair, Poe said he would be *good* at debate, not *better*."

"He would be though," Reg said. "Better at debate, better at theater, better at charming the teachers, better even in some of our coursework . . ."

I leaned forward, elbows on the table. "I'm not a relationship expert or anything, but it seems like you shouldn't be in competition with your boyfriend."

What I really wanted to say was that it seemed like he was pushing Poe away now to avoid a painful goodbye later, but I didn't dare voice that in front of Sal.

"Maybe you and Mr. Dupont have a little *too much* in common," Sal said to Reg. "Don't they say opposites attract?"

"You ought to know," I said.

Sal answered me with a sharp look before swiping up our bowls and retreating to the sink to do dishes.

Reg gave me a look behind Sal's back that clearly said, *Mind your own business*, then left the kitchen to hide out in his room with his homework. As if homework even mattered now.

It took a few seconds of the silent treatment before I dragged myself up from the table to stand next to Sal. I grabbed a towel to dry, and he silently passed me the first dish.

"Sorry," I said after a bit. "That was—"

"Rude? Out of line?"

"I was going to say—"

"Insensitive? Uninformed?"

"Not cool."

"That too."

I took a breath, dried another dish. "Anyway, I'm sorry, okay?"

He humphed and passed me a cluster of spoons. "Okay."

We washed and dried in silence for a few seconds.

"So have you heard of this Halloween Hoopla?" I asked.

"Of course."

"You ever been?"

"Once or twice. Not much for costumes. Or crowds."

"What about this year? Fiftieth anniversary and all."

"I'll pass."

I resisted the urge to cheer and instead said a silent thank-you to the old guy for making this part of the job so easy. And there was something else.

It wasn't just that Sal would not be there to interfere, I realized. I was also relieved that he wouldn't witness my betrayal, to know I played a part. I got a sick feeling imagining his disappointment and wondered briefly if memory fades worked on slayers.

"I'm on the planning committee, you know."

Sal lifted his bushy eyebrows and handed me more silverware. "Is that what you've been up to? And what do you get out of it?"

I feigned insult. "I get nothing more than the satisfaction of doing a good deed, of course!"

We both laughed, and I admitted, "Okay, I was pressured into it by Syd and Soph. And I get to ride on the float."

"You do? Maybe I should come, then—"

"No! I mean . . ." I made a show of rolling my eyes. "It's going to be totally lame, and I'll be super busy with committee stuff. I won't even be able to talk to you."

"You sure?"

"I'm sure."

It was almost too easy to get Sal to stay home. All the pieces were falling into place, and there was little doubt now— Halloween would be our last night as humans.

When the dishes were done, we sat at the table, Sal carving away at a block of wood and me, pretending to pore over a biology textbook. I turned to a chapter on human anatomy, and Sal reached over to tap the page with his whittling knife.

"Left a few things out, didn't they?"

"Ew. I hope you're not going to give me the *talk* or something, because I'll be immortal again soon, and we don't worry about the birds and the bees—"

"Relax," he said. "I just meant, they think a beating heart is the only thing that keeps us moving, keeps us alive."

"But isn't that what you believe too?"

He turned his wooden block in his hands, inspecting all the angles. "The way I see it, there's a difference between natural life and unnatural life. One is a gift. The other is . . . *stolen*."

I scoffed. "That sounds like something straight out of the slayer handbook."

"Yeah, maybe." He shrugged and started carving again. "And I suppose we're as unnatural as any immortal. Heck, we probably wouldn't even exist without vampires."

"Maybe neither would exist without the other," I offered.

Until now, I'd never thought of it that way: vampire and slayer, two halves of the same coin. It made a strange kind of sense.

"Yin and yang," Sal said.

"Black and white."

"Or more like the murky gray space in the middle."

"Yeah, I like that better." I pointed to myself. "That's kind of how it feels to be . . . *this*."

"To be what?"

I searched for a way to explain it. "To be human, but only recently. Like I don't fit in either the mortal or the immortal worlds, and I'm just stuck in some kind of purgatory. Is that what it's like to be a slayer?"

Sal paused his whittling, the hilt of his knife pressed to his lips. "Yeah, I'd say that's pretty accurate, especially for a retired slayer. Like you exist in both worlds but belong to neither."

"Sun or shadow."

"No twilight in between."

We exchanged a silent look of understanding. Who knew I could have so much in common with a slayer?

"We're very poetic," I said with mock sincerity.

He grinned. "If only there were a market for slayer-vampire-semi-mortal collaborative poetry collections."

"Not exactly the kind of thing you can pick up at the library," I agreed.

"Maybe a specialty bookstore, then."

"Hey, that's what Lina can convert her coffee shop to after—"

I choked on the words, lassoing them just in time to pull them back from my lips.

"After what?"

"After . . . after she gets tired of running a coffee shop. She can't do it forever, right? People would start to ask questions. She's already been there, what? Ten years?"

"Fifteen," Sal said, and his features arranged themselves in such a way that it was obvious the thought had not occurred to him—that Lina would have to close shop one day, would have to go away.

As much as he grumbled about her, it was clear he still had feelings for her. Maybe a part of him would be happy when the Blood Clan moved in and it meant Lina could stay.

Forever, if she wanted.

"So, what's that you're making?" I asked, changing the subject.

I reached for the wooden block, but he held it out of my reach.

"It's not your concern," he said.

His abrupt response surprised me a little, but I suppose a few minutes of bonding at the kitchen table didn't exactly make us BFFs. I couldn't blame him. I had my secrets too.

"Fine, don't tell me," I said. "But do me a favor and make something without pointy ends for once?"

Sal chuckled. "No promises."

THIRTY-ONE

PLAYING DEAD

Kachunk. Kachunk. Kachunk.

There is something so satisfying about wielding a staple gun.

I smoothed out the flyer I'd just secured to a power pole, halfway between Hope High and All Hours. We were papering the town with the updated Halloween Hoopla hours, the new times popping off the page in giant orange lettering. My hand slid over the awards for best floats and costumes and landed on the bottom line of text:

Biggest Hoopla in history—no more, no less.

Sophia sailed out the front door of the hardware store, where she had just unloaded a stack of flyers and fell into step with me and Sydney as we made our way to the next wooden pole to cover the old flyer with the new one.

Kachunk. Kachunk. Kachunk.

We crossed the street to plaster flyers on the boarded-up windows of the abandoned movie theater.

"This town is so pathetic," Sydney said, gesturing up at the empty marquee. "Look at this place. It's totally stuck in time."

Sophia sighed. "We definitely suffer from arrested development."

I tried to peek between the boards to see the theater lobby, but it was too dark inside. As I pulled back, I noticed a letter etched on the glass of the shuttered ticket window. I traced the letter with my finger, a capital *M* with swooping script. I recognized that particular *M*, and even though whatever came after it was hidden behind a wood panel, I knew the full word without a doubt.

Morgana.

No wonder it had never reopened. The current owners had no use for it.

I shook my head, disappointed. The least the Elders could have done is let the town have a movie theater. It seemed spiteful to keep it empty for no reason. It's not like this tiny theater was going to draw hordes of people from out of town.

I comforted myself with the thought that after the migration, the people of Nowhere would all have enough cash in their bank accounts to open their own movie theaters. Their memories would tell them the money came from insurance or government payouts, due to the loss of their property to flood. The logical part of their brain that could deduce the payouts were far too big to make sense would be muted. Memory fades were incredibly impressive when done well.

Sophia stapled a flyer to the last empty window board. "If these new hours help us top our fundraising goal, we'll have to start thinking about what to do with the excess."

"The band needs new uniforms," Sydney said as we continued down the street.

She affixed a flyer to the next pole.

Kachunk. Kachunk. Kachunk.

"Or maybe the theater could use a fund for sets and props," Sophia said. "I'll ask Poe."

"What's going on with him and Reg, by the way?" Sydney asked me.

"You can ask him yourself," I said, pointing up ahead to the turquoise awnings and bright yellow door of All Hours. Reg and Poe had just spilled out the front door, with Dexter following behind them.

No, wait. He was stepping between them, his arms stretched to keep them apart.

We dumped the rest of our flyers into a bag looped over Sydney's shoulder and raced up to the boys.

"Guys, chill!" Dexter said.

Poe tried to sidestep Dexter but was easily blocked by his tall friend, so he settled for craning his neck around Dexter's frame to point at Reg. "You're overreacting."

"I don't see why you are trying to keep me from rehearsal." Reg argued. "The understudy needs to know the part as well as the primary player."

His arms were gesturing in a wild way that was *so* not my brother. Human emotions were clearly more than he could handle, and our return to immortality could not come soon enough.

"Reg—" I started, but Poe drowned me out.

"I'm doing no such thing!" He held out his cell phone, screen aimed at Reg, like a weapon. "They specifically said they didn't need understudies for the pickup rehearsal."

Reg refused to look at the phone. "Just admit you are threatened by me."

Poe looked like he'd been slapped. "*Threatened* by you? Is that a joke?"

"No, *you're* the joke—"

"Hey!" the twins said at once, both moving to stand behind Poe.

I hesitated, then took a few halting steps to hover near my brother. Reg was being an ass, but only I understood what it was like to suddenly feel things—*really feel them*—after a century of barely feeling anything but thirst. I would tell him he was a jerk later. For now, I had his back.

Poe shook his head at Reg, tears in his eyes . . . and a little bit of pity too. "Jealousy does not become you."

I winced. That was not going to go over well.

"What did you just say to me?" Reg asked in a low hiss. If it weren't for the wall of Dexter, he looked like he might take a swing at Poe.

Poe swiped at one eye, then pulled himself up straight. "I said you're jealous. And unreasonable. It's not my fault the director only wants his primary Puck."

Reg's fists balled, his face reddened, and when he spoke, spit flew from his mouth.

"PUCK *YOU!*"

Then he stormed away, yanking his arm out of my grasp when I tried to stop him.

"Reg!" I ran to catch up. "Stop!"

His strides were longer, but I was faster, and I finally jumped in front of him and pressed a hand to his chest.

"You are so lucky I am wearing tennis shoes today," I said, huffing. "If you'd made me ruin my heels . . ."

"I could always outrun you when we were immortal," Reg grumbled.

I glanced over his shoulder to make sure the others hadn't heard him. Satisfied we were out of earshot, I smiled. "In your dreams."

He crossed his arms, forcing my hand off his chest.

"What happened?" I asked. I had a hard time believing the blowup I'd just witnessed was really about rehearsal, and when Reg didn't answer right away, I said so out loud.

"It's not just the play," he said. "It's all the things . . . all the *mortal* things. Relating to teachers and being popular with the other students. He's just so good at being human."

"Of course he is," I said. "They all are. It's all they've ever been."

I couldn't see why Reg cared so much. Why did he need to be a model mortal . . . unless he wanted to remain one? And now I was the one crossing my arms, shutting out the idea.

"The good news is, this will all be over soon," I reminded him.

He didn't meet my eyes. "Yeah."

"So can you just let it go?"

"Can you?" He looked up. "Let it all go?"

"What do you mean—"

"Never mind." He circled around me, tossing a glance back at where our friends still stood outside of All Hours. "You wouldn't understand."

"Oh, come on. Who understands you better than me?"

"Better than I." He smiled, to let me know he was teasing, but a sadness lingered in his eyes. He turned and walked away, and this time I didn't follow.

I returned to the coffee shop, where Sydney and Sophia comforted a now openly crying Poe. They tried to convince him to come into All Hours, but he waved them away, sniffling that he had to go to rehearsal, and took off in the opposite direction as Reg.

"What the hell is with your brother?" Sydney snapped.

She wasn't wrong to ask, but her tone set off my sibling defenses. "He's under a lot of stress, okay? You all have no idea what it's like to . . . be *us*."

"What you two have been through is awful," Sophia chimed in, softer than her sister, "with your parents and moving here and all. But it doesn't excuse the way he's treating Poe. I mean, you're both in the same situation, and *you* don't act like that."

My mouth fell open.

No one had ever accused *me* of being the nice one.

Dexter took a tentative step between me and the twins, as if preparing to break up another fight, but then he beamed one of his biggest smiles. "Men. Am I right?"

The tension of the moment dissolved into quiet giggles in response, and I had to admire the effortless way Dex could change the whole mood of a moment. He seemed to have control not only of his own emotions but the emotions of other humans as well. He made being mortal look easy. Reg was right about that.

Dex took my hand as the four of us poured into the coffee shop and occupied our usual table. I liked the feel of his hand in mine, but there was an extra weight to it now. What right did I have to hold his hand when I was part of a plan to upend his life? I had been avoiding Dex all week, but maybe that wasn't enough. I wondered if I should be pushing him away like Reg was pushing Poe. Still, I couldn't bring myself to let go.

I squeezed his hand.

Not yet.

Sydney dumped out the bag of our supplies, taking stock of the remaining flyers.

"More flyers?" Lina asked from behind the counter.

Sophia snatched up a stack and placed them on the counter. "To replace the old ones," she said. "Can we put a couple in the window too?"

Lina slid the top flyer off the pile, her lips pursing almost imperceptibly. I lowered my gaze before I could see the disapproving look on her face. I knew that disapproval was for the council, but I felt her judgment all the same.

"You can put *one* in the window," she said.

"Thanks!" Sophia snatched the one in Lina's hand and grabbed a roll of tape from our pile of supplies.

"Just one, Miss Carlone!" Lina called. "I don't need you cluttering up my windows."

"Because clutter is *so not her thing*," Sydney said under her breath, eyes shifting over the photos covering every wall.

I tried to smile in response, but I could feel my lips pulled tight.

Dexter touched my knee. "You okay?"

The warmth in his voice, the tenderness in his eyes. He might not carry around a big old bag of feelings all the time like some humans, but he had them.

"I'm fine," I said, taking his hand from my knee and clasping it in my own.

"Ew," Sydney complained. "Public displays of affection make me queasy. That's my cue to leave."

"Whatever do you mean?" I asked, climbing into Dexter's lap.

He wrapped his arms around me and stroked my hair. "Yeah, what are you talking about? There's no PDA going on here."

Sydney made a gagging motion and gathered up the spilled contents of the bag. "Soph and I will unload the rest of these. You two just . . . try not to slobber on each other too much, okay? People eat in this establishment."

We laughed and waved goodbye to her and Sophia. I stayed in Dexter's lap long enough to plant a kiss on his cheek, then returned to my chair. His bronze cheeks tinted with a blush.

Yep, still got it.

For a moment, I imagined all the colors of Dexter's face fading to the translucent skin of a vampire, his sunny-blond hair and green eyes turning black. But even in my fantasy, it didn't look right. He just wouldn't be Dex without that golden glow. And even if I were tempted to turn him instead of letting the Elders send him away, it would be a blatant violation of the Treaty of Annis. I'd be in a whole new world of trouble, and the Elder Seat wouldn't be so forgiving next time.

Dexter and I spent the next hour sitting as close as possible without actually sitting on each other's laps, and after a while, my cheeks hurt from so much smiling. Like laughing until your belly ached, it was just one more way human happiness actually caused physical pain.

I realized with a start that I would actually miss that, the mortal ability to feel something so much it hurt, even when it felt good.

Dexter eventually headed home for dinner (and I think to check on Poe), and I stayed, sipping coffee, until the rest of the shop emptied out. I wanted to check on Reg too, but I sensed he needed some time alone. When all the customers were gone, and darkness began to fall, Lina collapsed into a chair across from me, propping her feet up on the oak barrel that passed for a table.

"Tired?" I asked, as if vampires could tire.

She sighed. "Exhaustion comes in many forms."

"What will you do?" I asked. "When everything is done?"

"You mean when the good people of this village have had their minds violated, their homes stolen, and their futures forever changed?"

I shrank back in my chair, hiding my face behind my coffee mug. "Well, when you put it like that . . ."

"If you're going to do a thing, you should be able to talk about the thing."

"And if you feel so strongly about a thing, you should have tried to stop the thing."

We stared at each other for a long moment, and finally, Lina looked away, shaking her head.

"You're right."

"So why aren't you fighting it?" I asked. "I mean, not that I want you to—but I would understand. It's just . . . me and Reg, we don't have a choice. This is our one shot to get off death row."

She smiled. "You have a funny way of talking about life, princess."

"And you didn't answer the question."

"I've been around long enough to know that if the Elders want this town, they'll take this town. Without your help, they might send the Bloods in to take it themselves."

"That would be . . ."

Awful.

"Messy."

Lina agreed. "The alternatives certainly make the current operation look downright friendly."

"Will you stay?" I asked.

"And what? Turn the coffee shop into a blood bank?"

I wrinkled my nose. "Point taken."

"I honestly don't know what I'll do next," she said. "I never think that far ahead."

"Why not?"

"An endless road is an overwhelming prospect. When you've got eternity in front of you, the present becomes a lot more interesting."

"Well, I hope you don't stick around," I said.

Her eyes narrowed. "Oh yeah? Why not?"

"Because I don't want Sal stuck here with a bunch of Bloods, and I think if you stay, he will too. To be close to you."

Lina said nothing, but if she were human, she looked like she might cry.

I set my coffee cup down and tried to be gentle with my words.

"You know that thing people say about the thin line between love and hate? In a hundred years, I've never understood it until now."

Lina didn't answer, but a puff of air caused me to blink, and when I opened my eyes again, she was cradling a picture frame in her hands. It was the photo of her and Sal in front of the pyramids, under the bright Egyptian sun. She ran two fingers over the image.

"I wanted to turn him, so this could be us forever. But it would have taken millennia before he could walk in the sunlight with me, and it was against everything in his being."

"Really? He seems kinda dark, if you ask me."

Lina smiled. "Don't let the rough exterior fool you. That man is made of pure light."

I thought of Dexter's bright eyes and golden hair and skin, as if the sunshine was burning right out from his core. Now, that was a guy made of pure light. Sal? Not so much.

"You know, it's funny really," Lina said, moving to hang the picture back on the wall—this time at a speed I could see.

"What's funny?"

"He didn't want to be vampire, and I didn't want to be human, and yet we both turned against our nature anyway. He no longer slays, and I no longer feed." She adjusted the frame until it was perfectly straight. "And yet somehow, we still can't find a way to be together."

Just like Dexter and I would never be together. Not that we were some epic love story, but it was sad to know we never would be. At least Dexter wouldn't remember us, and I would have my thirst to distract me. Sal and Lina had to keep spinning in the same universe, and when I saw the pain in Lina's face as she stared at that photo, I decided it was probably for the best that Dex and I were going to end before it got any harder to say goodbye.

THIRTY-TWO

SO MUCH FOR THE SUN

The day of the Halloween Hoopla dawned gray and chilly, and the clouds remained thick throughout the morning, as floats and flatbeds clustered at the edge of town, lining up for the march down Main Street. I stared up at the sky, looking for any cracks of light, but the gloom was solid. I guess the sun just wasn't much for goodbyes.

"Earth to Charlie!" Sydney tugged on the hem of my fairy dress. "What's wrong, you not get enough coffee yet this morning? Need me to call Lina for a special delivery?"

Sydney was sitting on the bed of the float, at the edge of our paper-mache graveyard, gluing some fallen letters back onto their Styrofoam headstone. I dropped down beside her, perched on my knees, so that my fairy wings wouldn't touch the ground.

"Yeah, just need a caffeine fix," I said.

But that wasn't true. Sal and I had split a pot of coffee that morning, the two of us watching the sunless dawn break over the cornfields in total silence, both drowning in our own thoughts. I wondered what we would be to each other by nightfall. Friends or foes? When we reached the cold dregs at the bottom, Sal clinked his mug once against mine. *Friends*, I hoped.

But I was fooling myself. Unlike everyone else in Nowhere, Sal would remember us, would know what we did, and how could he ever forgive? Eventually, he disappeared into his wood-shed, and I went to cover myself in glitter.

Which I was regretting now that the glitter had seeped into a few very itchy places. I wiggled side to side, trying to scratch without being obvious about it. *Itching* was, by far, the worst part of being human. I would not miss it in the slightest.

"Have you seen Dex, yet?" Syd asked, eyes on her headstone repairs.

"Not yet," I said. "The Future Farmers float is way up at the front."

"He is *so* Iowa."

Sydney put the last letter in place and adjusted her horns. Somewhere nearby, her mirror image was sporting a halo.

"You know," I said. "If you and Soph really wanted to come in *costume*, you should be the angel and she should be the demon. Because we all know which of you is the good girl."

Sydney feigned offense. "I can be good!"

"You can be no such thing!" Poe declared, appearing alongside our float in a top hat and vintage suit.

I slid down to the street and gripped Poe's lapels. "This is amazing, and you did not get it in Iowa."

"Special order from a costume shop in Hollywood." He removed my hands from his fabric and pretended to brush off my dirt—or maybe he was brushing off actual glitter. "When it comes to Halloween, Poe doesn't play."

"But what are you supposed to be?" Sydney asked.

"Not *what*," he corrected. "*Who*."

He lifted up a large, ornate picture frame, entirely empty in the center and positioned it around his upper body.

I frowned. "You're a painting?"

"I don't get it," Sydney said.

"He's Dorian Gray." Reg strolled into view around a passing group of parade preppers, startling Poe. The two of them had not spoken since their fight. I had tried to ask him about it, but he'd only told me to leave it alone, and, eventually, I did.

Poe lowered the frame. "Well, the *portrait* of Dorian Gray, but yes. That's right."

Reg smiled, but the rest of his face was stiff. "It's really good."

"Thanks." Poe's smile was warmer than Reg's—more hopeful. "I knew you would get it. And you're a—"

"Vampire," I finished, treating my brother to one of my most withering looks.

Reg, to my total annoyance, had chosen to dress like so many of the masses . . . as the humans' cartoonish idea of a vampire. He'd claimed it would be funny, except he wasn't laughing, and it seemed to me that he was being deliberately disrespectful with his white plastic teeth and his black-and-red satin cape. I hoped he would de-accessorize before the night's events.

"Charlie, can I talk to you?" Reg said, turning from Poe and gesturing for me to follow him to the end of the float.

I trailed him to a quiet spot between the cab pulling our float and the bed of a long tractor trailer covered in fake cobwebs with a sign that read, "Haunted Hayrides, Morgana Farms."

"I'm skipping the parade," he said. "It's . . . too difficult."

I hurt for Reg, for both of us. I just wished he could see that we would feel better when we shed our human emotions . . . or at least had them dulled by the desire to feed.

But who are you to decide for him? A little voice asked me.

I pushed that question down, and another one rose in its place, more pointed than the other.

If not for me, would Reg stay mortal?

The question was right there on my lips, but I couldn't ask it. I was too afraid of the answer. Instead, I asked out loud, "Why don't you just talk to Poe?"

"And tell him what? The next time you try to kiss me, I might bite you?"

"He might like that."

"Everything's a joke, isn't it?" Reg said.

"Hey, once upon a time, you would have liked that joke."

"Well, once upon a time feels like a lifetime ago."

He had me there.

"Look, Reg. If you're not in the mood for a parade, I understand, but this is it—our last day in the sun." I shot the gray sky a dirty look. "Sort of. And you're already in your awful costume."

"I just can't. You have fun though, okay? You've earned it. I mean that."

"But, Reg—"

"I'm fine. I promise." He popped the ridiculous teeth into his mouth, raised his arms, and in the loudest and most embarrassing way possible, shouted, "*I vant to suck your blood!*"

I managed a laugh and pushed him away. I watched him weave through the parade lineup, skirting floats and circling a pickup truck full of fat little puppies. The sign on the side of the truck declared the parade entry was for the Northern Iowa Pug Rescue. When I looked up again from the sign, Reg was gone.

Weeks of building a float, hours of sitting around in the staging area, and yet the start of the parade seemed to come all of a sudden. We made the short trek through the village, with most of the freshmen and sophomores desperately propping up gravestones that toppled over with every bump in the road, while the rest of the committee members waved from the edges of the float. Sydney and Poe lounged against a railing, making judgy comments about costumes. No one pointed out that Poe quit the committee and shouldn't be on the float, because that was the power of Poe and the Carlone twins. Sophia beamed as parade announcers barked over the megaphone that we were the Hope High Halloween Hoopla party and parade planners, and the crowd cheered.

What little crowd there was. It seemed most of Nowhere was *in* the parade, leaving only a smattering of people to populate the sidelines. In front of us, a float decked out with stained glass and a steeple trailed a banner that proclaimed, "The only path to immortality is through Him and His church." Behind us, a

small tractor pulled an actual bar, with barstools and everything, and the burly group of guys filling the stools all donned
shirts that read, "The Bar Drove Me Home."

I leaned on the back rail of the float, watching the tail of the
parade snake down Main Street. One of the bar patrons lifted a
mug of beer to me.

"Nice job, kids! Best parade in fifty years!"

I waved back but could not speak, as I was hit with a spasm
of nausea. *Fifty years.*

This village had fifty years of parades and ages of history
before that—more than the people of Nowhere even realized.
And it would all be wiped away in one night. I shuddered, trying
to shake away the thought, but it clung to me, like cobwebs.

The parade trundled past the only real crossroad in
Nowhere, and from down the street, the loud, bright storefront
of All Hours seemed to scream out at me not to strip the color
from this community. Under one of the coffee shop's turquoise
awnings, Lina hovered, arms crossed. I wondered if she still
planned to hock coffee at the party, or if she couldn't bear to
watch it all go down. I lifted a hand to wave to her, but she only
ducked her head and disappeared back through the shop's yellow front door.

"Guess she didn't see you," Poe said, joining me at the back
of the float. His portrait frame was slung over one shoulder, and
he set it to lean on a gravestone.

I lowered my arm, hand clenching to a fist. "Yeah, guess not."

Poe slumped against the rail, and he looked so sad, I couldn't

291

even chide him for wrinkling his vintage threads.

"Poe," I said. "You know how much Reg cares—"

"Don't."

"But . . ."

"He already told me."

I stilled. "What?"

"I know you guys are leaving."

"Uh-huh," I said, because I was afraid to say more.

"Back to New York," Poe said. "Can't say I blame you. This place must seem so boring to you."

I placed a hand on the rail to steady myself. I felt off-balance, and it wasn't from the float rocking down the road. It would have been nice for Reg to keep me in the loop on the tales he'd been telling. But I couldn't blame him for his little fib. At least making up a story gave him a chance to say goodbye.

"It's not boring," I said honestly. "Thanks to you. Thanks to all of you."

Poe grabbed me up in a surprise hug, and I had to swallow a lump in my throat.

"Reg doesn't want to leave, you know." I pulled back to meet Poe's eye. "It's me who wants to go home. Reg, he . . . he would probably stay here if . . ."

If it wasn't for his selfish sister.

I gripped the rail until my knuckles bleached white. Funny how much I disliked that pale shade on my skin now, compared to the warm olive of the rest of my hand.

"He asked me to come with," Poe said.

I stifled a gasp. It wouldn't surprise me if Reg fantasized about turning Poe the way I'd thought of turning Dexter, but did he actually make an offer? Was he trying to get permanently stuck here?!

But of course. He was. That must have been his plan, exactly.

"I turned him down," Poe went on. "I'm sure he told you."

I nodded. It was all I could do; I was so tired of giving voice to lies.

"You don't want to leave Nowhere?" I asked.

Poe shrugged. "Someday, sure. But it's not such a bad place to be from."

He waved at someone behind me, and I looked over my shoulder to see Sydney and Sophia coming our way, faces lit up with identical smiles.

Not a bad place at all.

"This is the end," Sydney called as they approached.

Hope High loomed up behind them, and the parade line scattered, floats and flatbeds veering off to claim various parking places around the school.

The end . . .

Sophia pulled off her halo and ran a hand through her blond tresses. "We're going to park around back by the gym and start decorating. Poe, you in to help?"

Poe faked a groan. "Fine, but I don't stand on ladders, and I don't do *glue*."

The twins laughed in their harmonious, infectious way, and I couldn't believe I would never hear that sound again. Would never share another coffee with this crew at All Hours, never drive down another sun-soaked dirt road with Dexter, never again spar with Sal across the kitchen table.

It wasn't just the people, I realized with a squeeze in my chest. It was this *place.* I had convinced myself that it was worth sacrificing the village to spare the villagers, but tearing the people and the town apart would mean taking more than their blood and their memories. We'd be stealing a piece of their very soul—the piece called Nowhere.

Our float lumbered into its assigned spot alongside the school, just below a giant banner, slung between second-story windows:

NOWHERE ANNUAL HALLOWEEN HOOPLA
NO MORE, NO LESS THAN HORRIFICALLY FUN!

Except the second half of the banner had sagged, the top edge folding over the bottom, so that only the words on the far left still stood tall.

NOWHERE
NO MORE

The flatbed under my feet lurched to a stop, and my heart lurched along with it. I still didn't know what the hell that stupid motto meant, but I knew this much: if Nowhere was no more, the world would definitely be a little less.

After all these weeks, Nowhere finally felt like *somewhere.*

Sophia barked an order to head to the gym, but my feet didn't move. I had somewhere else I needed to go first.

"Charlie, you coming?" Sydney asked.

Poe's hand fell soft on my shoulder, turning me around. "Hey, what's wrong?"

I swiped at my eyes, but they were dry. The time for tears was done.

"Poe," I said in a rush. "Listen. Whatever happens tonight, promise me you won't forget us—me and Reg."

"As if I could ever forget—"

"Promise!"

He backed away a step. "Oh. Okay, promise."

The twins appeared at his side, then moved past him, reaching for me.

"Charlie?"

"Are you okay—"

"I'm sorry, I have to go!"

I leaned away, even though all I wanted to do was fall into their outstretched arms. If I worked fast enough, with any luck, there might still be time for that later. But I needed to move.

I hauled myself up over the float's back railing and climbed down to the street.

"Where are you going?"

"What's happening?"

"Is this about New York?"

My feet hit the road, but my fairy wing was caught on the rail. I ripped the wings from my shoulders, leaving them dangling from the back of the float, beneath the concerned faces of my friends.

"I have to go," I said again.

I turned and ran straight into Dexter.

"Found you guys!" he said. "Been looking every— Whoa, Charlie, what's—"

I stood on tiptoes, grabbed his face, and planted a kiss on his lips before he could finish the question.

Then I raced away, hoping there was time for what needed to be done. Time to even *figure out* what needed to be done—what it would take to stop a vampire invasion and the mass memory wipe of an entire community of colorful, kind, not-at-all-boring people. I had no idea if it could be done, but I knew I couldn't do it alone.

I needed my brother, a slayer, and a certain white picket fence.

THIRTY-THREE

OVER MY DEAD BODY

The trip from town to the cottage went by in a blur—not the kind of blur I used to experience running at immortal speed, but the kind where you are so focused on the thing in front of you, all the rest just fades away. And soon, the thing in front of me was the cottage gate. I flew right through it, barely registering as it banged open against the rest of the wooden fence.

"Careful, there!" Sal called from the front porch.

I hadn't noticed him slouched down in his favorite porch chair, whittling knife in hand, working away at the mysterious wooden block.

No, "block" wasn't the right word. It was looking more like a box.

"You almost knocked down my fence," he said.

"It'll be down soon enough," I panted.

His hands paused. "Is that right?"

"That's right."

"And who, exactly, is tearing down my fence?"

"We are. You and me. And Reg too."

Sal looked up from his work, messy gray eyebrows so high

they were almost in his hairline. "And why would we do that?"

"Because we need weapons."

He set his box and knife to the side.

"Well, now, *that* is interesting."

"What's interesting?" Reg emerged from the cabin, still in costume.

It didn't take long to fill them in on my plan, and when I was done, Sal sat stroking his beard, and Reg asked, "So, you want to scatter the crowd, even though no human can outrun a vampire, and you want to fight off the rest with our army of three?"

"Basically," I said. "You in?"

Reg didn't answer, but he stepped down into the front yard and picked up an ax Sal kept leaning against the front porch. And that told me everything I needed to know.

Whether we were pleading for immortality before a council of the most powerful vampires in the world, or planning to take them down with a measly couple of fence posts, Reg's side was my side. Always.

Soon, we were dismantling Sal's white picket fence, one stake at a time. Reg ripped each stake off the fence and yanked it out of the ground; Sal hacked them to a handheld size and shaved the triangular tips into a more lethal point; then I piled them into duffel bags Sal had unearthed from a closet, each one falling onto the rest with a hollow clunk.

Rip.

Yank.

Hack.

Shave.

Clunk.

The posts made for some pretty sad stakes, and the squared-off shape was uncomfortable to hold, but it was the best we could do on short notice. Retired slayers didn't exactly keep an armory of stakes stashed around.

I turned one of the posts over in my hands, remembering what Sal had said about the first time he transferred his healing power into wood—particularly the gory bit about what happens to vamps who turn human only to find a stake sticking out of their chest.

"Sal, are these going to like, *maim*?"

He passed me a newly shaved post. "If you're asking whether these sticks will smoke 'em or stake 'em, the answer is smoke."

"How do you know?"

He threw his hands up to the sky and did his best impression of a TV evangelist. "Because I didn't lay my healing hands on them."

"But—"

"It's just the gate, kid." He pointed to the gate, which was hanging a little lopsided after my aggressive homecoming. "No need to charge up the whole fence when just the gate posts will do the trick."

I had not slowed down for even an instant to really picture what was to come, but I imagined it now and felt a twist of anxiety. I was not thrilled about the idea of vaporizing vampires, but I reminded myself that it was just the Elders, and after what they'd done to us, they could definitely bite it.

"Hey, less talking, more working," Reg said, pointing to a pile of newly uprooted fence posts. He was sweating through his vampire costume and giving off a very human smell, but he moved with determination and almost seemed to be smiling.

"What happened to your ridiculous plastic teeth?" I asked.

He ran his tongue over the top row of perfectly even human teeth, pausing on the incisor. "I'm getting used to these."

"Good thing," Sal said. "Because after this move, you'll be stuck with them."

My heart stuttered, and I forced myself to breathe through it.

I knew what I was giving up—and giving up for a mission that would likely fail—but if I let myself stop to think about it, I might lose my nerve. And then Nowhere would lose everyone.

Rip.

Yank.

Hack.

Shave.

Clunk.

We worked in silence for the better part of an hour, and soon the sun was sinking toward the hills behind the cottage. The barbecue would be winding down by now, the band taking the stage. Full dark was less than an hour away.

When the fence was nothing but splinters and the gate had fallen, flat and harmless, to the lawn, I zipped up the last duffel bag and hauled it over my shoulder, sagging a little under its weight.

Sal saw me struggling and told me to wait. A moment later, he returned with a long, wide loop of leather in roughly the shape of a beauty queen's sash. Except, where "Miss Congeniality" should be, there were smaller loops of leather just right for holding stakes. Sal draped it over me, dropped a few stakes in the holders, and relieved me of the duffel.

"Suits you," he said, mustache twitching. It was the first hint of a smile I'd seen on his face since I'd explained to him, at a rapid-fire pace, what was about to go down in Nowhere and the part Reg and I had played. "Come on, let's load up the truck."

"Streets are blocked," I said. "We have to go on foot."

Sal squinted at the western sky, now blazing with sunset orange and red. "We'll take it as far as we can, then walk the rest."

But it was more like running than walking, as Sal's truck only got to the line where cornfields met tree-canopied streets before the glut of parked cars made travel on wheels impossible. We emptied the flatbed of all the stakes we could carry, and then the three of us—sister, brother, slayer—charged into town, racing against the coming dark.

The streets outside of Hope High were thick with people when we arrived. Ghosts, zombies, and other supposedly immortal beings licked the barbecue from their fingers and grooved to the music blasting out of speakers set up along the curb in front of the school gymnasium. We squeezed down the narrow gap between two floats to join the action and took quick stock of the scene.

The sun was below the treetops now, and shadows grew long on the street. There was more light pouring from the open gym doors than the sky.

"Do you see Poe?" Reg stood on his toes, scanning the crowd.

I shook my head. No Poe, no Dexter, and no twins.

I started to look around for Lina too, but a tall boy, vaguely familiar from the halls at school, stepped into my view. He held a red cup, and, judging by the way he was weaving back and forth, I suspected it had more than soda inside.

"I get it!" he said, waving his free hand toward my bandolier of stakes. "You're like . . . a fairy princess meets Chewbacca!"

"Uh-huh, sure."

We stepped around him and didn't look back as he called out, "But wait, was Chewie immortal?"

"Reg," I commanded. "Look for Lina. She's supposed to be running the coffee cart. We'll need her help."

Sal sniffed and shifted the backpack full of stakes on his shoulders, but he made no comment on Lina.

"I'll walk the perimeter," he said, sounding more soldier than senior citizen, for once.

When they were both gone, I searched the faces around me. I spotted a Peter Pan, a few leprechauns, and a ton of vampires—just not the real variety. The sun was setting, but it was possible we still had time to disperse the crowd, let them at least get a running start. We just needed to create an exit path.

Most of the floats were parked on the side streets, but a dozen or so had been arranged to create a kind of wall around the street party. I knew from my time on the planning committee that this was intentional: use the floats and trucks to keep cars off the road, so it's safe for pedestrians. Unfortunately, all it had done was create a neat little pen for all the human prey. Getting out would be slow and cumbersome, with people scrabbling over the tops of floats and bottlenecking at the skinny pathways in between. I had chased enough humans to know when their escape routes did not look good.

My searching gaze landed on the pickup full of pugs. During the parade, they had been yapping and panting and scrambling to get a view over the side of the truck walls. But the lot of them must have been dozing now, because just one lone pug with a fat, wrinkled face and gray whiskers poked his head over the truck rim, drool sliding from his long tongue onto the Northern Iowa Pug Rescue sign.

Sorry, pug. I'm in the people-rescuing business tonight.

Actually, I wondered if I could do both. What were the odds the pug truck driver left the keys in the ignition? Or any of these other floats and trucks? We only needed to move one or two to make an exit big enough for a crowd to fit through. I was about to jump behind the wheel of the nearest float, when the last rays of sunlight blinked out.

THIRTY-FOUR

FIGHT OR FLIGHT

It was too late for a clean escape. Twilight was here, and the Elders would not be far behind. I needed to end this party. Now.

I noticed one of the AV club's supersized speakers nearby. It was nearly as tall as me, but I managed to scale to the top of it and stood to look over the sea of Nowhere residents. It had to be absolutely everyone in town—*no more, no less.*

I took a deep breath, summoning all the air in my lungs and all the power in my vocal cords, and screamed:

"RUN!"

I voiced it. I know I did; I felt it scratch my throat as the raw sound escaped. And yet, I could not hear it. And neither could anyone else.

Because at that exact moment, I was drowned out by the PA system, and the sound of a girl with a microphone and an amplifier.

Sydney.

Her voice reverberated from the speaker beneath my feet.

"Okay, everyone! Let's take this party inside!"

Sophia joined her on the mic. "It's time to announce the winning float and the best costume. Come on into the Hope High gym to hear the winners!"

No!

"NO!"

But this time, it was the music that drowned me out as someone cranked up the volume on "Monster Mash." The song erupted from the speakers as people crushed into the gym. I jumped down to the sidewalk, right in front of a young couple, waving my arms and urging them to turn back, but they only flowed around me like water, as if they didn't even see.

The monster mash, it was a graveyard smash!

A group of guys from the barstool float were next in my path, and I opened my arms wide.

"Wait! Don't go in there!"

"Hey, kid, it's just a costume contest," one of them said. "Don't worry. If you don't win, you can go for Miss Congeniality."

"What's that?" one of his buddies asked. They both sounded tipsy.

"Congeniality! You know. Like nicest or most popular or something."

I was pretty sure I was going to be nobody's most popular after tonight, but for the first time since I had arrived in Nowhere, I did not care.

Okay, I cared a little, but I so did not have time for that right now.

They did the mash, they did the monster mash!

As person after person moved around me or tried to push right through me, I found myself swept up in the sea flowing toward the gym.

"Stop!" I cried.

But they didn't even slow.

Lambs to the slaughter, Reg would have said.

I tried to spot him in the mess of humanity, but everyone was so close together at this point, I could barely see over the heads of the people right next to me. Too soon, the crowd had narrowed into a funnel at the doors to the gym, and I was right in the middle of the bottleneck.

Desperate, I pressed my hands into the chest of the person closest to me, as if I could physically stop the force of humanity pushing into the school.

"Chewbacca fairy! Where you been?"

I looked up to see the chest belonged to the tall boy with the red cup. He grabbed one of my hands and tried to hold it.

Gross.

I was tempted to toss this one to the Elders.

Instead, I snatched my hand back and warned him, "Don't go in. You'll be trapped."

He squinted at me. "Is this some kind of role play?"

"Oh my God! I swear, some of you aren't even worth saving!"

With that, I gave up and let the tide carry me into the gym for plan B. Once we spilled through the doors, the crush lifted, and I could breathe.

And I could run.

I headed straight for the platform in the corner of the gym, where I knew Sydney and Sophia were holding court with the AV kids and the audio system.

"Charlie!" Sydney called as I approached. "Where have you been?"

"And why are you running?" Sophia added, her halo slipping as her head tipped to one side.

"Give me the mic!" I snatched it from Sophia's hand without waiting for an answer. "Turn off the music."

A timid-looking boy did as I commanded and cut the tunes, but when I spoke into the mic, nothing happened. I tapped my foot impatiently as he fiddled with a soundboard.

"Charlie, what's going on?" Sophia asked.

She looked scared.

Good.

It was about time someone looked scared.

"Kid," I said to the boy. "I don't have time for this. Turn the DAMN MIC ON."

The last few words boomed out over the gymnasium, echoing through the space and causing a hush to fall over the crowd.

I did not let the opportunity pass.

"Everyone," I said into the mic. "You need to leav—"

BANG!

The outer doors of the gymnasium slammed shut, followed by the smaller slams of interior doors closing.

Locking.

The lights flickered.

It had begun.

I took a single shaking breath and tried the microphone once more.

"Prepare to fight."

I dropped the mic and pulled two stakes from my bandolier, handing them to the now slack-jawed twins.

"You're going to need these," I said, rearming myself with another set.

If we made it through the night, I would have to thank Sal. His little stake sash was coming in handy.

The AV boy rescued the mic from the floor and, standing, caught sight of my stakes. He dragged a hand through his hair and groaned.

"Oh man, is this another vampire attack?"

Before I could even process his question, the windows high above the gym floor shattered, all at once, on every wall, like an explosion. Glass rained down on the packed gymnasium, and right behind, dropping from each window, an Elder vampire, clad in black hunting gear—though this was less of a hunt than an ambush.

For a moment, there was only the tinkle of glass, followed by an instant of silence. Then someone screamed.

THIRTY-FIVE

SOMETHING STRANGE & FAMILIAR

The gym was filled with screaming, scrambling humans, and the Elders slid easily among them, biting, drinking, dropping them into comas. It was a punch in the gut to see how effortless it was, and my stakes felt small and stupid in my fists. Still, I clutched them tight. I might be powerless. But I wasn't alone.

"Fight," I ordered the twins. "Aim for the chest."

"But shouldn't we get out of—"

"They barricaded the door," I said. "I guarantee it."

"Our parents are outside," Sophia said, tearful.

"Then maybe they got away," I lied. There was likely a much larger group of vamps outside, taking care of any stragglers. This was a strategically planned operation. The Elders would not be sloppy.

"Don't worry, Soph." Sydney reached for her sister, but Sophia was yanked suddenly, violently backward. A vamp had her by the neck, fangs out and poised to strike.

Sydney let out a wail so primal, the sound of it carried above the others, standing out in the cacophony of screams. Then she lunged at the vampire holding Sophia, hands clawing at his face. But instead of scraping down his skin, her nails caught only smoke.

Through the smoke, Reg's face appeared, his stake still raised where he had struck.

Next to him, Lina was similarly armed, her coffee shop apron still on, the front pockets filled with stakes.

Reg blinked as the smoke evaporated. "Found Lina."

"Your idea?" she asked me.

"Yep."

"'Bout time."

"What is happening?" Sydney asked, arms wrapped tight around Sophia.

"There's no time to explain," I said.

"It's vampires," Reg said.

Okay, so maybe there was time for that.

More Elders were sailing through the high windows, and one landed right next to Lina. She stuck one arm straight out to the side, her stake landing square in his chest, without even sparing him a glance. He was gone in an instant, his smoky remains floating right back out the window he'd come in.

Lina twirled the stake in her hand. "So, you got a plan here, princess?"

"I didn't really get past the *show up with lots of spiky things and hope they hit the road* step," I admitted.

"They're so fast," Sophia exclaimed as one sped by.

"If you can see them, you can stake them," I said.

Lina added, "Fighting and feeding take precision. Most of us have to slow down—"

"*Us?*" Sydney cried. "Lina, are you . . . ?"

A body dropped in front of us, so close it skimmed my fairy skirt on the way down. It was a woman, and she hit the floor with a heavy thud.

"Oh my God!" Sophia wailed. "She's dead!"

"Not dead," Reg corrected. "More like a temporary coma—"

"Less chatting. More staking," I snapped.

Then, without any further explanation, we leaped into the fray.

Fighting was clunky in my human form, but I was surprised to find myself a worthy opponent for the Elders. I knew their moves, so I knew how to dodge, how to throw my neck out as bait, then duck just in time, sliding the stake home.

One grabbed my arm, and I spun into him instead of away. *Dust.*

Another caught me from behind, and I went with the momentum, rolling backward, right over his head, and catching him in the back. *Vapor.*

I tried not to look in their faces. I knew I was on the right side now, but a small part of me didn't want to recognize any of the Elders, didn't want to look them in the eyes before they disappeared.

They sealed their own coffins, I reminded myself.

And nobody crashes a party I helped plan.

All around me, the people of Nowhere were fighting back.

No longer scrambling, they were now working in teams to ward off attacks. An equipment closet was open, and someone had smashed a few baseball bats against the wall until they splintered. Several people were running around with sharp sticks from the bat's remains, their screams now changed to guttural war cries.

I had lost the twins, but in the middle of the gym, I found Sal, both of us staking the same vamp at once.

"Having fun?" he asked with a wink.

It seemed like a strange question until the answer came bubbling up inside me, even stranger.

"I'm having . . . something," I said.

A group of vamps surrounded us, and we whipped around, fighting back-to-back.

"I can't explain it," I yelled over my shoulder to Sal even as I sparred with the pair of unfamiliar Elders in front of me. "I'm all amped up. Jittery, kind of, but powerful too. Like how coffee makes me feel, but times a hundred."

My stake landed in the first opponent. *Poof.*

"I'm just so . . . *buzzed!*"

The second vamp came in for a bite, and I feinted left. She followed my movement, and I snagged right, my weapon finding her exposed sternum.

Sal ended his vamps at the same moment, and we turned back to one another.

"So, what is it?" I asked. "This feeling."

"Adrenaline," he said.

Then he was gone again, lost in the crowd with a new foe.

I reveled in the tingle of my skin, the pounding of my heart, the energy that threatened to lift me right off the ground.

Adrenaline might just be the best part of being human.

"Charlie!"

Dexter came flying through the melee, knocking both humans and vampires aside as he beelined for me. I noticed one of the bat slivers in his right hand and a cut of some kind on his left arm, but soon both hands and arms were out of sight and wrapped around me, as he scooped me up in a bear hug.

No, not just a hug. Dexter closed his green eyes and smashed his face against mine in a sloppy, too-wet, aggressive, all-over-the-place kiss. His energy collided with mine, and we exchanged heat and saliva and oxygen and a whole lot of unsaid things. It was a total mess . . . and the greatest kiss I'd had in more than a century.

Sorry, adrenaline. Make that second *best part of being human.*

"I want you to meet my parents," Dexter said as he pulled away, one hand still in my hair, the other using his makeshift stake to gesture at a middle-aged couple clutching their own baseball bat shards.

I wiped my mouth. "Right now?!"

"Mom! Dad!" He waved them over with his wounded arm.

"Are you okay?" I asked.

"Yeah," he said. "It's actually kind of weird how *okay* I am. How okay everyone is."

A woman raced past us just then with her hands in the air,

shrieking for help at a glass-shattering pitch.

"Okay, not her," Dex said. "But a lot of people seem okay with all this. You too, right?"

I coughed. "Uh, yeah, me too. Totally okay. Super weird."

His parents had nearly reached us when a couple of humans tussling with a vampire slammed into them.

"I've got them!" Lina appeared, charging out from the crowd, but she was too late.

The dark smoke that used to be an Elder rose up before Dexter's dad, his stake still outstretched and a look of wonder on his face.

"It's all so familiar," he said. "Like we've done this before."

Lina took his splintery stick and replaced it with one of her own stakes from Sal's fence. "You *have* done this before."

What?

"I knew it!" Dexter's dad exclaimed.

Introductions forgotten, Dexter dropped one last kiss on me with a command to be safe, then he joined his parents as they engaged a new group of vampires.

Cleanup outside must have been nearly over, because more Elders were flooding in through the windows, their faces already slicked with human blood. Not a good look, I thought, but then I remembered my face was still partly covered in Dexter's spit, so I probably didn't have much room to talk.

I spun through the room again, helping people keep their attackers at bay. Vampires were at their most vulnerable when lost in the feed, so I smoked a few right where they stood, sucking the life out of someone.

No, not the life, I reminded myself. *Not even the memories yet.*

This was just the first wave—the takedown team. Once everyone was knocked out with venom, a second crew would come in and do the complex job of erasing and replacing the memories.

"Not on my watch!" I cried, leaping, stake out, toward a nearby figure in black.

"Whoa!" The figure's hands flew up. "Charlie, it's me!"

The stake dropped from my hand and skittered across the floor. "Poe?"

"You almost stabbed me," he said. But then he wrapped me in a hug.

"Are you okay?" I replaced my stake and handed him another from my bandolier.

He tested the weight of it in his hand. "I am oddly unflummoxed."

"Huh?"

"I'm not as freaked out as I should be."

"Yeah, there seems to be a lot of that going around," I said. "It's kind of freaking *me* out."

"Charlie!"

It was Reg's cry, but it echoed across the chaos in the gym, so I couldn't tell which direction it came from.

"Charlie!" he called again, and this time Poe spotted him.

"There! He's over there."

Reg was pressed against the far wall of the gym, waving frantically, and we pushed through the scrum, trying to reach him.

A fresh spray of glass rained down from above as a new wave of vampires leaped through the high windows. One pair dropped right next to us, a man and a woman. I smoked the guy before he'd even straightened out of his crouch, but the woman—no, the *girl*—caught me off guard. It was the doe-eyed Elder, the one representing the Blood Clan. I wasn't exactly her biggest fan, but seeing a face I recognized made staking the heart below that face feel . . . wrong. It took me out of autopilot, interrupting my fight-or-flight response.

Basically, I hesitated.

And she did not.

"I knew we couldn't trust you," she snarled, fangs out and glinting.

She darted in for the bite, but all that grazed my skin was smoke, and in the small space between me and where she had once stood was Poe's hand, wrapped around his stake.

"Friend of yours?" he asked.

Before I could answer, Reg shouted again.

"Charlie! Come on!"

I dragged Poe behind me as we dodged the throngs of humans and vampires still sparring. Damned if this little village wasn't made up of some decent fighters.

Reg moved down the wall as we neared, motioning for us to follow. "This way. I heard them."

"Heard who?" I asked.

"The Elders," he said, breathless. "There were two of them talking. They didn't see me, but I heard them, and then they went this way. Hurry!"

"Wait! I don't understand."

But he only ran faster, leading us toward the back corner of the gym.

"Reg, slow down! You heard the Elders talking about what?"

Finally, he stopped next to a small door along the side wall, under an inconspicuous red exit sign.

"About this," he said, pushing against the bar that spanned the door.

It opened with a metallic bang, followed by a whoosh of crisp night air.

THIRTY-SIX

CHOOSING SIDES

There was this tiny moment—just a fraction of an instant—
when I felt like a star making her debut onstage. Bright lights
poured in through the doorway like a spotlight, and a hush fell
over the room.

Except the spotlight was actually the glow of stadium lights
from the football field at the end of a long, topless tunnel, and
the hush was not for me but a reaction to the sound of the door
slamming open.

And then the instant was over, as the crowd stampeded
toward the tiny exit. I had to move or get trampled, and I was
moving. I tried to stay within sight of Reg and Poe, running on
either side of me down the broad patch of grass between the two
towering walls that led to the field. But the swell of escaping
humans soon overwhelmed us, and Reg and Poe were lost in
the waves.

The walled path between the gymnasium and the football
field had seemed comically wide the first time I'd seen it, but
with hundreds of people trying to cram through it all at once,

the space seemed claustrophobic, the sheer brick walls endless and inescapable.

Our best hope was to run for the opposite end of the football field, where the public usually came and went through the high archway. The people of Nowhere moved instinctively in that direction, and my feet pounded the grass alongside them. Beyond the archway was a wide-open parking lot and escape in every direction. The Elders could not chase us all, and if they couldn't catch everyone, they would have to abandon the plan.

But as we spilled out into the end zone and got our first full view of the field, my vision of escape, that bright light at the end of this night, winked out and turned to blackness. At the other end of the field and all along the sidelines, awaited an entire army in black hunting gear.

I didn't have time to wonder why the Elders had unblocked the door or why they'd talked about it in the open, where Reg or anyone could overhear. And now I didn't have to wonder at all, because the answer was obvious. The arena wasn't a way out. It was a trap.

I knew this move.

I had *played* this move.

"Stupid!" I chided myself aloud, skidding to a stop on the turf.

The vampires ringing the field were not Elders. They far outnumbered the council members I had seen crammed into the basement of the theater in Minneapolis. And that didn't even include the countless number that had already been turned to smoke tonight. It was clear, there under the blazing lights of the Hope High football stadium, that it wasn't just the Elders here to take the village. With a shiver, it occurred to me that these additional vamps might be members of the Blood Clan, already come to claim their new territory.

But as I looked around, I saw it was worse than that. It was all the clans, called by the Elder Seat to act. There were Bloods, yes, but also Shadows and Starlights and even Bones. So many familiar faces, I nearly collapsed to the ground.

This was wrong. This was all wrong!

I had come prepared to fight the Elders—to smoke them, if necessary. It was as much as they deserved. But this . . .

Feelings were at war inside me, my earlier determination unraveling into an inner chaos that mirrored the chaos on the field. The realization that we were surrounded had hit the crowd, and people were running in all directions.

I had to get everyone off this field, but the archway to the parking lot and the great beyond was completely blocked. Even if it wasn't, humans were all over the place—scrambling into the bleachers or behind the concession stands. Immortals were taking them down even as they moved, dropping them mid-stride. One minute, a human was running. The next they were on the ground, until the field was littered with bodies.

Other mortals held their ground, crouching midfield like a starting line, armed with shards of wood or other makeshift weapons. Those who fought back were landing their stakes. Here and there, small tornados of black smoke swirled up past the stadium lights and disappeared into the inky sky.

Not far from me, a man dressed as Thor snapped the paper-mache head from his homemade hammer, exposing the handle, which appeared to be the smooth, rounded end of a broomstick or a mop. I winced as a vampire vaulted toward him, sailing down from above, fangs out. Thor swung his mighty mop handle and, with the sheer force of will, drove that super dull end of the stick right into his attacker's chest.

And then the flying vamp was just a shadow, floating away.

But moves like that were in the minority, and the human herd was thinning. The number of people lying on the grass would soon surpass the number of people standing on two feet.

Fending off attacks with my two-fisted stakes and trying not to fatally stab any vampire I didn't recognize as an Elder, I searched around to see if any of the humans still standing were *my* humans.

Eventually, I spotted Dexter across the field, holding up his mom, who looked exhausted. Not far away, the tall boy from school, still holding his red cup, sank to his knees as a vampire finished with him. The humans were tiring. The vampires would not.

At opposite ends of the field, Sal and Lina were the only two still fighting with any stamina, and soon, they would be overwhelmed by sheer numbers. The one thing the humans had on their side was that, at nearly one thousand strong, they at least outnumbered their attackers in the beginning, but between this unforeseen trick of the Elders calling in backup and the fact that the football field was now carpeted in coma victims, prospects were looking grim.

And where was Reg? Poe? The twins?

Were they flopped on the ground with the rest?

My heart skipped a beat.

I chose the wrong side.

By encouraging Nowhere to fight back, I had only delayed the inevitable and given everyone a night full of fear when they could have simply been put to sleep. And now my former kin were paying the ultimate price for my betrayal.

As I spun in the center of the field, surrounded by familiar immortal faces, I felt the full, crushing weight of it. Every wisp of smoke winding upward was hundreds or even thousands of years of life lost. Many of those smoky remains belonged to immortals who still believed their methods were humane, that fear was temporary and easily erased to prevent long term trauma. They probably saw tonight as a simple acquisition of a new home and not a bloodbath. Most of them probably didn't even know what they were even here for—just following Elder orders like good immortal soldiers. The Elders had this coming, and maybe the Bloods too, but the rest? They were dying for nothing.

In that instant, looking out over a field of humans falling down and vampires floating up, I felt certain that there were no winners in this arena.

My shoulders sagged, and the stakes slid from my slackened grip. When a hand gripped the back of my neck, I closed my eyes, ready to give in. It was as much as I deserved. With any luck, they'd erase the memory of this disaster as a small kindness.

But then the hand turned into an arm . . . two arms . . . wrapped all the way around me in a rough hug.

Sal.

I sank into him with a ragged, sobbing breath.

"It was an ambush," he said, his voice like gravel in my ear. "We've lost."

"This is all my fault," I mumbled into his flannel shirt.

"Yep."

I pulled back, swiping the tears from my cheeks. "Excuse me?"

"You could've stopped it, could've warned everyone. Instead, you made your deal. Traded away this whole town for your chance at forever."

"I didn't mean for—"

"And then you told all these mere mortals to take up arms against a superpowered foe."

"Right, but—"

"So, yeah, I gotta concur this scene here is pretty much all your fault."

Hmph.

"Well?" he prompted, eyes piercing into me. "What are you going to do about it?"

I was about to protest that I had already done everything I could think of, but then I spotted the single stake he had stashed in the front pocket of his shirt. My eyes flowed over his shoulder to the pack full of stakes on his back, while my hands ran the length of my bandolier. An idea was forming, one that didn't require me to choose sides at all.

"How many more stakes do you have?" I asked.

Sal shook his head, a look of pity on his face. "Not enough, kid. Not enough."

"That depends," I said. "How many does it take to build a fence?"

THIRTY-SEVEN
A MATTER OF LIFE AND DEATH

Just minutes later, we were on our knees at the entrance of the broad tunnel that led back to the gym, the battle for Nowhere still raging on the field in front of us. Sal's backpack and my bandolier were cast to the side, the stakes they once held dumped in a pile between us, as Sal and I feverishly worked them into the ground, turning them back into fence posts. There weren't enough stakes to stretch all the way across the wide opening, and Sal wasn't confident that he could re-create what he'd built back at the cottage, but I urged him to try.

Soon, we had a kind of miniature, makeshift fence reaching from either side of the tunnel opening but not quite meeting in the middle. It was a short fence, no higher than our shins, and there was no gate, but something about those little white stakes sticking out of the ground like fangs gave me the same shudder as when I'd first seen them surrounding the cottage, and I had a feeling in my gut that this just might work.

I was shoving my last stake into the ground when Poe and the twins ran up, panting and disheveled.

"You're okay!" Sydney cried, dropping to her knees beside me and throwing her arms around my neck.

"What's your uncle doing?" Poe asked.

At the other end of the tunnel opening, Sal was gripping each stake, one at a time, head bent low and muttering some kind of chant.

"I'll catch you up later," I said, standing. "Right now, I need your help. I need you to round everyone up—get them to come this way, back toward the gym."

Poe gaped at me. "But we'll be trapped. The gym doors—"

"Just do it!" I cried.

The twins moved in unison, racing back into the melee and dragging Poe along with them.

"And find Reg!" I hollered at their backs.

Sal wrapped his hands around the last two stakes, muttered his enchantment, and then sat back on his knees. "That's it, then."

And it really was it. Because either this was how we won, or this was the most colossal mistake I'd made yet. One way or another, the night was about to end.

"If this works, there are going to be a lot of pissed-off vampires," Sal said.

"At least they won't be *dead* vampires."

"The girl I met just a couple of months ago would have said passing through my fence *was* a death sentence."

I put my hands on my hips and looked out toward the field. A crowd was gathering under Sydney and Sophia's command.

I blew a stray hair out of my face. "That girl sounds kind of awful."

He stood up, brushing the dirt of his hands. "Eh. She's not so bad."

"Don't go soft now, old man. If this doesn't work, we've just drawn targets on our backs."

"Guess we're about to find out," he said.

The swarm of people was surging toward us, a single amorphous entity, backlit by the stadium lights. I had never been more impressed by the influence of the Carlone twins, the true queen bees of Hope High.

We stepped aside as the first tendrils of that swarm sprinted into the tunnel, racing toward the gym. As quick and as confidently as people were moving, I could only imagine Sydney and Sophia had told them the gym's front doors were open. I hoped they would forgive the lie if this plan panned out.

And if it didn't . . . well, I guess they wouldn't remember anyway.

"Stay to the middle!" I shouted, pointing out the fence stakes, so people wouldn't trip. "Get to the gym! It'll be safe inside!"

Most folks ran through the gap Sal and I had left in the fence, while a few jumped right over the stakes. More than a dozen humans had passed by before the first vampire crossed the line. It was an Elder, vaguely familiar from the council gathering, and I held my breath as he sailed over the fence, just above the gap . . . and immediately crumpled to the ground.

Another vamp passed through and dropped next to the first.

Then another.

And another.

My human heart pounded as I watched them fall.

They writhed on the ground, clutching their chests and gasping for breath. A breeze rustled the grass around them, the force of Sal's slayer magic. I remembered the power of that little personal tornado from the first night I'd stepped through the cottage gate.

"It's working!" I cried actual tears of relief. "Sal, it's working!"

Laughing through my ridiculous human tears, I slammed into Sal with a hug that nearly knocked him off his feet—as much from surprise as from the force of it.

One more vampire, on the heels of her human prey, hit the ground.

Two more.

Three more.

The humans flowed around the growing pile of vampires, few even stopping to register what was happening. I gasped as one desperate man climbed right over the top of an Elder, his boot leaving a muddy footprint on the chest of the Elder's black shirt.

The crowd was more stretched out now, arriving at our fence in pairs or even individually. Soon, Poe was barreling toward us, and running next to him . . .

"Reg!" I grabbed my brother into a bear hug as he entered the tunnel. I had given out more hugs in the last hour than I had in the entire last century.

"Sydney and Sophia said to come back to the gym," Reg said. "Did you get the other doors open?"

His gaze slid down to the tiny fence posts and around to the dozen or so vampires—*former vampires*—rolling on the grassy tunnel floor. Then his eyes widened in understanding.

"Here come Syd and Soph!" Poe shouted.

He waved down the twins as they approached, and we were all so happy to have our group back together again that we didn't even notice Lina running up right behind them.

She was keeping pace with the twins, to cover their backs, so she wasn't moving at immortal speed, but she was still fast, and by the time I looked up, it was too late. My scream of warning would not be enough to stop her.

She was just inches from the edge of the fence when an arm shot out in front of her.

A flannel-clad, rough-handed, stubborn old arm that caught her right around the waist, and flung her back toward the field.

Lina landed like a cat and skidded around in a crouched position, ready to strike. When she saw the arm that had cast her backward belonged to Sal, she looked downright murderous. But then her eyes drifted left and snagged on the fence posts. She looked back at Sal. Back at the fence posts.

Then she stood, charged right up to Sal, and planted a kiss on him.

I looked away, partly to give them privacy and partly because, whether human or vampire, grown-ups kissing was just universally *yuck*.

"Why did you do that?" Lina asked Sal.

He rolled his shoulders, face beet red.

"It just oughta be your choice," he said. "And if you think—"

But whatever he was going to say next was smothered by another kiss from Lina.

A new group of humans hit the tunnel, but this time, the vampires chasing them pulled up short. They looked at us, recognizing Adelina the Ancient, Salvador the Slayer, and me and Reg, the two former immortals who were supposed to be the planners of this party. I watched the questions surface on their faces as they noticed the former vampires behind us, now sitting up with slow, clumsy movements, their chests heaving with deep human breaths.

The immortals hovering just outside the tunnel began to slowly back up, even as another vampire sped our way, a blur of movement I could barely make out until he froze, instantly, as if suspended in midair.

Adante.

His feet were still on the grass, but his body was half arched over the fence posts, eyes locked on them in suspicion. Inch by inch, he pulled back, as realization dawned. The other vampires had halted their retreat with Adante's arrival, and they watched the scene now with a mix of curiosity and fear. But Adante's face was pure murder. He raked his gaze from the stakes to Sal to Lina and, finally, to me.

"You betrayed us," he snarled.

"I believe it was *you* who put us on this side of the fence." I lifted my chin, even though my heart was hammering.

"As punishment for a crime!" Adante was spitting, fangs bared. "What you've done to your kin is—"

"You want them?" I stepped to the side, offering him a clear path to the pile of former vampires. "Come and get them."

He did not even spare them a glance. "How dare you?!"

But the rage he felt was clearly not for them. It was for himself—at having been outplayed. He hissed, tongue darting through his fangs, and for a moment, it looked like he might risk crossing the fence just to rip out my throat.

But then he carefully reorganized his features, dabbed away the blood at the corners of his mouth and tugged on the ends of his sleeves. With effort, he turned his stare away from me to address Lina.

"Adelina," he said, voice strained. "At your convenience, the Elder Seat requests a word."

She nodded once in response, and I saw Sal's shoulders tense.

Composed now, Adante gestured to the vampires behind him, waving for them to leave. With grateful faces, they turned and ran. Adante followed, and soon, all the remaining vampires were doing the same.

One by one, they disappeared into the shadows of the night, until only mortals remained under the sun-bright glare of the Hope High stadium lights.

THIRTY-EIGHT

DÉJÀ VAMPIRE

It took only a few minutes for word of the vampires' departure to spread, and Nowhere shifted quickly into a new mode. Incredibly, very few people ran away. Instead, they worked together to smash open the barricaded gym doors and to locate fallen friends and family.

The people of Nowhere were heroes, *no more, no less*, and as I watched them help one another, I knew I had made the right choice. Still, in the quiet aftermath of the attack, I felt the stinging sensation of loss. We had one chance to reclaim our immortal lives, and we had thrown it to the wind for this tiny town. Charlotte Drake, House of Drake, Clan of Bone, thought Charlie Smith of Nowhere, Iowa, was a fool.

Reg and I wound our way through the gym and field, letting everyone know that the coma victims would wake when the vampire venom wore off. Out in front of the school, we found the people who had not made it inside the gym. Their prone forms were scattered on the lawn and in the street, surrounded by overturned chairs and abandoned food carts, as a dozen or so pug puppies scampered this way and that.

We helped Poe load his sleeping parents into a car while Sydney and Sophia searched for their own mom and dad. The people of Nowhere seemed as unrattled in the aftermath as they had been in battle. I knew the town had ancient history, but it was clear now that it had more recent history as well.

Back in the open-air tunnel, we found Sal and Lina tending to the group of new mortals.

One of the former vamps raised a shaky finger to point at me and hiss, "You chose the wrong side."

But in the end, I hadn't chosen a side at all. I'd managed to protect the village *and* stop immortal lives from going up in smoke. For once, the only side I didn't choose was my own.

"Better human than dead," I said.

He sneered. "Debatable."

As Reg and I circled the group, another new human—formerly an Elder—kept touching his fingers to his wrist, then to his throat, and back again, feeling the pulse of his own blood flowing for the first time in centuries. His eyes were wide with wonder.

I winked down at him. "You get used to it."

Reg surveyed the lot.

"Do you think they're all coming back to the cottage, then?" he asked.

"Ugh, I hope not." I pointed to a skinny former vampire who looked close to our age. Pimples were already sprouting on his face, and his hair was taking on a greasy sheen. "I am so not sharing a bathroom with that guy."

Hours later, Reg and I dragged our tired human bodies home, down the dark, tree-lined streets of Nowhere, through the fields yawning open under a starry sky, and back to the cottage, where Sal was waiting for us.

He was furiously scribbling in a notepad and barely glanced up.

"You two get your friends off all right? They all find their parents?"

"Everyone's accounted for," Reg confirmed.

"Where's Lina?" I asked.

Sal's pen paused. "Still with the council."

"Did we get her in trouble?"

"Not any trouble she didn't dive into willingly. I wouldn't worry." His mouth twitched. "That woman can handle herself."

We collapsed into the closest kitchen chairs, and I might have fallen asleep right there at the table, if I hadn't been curious about Sal's scribbles. "What are you doing?"

"Cover stories for our newly human friends. I've called in some favors to put them up for a few nights, but that won't last, and I don't have room for them here. I need to get them acclimated, ID'd, and on their way pretty quick."

I grimaced. "Sorry about that."

Sal's head snapped up, and he jabbed his pen in my direction. "Don't you ever say sorry for what you did tonight."

A firework of pride exploded in my chest, but I only nodded.

"Sal," Reg leaned forward, weary. "The town, the people . . .

so many of them tonight were . . ."

"Unfazed?" Sal offered.

"Alarmingly so."

Sal pushed his pen and pad to the side.

"I've been wondering about that too."

"A boy from the AV club called tonight 'another' vampire attack," I said. "And Lina told Dex's dad he's done this before."

"He likely has," Sal said. "Bunch of 'em have. But what I can't figure is how they almost seem to remember things."

"Remember what things?!"

"The Elders have been meddling in the matters of this town for centuries." Sal waved a hand as if this should be no surprise. "I told you how they own most of it. You think they managed that without interacting with the humans?"

"Dexter's family farm," I said. "Dex said his dad almost sold it a couple of times but couldn't do it. When he finally sold to Morgana, it was a big shock."

Sal pointed a finger. "Bingo. My guess is those first deals fell through with the help of a little mind manipulation. Who knows how many encounters your boyfriend's dad has had with the Elders and their brain poison?"

I hated the idea of vampire venom coursing through the veins of my friends and their families, of ideas being planted into their minds. It was what we'd fought against tonight. And for what? Only to learn it was already happening anyway?

"'It's for the best, and we should all be grateful,'" I said.

"Excuse me?" Sal knit his thick brows together.

"It's something Dex's dad says a lot. About selling the farm. I wonder if those aren't his words."

"Probably not. How do you think they keep this place small? Chasing away developers and whispering in people's ears that their ideas are too grand and they should just give up. One vamp who came through here was fit to be tied about his mortal punishment, and he spilled his guts about all kinds of things. Told me the Elders regularly attend town chamber meetings with their fangs out, poisoning everyone with their venom and wiping out deals. He said one time they even crashed a ground-breaking event to stop a strip mall from being built. Maybe your AV friend was there. Or maybe at some other event that got attacked and erased from everyone's minds."

"The movie theater," I said. "Downtown. There was a fire on opening night. And now the council owns it. Do you think they started it?"

"Hell," Sal snapped his fingers. "Maybe there wasn't even a fire at all, and they just planted that thought in everyone's head."

I gasped. "You think?"

"Who knows? I knew they were interfering, but I didn't really guess the extent of it until I saw how many people tonight seemed to be having déjà vu."

"That's not how the fade is supposed to be used," Reg said in disapproval. "It is always to be for the benefit of the recipient—to protect them from the trauma of memory—not for our personal gain."

"What about Dex?" I asked. "And Poe? They were unfazed

too." I swung my gaze over to Reg. "Or 'unflummoxed,' Poe said."

Reg gave a soft, sad smile in response. "Sounds like him."

Sal shrugged. "Probably a case of wrong place, wrong time. Maybe saw something they shouldn't have. But the real question," he repeated, "is why do they seem to remember?"

Lina burst through the front door just then, a scatter of fall leaves around her feet, chased into the cottage by the wind she created with her speed.

"That is exactly what the Elder Seat wants to know."

"How did you get past the gate?" Sal asked.

"What gate?"

"Oh yeah."

They smiled at each other, and he pulled out a chair for her. I noticed that he also pulled it a little closer to him. I'd had a hard time before, picturing Lina living in this place, but the way she flung her scarf over a hook on the wall, helped herself to a cup of coffee, and sank into the seat next to Sal . . . she was right at home.

"I've been conferring with the Elders. Those who are left."

"Are they mad?" I asked.

I knew it was a childish question, and the answer was so obviously yes, but I couldn't stop myself from asking it.

"You may have inadvertently done them a favor, actually," Lina said.

Reg and I exchanged quizzical looks.

"The council is disturbed by the number of humans who

took tonight's events in stride. They're worried a migration will fail if the necessary memory work involved does not hold. It could present a serious risk of exposure for our kind." She sipped her coffee and smiled. "I may have helped them to this wise conclusion."

"No migration?" I asked, my heart lifting. "They won't try again?"

"Not until they figure out why the fade isn't working as it should here."

"I'll tell you why." Sal dropped a fist onto the table with a thump. "Too much monkeying with their minds! Over and over again. At some point, the system breaks down. Like a screw stripped of its grooves, the brain zaps just aren't holding anymore."

"Interesting hypothesis," Reg said. "Perhaps the people of Nowhere are building up an immunity to vampire venom."

No, that wasn't quite it. I doubted Dex and Poe or even all the adults had endured multiple memory fades. A few, maybe, but not all.

Lina set her mug down and spoke almost as if to herself, alone. "It could be their lineage."

"Like, what? Their DNA?" I didn't follow.

She looked up, and I noticed a spark of curious excitement in her eyes. I guess when you'd lived long enough to see it all, anything remotely new was interesting.

"This town is full of mortals with immortal history."

Reg and I responded with blank stares.

"Nowhere isn't a place people move to," she said. "It's not the kind of town that grows from outsiders coming in; it's the kind of town that grows generation after generation."

The kitchen fell silent as she let that sink in.

I was the first to speak, in a hush. "The people of Nowhere are the descendants of vampires turned human."

"It makes sense," Reg said. "I hadn't thought of it, but of course newly turned mortals would just settle here in town, lacking anywhere else to go."

Sal said, "Most of them move right along nowadays, but it would have been different back then."

"I'm sure there are exceptions," Lina said. "But most of the population could tie their family tree back to a vampire house, if they knew of such things."

"None of them know their own history?" I asked.

"I suspect the first former immortals to inhabit Nowhere did not pass down their stories out of fear that their human families' minds would be manipulated. They likely kept our vampire secrets, not to protect *us* but to protect their mortal children. And after a few generations, the memories were lost the natural way . . . because there was no one left who remembered."

"And that's why the memory fades work differently on them?" Reg asked.

"It's only a theory." Lina refilled her coffee.

I was struck by sudden indignance. "But the Elders must at least know that the humans here are, like, the great-great-great-grandkids of former immortals. And they still tried to take their homes?"

Lina sighed. "To the council, a vampire twice removed is no vampire at all."

But that was the whole problem, wasn't it?

The truth was unfolding before me. I thought of the furious way Adante had spoken of the human "invaders," when he knew their history all along. It was an unreasonable amount of hate for a species that posed no threat. But I could see now that their very existence posed a different kind of threat, the kind that called into question the one thing vampires prized most—their immortality.

It must have been painful for the Elder Seat to see vampires who were "punished" with mortality . . . go on to live and thrive and, worst of all, have children. Because if former vampires lived on through generation after generation of their descendants, it proved there was more than one way to be immortal.

"Shh," Lina said suddenly.

I looked around. "Uh, nobody's talking—"

"Shh!"

She tipped her head, listening to something the rest of us couldn't hear, then she leveled her gaze at me and Reg.

"There's someone outside."

THIRTY-NINE

THE WORST PART OF BEING HUMAN

Adante waited on the sidewalk, in the same spot where he'd first left us to our mortal fate, as if still standing outside a fence. Only now the fence was splintered all over the yard and nothing at all stood between us—nothing to stop him from tearing our fragile human bodies to pieces. And maybe that's what he wanted to do, but he kept looking over our shoulders to the cottage, where he knew both a slayer and an Ancient waited inside.

"Well, that was certainly unexpected," he quipped.

"Sir, if we could explain—" Reg began, but Adante held up a hand to silence him.

"Tonight was full of surprises. And your betrayal was only one of them."

I kept my breathing steady and my expression unmoved. If Reg and I made it back into the cottage alive, I would consider that the biggest victory of the night.

"I'd like to tell you a story."

Oh, goody, story time. I stifled a sigh.

"Once upon a time, there was a little town, and this town's

purpose was to be a way station for immortals returning to humanity. But some of the humans made the way station their home. They tended the land and built themselves little shops and had . . ." His mouth twitched. "Families."

I was certain now, seeing the distaste in Adante's face, that this was the real objection to Nowhere—not that it threatened sacred land but that it proved there was life after death. The former immortals here lived on through their children, and their children's children. And then those future generations kept hanging around, just rubbing the Elders' noses in it.

"We've spent a great deal of time over the years trying to keep Nowhere small, to protect our interests, but tonight we witnessed what may be adverse effects of that work."

He was talking about the memory fades, and it sounded like he agreed with Sal that too much messing with people's minds had somehow stopped the fade from working. He did not seem to suspect, as Lina did, that it had anything to do with their ancestry. Of course not. That would mean admitting that even a trace of vampire might still exist within the humans of Nowhere.

"We will take time to study the population further . . . from a distance."

"You won't interfere anymore?" I asked.

"We won't let things get out of control, of course, but perhaps our energy is best directed elsewhere for the moment." He rubbed his eyes in a way that almost made him look tired. "Such as finding a location to settle our Blood brethren."

"And what of us?" Reg asked. It was only because I knew my brother so well that I heard the small shake in his voice.

Adante narrowed his eyes. "The council has determined that your decisions tonight were made under the influence of human emotions, of which you naturally have no control. Further, the Elder Seat recognizes and respects the allegiance paid to you by both an Ancient and a slayer."

That just sounded like a fancy way of saying the council was scared witless of Sal and Lina.

"No further penalties will be issued for your latest actions." He paused to look down his nose at us. "The vote was not unanimous."

I had several snarky retorts, but I held them back. Or rather, Reg's hand on my arm and his warning side-eye held them back.

"Thank you," Reg said to the Elder.

Adante pressed his fingers together in a little triangle under his chin and closed his eyes, as if to steel himself for this next part. "Now, then. To the final bit of business. The Elder Seat laments the senseless loss of so many immortal lives, the countless years of history up in smoke along with them."

I squirmed and looked down at my feet, feeling responsible for those lost lives.

"So many of our kin now gone, and two individuals with a century of immortal experience wasting away as humans."

I felt a grating irritation at the implication that humans were a waste and fought the urge to remind him that our humanity was his own doing.

"We have discussed the matter at length and reached a decision. Charlotte and Reginald, should you still wish to return to your immortal lives, House Drake and the Clan of Bone are ready to welcome you home."

Our jaws dropped in unison.

"You'll give us—you'll make us—" I stuttered. "We can be vampire again?"

"You're serious," Reg said.

"Unfortunately, yes," Adante answered. "Against my better judgment, this offer is valid. Though it expires at dawn, which by my calculations is only a few moments away, so I suggest you decide quickly."

It was everything—*everything*—I wanted. A return to our immortal lives, without harm to Nowhere. I should have been flying toward Adante.

But I was struck by a sudden paralysis.

An image of the sun setting on the hills behind the cottage crossed my vision, and my stomach did a little flip. The taste of coffee glided over my tongue, my mouth salivating even at the memory, and the turning in my stomach rose like acid up into my throat, as I pictured the faces of my friends, of Dex, of Lina and Sal.

While sunsets were spectacular and coffee even better than blood, I could still let them go for the promise of eternity.

But the people.

My people.

"Will our memories . . . will we . . ." I cleared my throat. "Will we remember? Nowhere, the humans—will we remember all of this?"

"Your memories will be gone." Adante said it with an air of assurance, as though this was yet another gift he was giving us.

"It will be as though none of this happened."

"What if I *want* to remember? Can I choose to keep these memories?"

Adante eyed me with a mix of confusion and distrust. "Absolutely not. As you well know, human memories are complex and can interfere with the immortal mind. You might lose the will to hunt, to feed. Lesser immortals have wasted away, driven mad by the human poisons of morality and memory."

He recited from a script, one I had heard before and once deeply believed.

"Are there no exceptions?" I pleaded.

Adante's answer was cold. And final.

"It is nonnegotiable."

And so were my memories—my humans.

"For me, as well," I said, the words coming out slow and broken. "I'm afraid . . . I must decline the council's generous offer."

I reached for my brother's hand, clutching it in my own. This offer would not be repeated and turning it down was gut-wrenching, but at least I knew Reg and I would be together in this mortal life.

Reg's hand slid from mine.

"And I accept," he said.

His voice was soft, but it echoed down the road.

Adante leaned back a bit, his mouth bent in a cruel smile, amused by this unexpected conflict.

Reg moved to stand in front of me, his back shutting Adante out so it was just the two of us.

"I don't understand," I whispered. "You said you were fine

being mortal, you said—"

"I said I was fine with a human *vacation*." He cast his eyes down, unable to look at me straight. "It was always meant to end."

"But tonight . . . Reg, we fought back. We won! What was the point, if—"

"The point was to save them, save their town. I didn't want any part of that treacherous plan to rob them of their homes, their memories." He looked up finally, human tears shining in his eyes. "I am so proud of what we did tonight. I am so proud of *you*, Charlie."

I spluttered. "Everything we've done here—the people we've met. You'll lose them all. What about Sal? What about Poe?"

A different kind of pain flickered across his features, and I could see then that Poe was part of the problem. What had ignited between them, fast and furious, had burned out almost as quickly. I could imagine Reg was anxious to be rid of those feelings.

He forced a smile through his tears.

"There is only one human I am truly worried about, and she still has a chance to change her mind."

"Reg, I can't—"

"I know you've grown fond of the humans," Reg said. "I have too. But consider all you are giving up for them if you stay. Your youth and beauty, your strength and speed . . . your immunity to heartache."

Yes, this was at least partly about Poe.

But Reg was wrong about heartache.

I had witnessed Lina's suffering over Sal and the two different paths they'd chosen. Immortal feelings might be dulled by thirst, but they were not erased.

A heart doesn't have to beat to be broken.

"It hurts to be human," I agreed. "But I think maybe they are worth it."

Reg placed his hands on my arms, grip tight, as if ready to shake sense into me. "Charlie, if you stay here, you will age. You will . . . you will . . ." He cast around, desperate for something that would change my mind. "You will have to get a *job*."

I responded with a small, sad laugh. "I hear we have a few new mortals in town. Maybe the slayer will need an assistant to help run his human halfway house."

Reg let out a guttural cry that was a cross between laughter and anguish. "Don't joke, Charlie. House Drake is waiting for us."

I took his hands and wrapped them in my own.

"I'm not a Drake," I said softly. "I'm a Smith."

It was devastating to say aloud, and I felt as though I was choosing between my brother and life itself. But it wasn't really a choice at all. The decision was inside of me, already made. And I could tell by the resigned look in Reg's eyes that he knew. It was the real reason he'd been so moody and distant lately. He knew what I would choose before I did.

"Sal, Dex, Poe, the twins . . . I can't lose them. Not even the memory of them." Tears slid down my cheeks. "But I can't lose you either. You're my partner in crime."

"Oh, please, no more crimes," Adante complained from a distance, and Reg had to physically hold me back.

"You don't need a partner anymore. You have a whole team now." Reg forced a smile. "Though, I'll have you note that it took half a dozen people to replace me."

I rested a hand on Reg's chest, to feel his broken, beating heart.

"No one could ever replace you. It's not just about them," I said. "I don't want to forget . . . *me*."

The truth of it hit home even as I said the words. It wasn't only our mortal crew I was afraid to leave behind; it was who I was when I was with them. They had a way of making me think of others instead of just myself, making me want to have friends, not followers. I liked that version of me, and I wasn't ready to let her go.

The human I was most afraid of losing was myself.

"I don't want to forget you either," Reg said. He spun to Adante, who was off to the side, looking utterly disinterested. "I will remember Charlie, at least, right?"

"You'll remember the century or so you were immortal together," Adante confirmed. "The details of this time will be gone, but you will be informed of what happened to her, that she chose to remain human."

"And we can keep in touch?" Reg asked. "I'll know where she is?"

"That would be an unprecedented exception—"

"Then make it," I growled. "I will find him anyway. I will use Lina and Sal and any other favor I can call in to find him and tell him where I am. You can't keep me from my brother."

Adante considered my words for a moment and must have

seen the truth in them. "We'll allow it."

"Thank you," Reg said.

Adante gestured out at the horizon. "The sun approaches. Are your farewells nearly finished?"

I shot him a disgusted look. "Excuse me, did you just tell us to *wrap it up*?"

"Charlie," Reg warned, but I ignored him.

"So sorry if our big goodbye is boring you," I seethed. "I know a fence you can sit on while you wait!"

"Okay, enough," Reg said, sliding to block Adante from my view once more. "He's right. It's nearly dawn. It's time."

My chest heaved. I was on the verge of hyperventilating.

But I knew they were right. The black of night had already bled out of the sky, and a new purplish blue hue announced the coming day. If they waited any longer, Reg would be turned just in time to get burned to a crisp.

Better an immortal brother than a dead one.

"Do it now, before I put up a fight."

I looked away as Reg moved toward Adante, unable to watch, but I knew the ritual well. Two bites, an exchange of blood, mortal for immortal, and then the transformation was complete. It was quicker than death and much less messy.

My tears had barely dried when I felt Reg's hand on my shoulder. I closed my eyes at the touch—powerful, though he was trying to be gentle, and ice-cold, even through my sweater. When I faced him, the eyes that met mine were pitch black, set into pale white skin.

He was the brother I remembered, but also someone new.

There was a warmth still there in his eyes that I had not known in our immortal lifetime—a little human still lingering. But maybe that was only because his memories were not yet gone. That ritual was longer and still to come. I wondered how much would change in his eyes when Nowhere, Iowa, was wiped away.

"One final chance," Adante sang. Behind Reg, he was dabbing a black cloth to the corner of his mouth, his lips stained red with Reg's blood. "Join your brother. Reclaim your immortal identity of Charlotte Drake, proud member of the Clan of Bone."

I marveled at the way those words—that were all I longed to hear just a few short months ago—did absolutely nothing for me now.

I ignored Adante and spoke only to Reg.

"Try to remember," I whispered. "Try to remember me here, what we did tonight."

"You know I can't—"

"Just *try*," I pressed. "Otherwise, you won't know why I made this choice. You'll think I abandoned you, and you'll never forgive me."

"Is that how *you* feel?" he asked. "Abandoned?"

I didn't want to answer that . . . not to Reg, not even to myself, and definitely not now, when we were saying goodbye.

"At least I will remember why you did it," I said. "You won't remember anything about my choice."

I was crying again, and Reg brushed away one of my tears with his icicle finger. "All right, Charlie. I will try to remember."

We clasped hands, me squeezing as hard as I could and Reg

being deliberately delicate, as the final remains of night lifted. The thin gray light of dawn was bloodless, nothing like the splendor of sunset, and while I had chosen a life in the sun, I might hate daybreak forever after this.

"Time to go," Adante called.

My heart pounded, panic setting in as the clock ran out.

"Reg," I said, tearful. "If you're a Drake, and I'm a Smith . . . are we still family?"

He pulled me into a hug so tight it nearly pressed all of the air from my lungs.

"We will *always* be family," he promised.

His cold embrace lasted longer than it should have, with the sun on approach, but still not long enough. Because all at once I was standing alone, bathed in sunlight, with my arms folded only around myself.

I collapsed to the ground, gravel biting into my knees, and sobbed.

This is it.

My hands clutched my chest as if I could reach right through it and hold my own beating heart, its *thump thump* now so intimately familiar.

This.

Is the absolute worst part of being human.

FORTY

THE COLD LIGHT OF DAY

It was more than a week before I could crawl out of bed and another week before I was willing to eat or speak. Sal made every recipe in his arsenal, but most days I just sipped at the coffee Lina brought by—as much to visit with Sal as to check on me, I think.

The slayer, through forgery or bribery or some other trick, convinced the school I had contracted something contagious and needed to learn from home indefinitely. The twins came by after school a lot, talking constantly about the events on Halloween and then clamming up when the conversation veered too close to Reg. Dexter was over more than the twins, but he knew better than to chat me up. He just held my hand and let me cry. Though Sal said no crying and handholding in the bedroom, so we had to take my pity party out to the hill behind the cottage, which only led to more sobbing, because it was the exact spot where Reg had shared all his excitement over being human. The sound of his voice still echoed in my brain like a ghost gliding over the hillside.

It's almost enough to make you want to stay, isn't it?

By the third week, a deep winter chill forced me to make a trip to the mall to shop for a winter coat and boots. That first outing became two, then three, and in late November, I found myself at All Hours one night, crammed in with my fellow humans around our favorite oak barrel table. The coffee shop was decked out for Christmas, and Lina had spiked my coffee with a shot of peppermint. It was difficult to mope under such festive circumstances.

I was tucked securely under Dexter's arm, Poe wedged in close on my other side. Across the table, Sydney and Sophia hammered Sal and Lina with questions. *Why do vampires turn to smoke? How does slayer magic work? Can vampires have kids? Do they go to the bathroom? Why do they all have black hair? And why doesn't Lina?*

I almost wished the Elders had wiped their memories.

They'd already performed the memory fade on nearly everyone else in town. The council had agreed not to attempt another takeover, but they couldn't have all these humans running around sharing wild stories about Halloween and turning us into the paranormal version of Roswell, New Mexico. The Elders had dispatched teams to the village over the last few weeks, performing as much memory work as possible, in the quiet of night, while people were sleeping. But some folks were on their guard, sleeping only in shifts, and a few more vampires had met their end in Nowhere.

The Elders caught up to most everyone, but in the meantime,

it had apparently made for some interesting arguments around town between those with total recall and those with imposed amnesia. Eventually, only our small crew would be spared the memory fade. Or so Lina told me. The Elder Seat did not communicate with lowly humans like me.

Lina answered the twins' questions patiently, but Sal got grumpy after a few minutes and futzed with a small wooden box in his hands instead.

"Hey, I recognize that," I said.

His mustache twitched. "Told you it wasn't a stake."

He tried to hand it to me, but I refused to take it. "Last time you gave me a box, it had my whole future inside."

"And that wasn't so bad, was it?"

"You named me *Smith*."

He chuckled and set the box down in front of me. "Take a peek."

Gingerly, I set down my coffee and picked up the box. It was amazing to see how it had transformed from a raw hunk of wood to the ornately carved piece of art I now held in my hands. Sal had certainly been busy while I'd been mourning.

Dexter's arm, still slung over my shoulders, gave me a little squeeze.

"That's cool," he said. "What is it?"

"Probably a trick," I said, sticking my tongue out at Sal as I lifted the lid.

Inside, a small stack of photos lay flat on the bottom of the box.

"Hey, it's me!" Dex said, reaching a hand in to pick up the first photo.

And it was him, inside his Jeep, parked outside of Sal's front gate, wearing . . .

"It's our first date," I said. I shot Sal a look. "You took a picture of Dex when he picked me up? Creepy, much?"

Sal feigned a serious expression. Or maybe it was an actual serious expression. It was still hard to tell with the old guy sometimes.

"You should always take a young man's photo when he takes a girl out for a date. Makes it easier for police to go looking for him later when the girl doesn't come home."

The twins exchanged a look like Sal was an overprotective conspiracy theorist, but Lina nodded in agreement. "I remember a time, before the council created rules to protect the balance of mortal and immortal life, a lot of young girls did not come home."

I shivered, realizing I was once one of those girls. I would never know where I originally came from, but after more than a century, I had still found my way home.

"Poe, you're here too," Dex said. He reached across me to hand the next photo to Poe. "With . . ."

"Reg," Poe finished. He ran a hand over the photo and then pulled off his glasses to swipe at his eyes.

"You can keep it if you want," I said. But he shook his head and passed it back. "You miss him even more."

The next picture was of Sydney and Sophia, then one of Sal, and finally a photo of Reg and me together. We were inside the cottage kitchen, heads bent low over bowls of Sal's chili, and we were laughing about something. Whatever it was, it had been funny enough that we hadn't even noticed Sal snapping our picture.

I placed the photos, one by one, back in the box, the photo of me and Reg on top.

"Why pictures?" I asked Sal.

He leaned forward, rubbing his rough hands together. "I knew, if you got your immortality back, that you would be made to forget. So, I intended to give you this box full of photos before you left, as a memento of your time here."

Lina rested a hand on Sal's arm. "How thoughtful."

"Didn't have the chance to give it to Reg . . ." Sal's voice cracked, and he had to clear his throat to go on. "So, I suppose you can do what you want with it now. Use the box for jewelry and put the photos in a scrapbook or something. Maybe put the picture of Dexter under your pillow or whatever the girls are doing these days."

Dex slowly lifted his arm from my shoulder.

"Awkward," he muttered.

"Reg really doesn't remember us?" Poe asked. "Wherever he is, he just . . . like we don't even exist?"

"He will remember only his sister," Lina said. "But not his time with her here."

"He'll know I chose this," I said, fighting a lump in my throat. "But he won't know why . . . because he won't know all of you. I'm sure it's why he hasn't contacted me. Wherever he is, he must hate me now."

Lina leaned across the table to touch my knee, but she didn't bother disagreeing. She knew I was right.

Sophia's face scrunched. "I don't understand why this 'memory fade' thing would work on Reg when it clearly doesn't even work well on simple humans right here in Nowhere."

Sal and Lina and I exchanged looks. We had agreed not to share with the group their lineage and Lina's suspicions. There would be too many questions, and we still had too few answers.

"I'm just glad they didn't force *us* to forget," Sydney said. "Not this time, anyway."

I set Sal's box back on the table, leaving the lid open to Reg's smiling face, and retrieved my coffee.

"You can thank Lina for that," I said. "She has a lot of influence with the Elders."

Sydney and Sophia gazed at Lina with awe—the same way they'd been gazing at her ever since they learned she was one of the oldest beings walking the planet and that she defied all rules of both human- *and* vampire-kind. If they thought she was cool before, they now thought she was a literal goddess.

"I don't know how much influence I have anymore," Lina demurred. "I merely called in a favor."

It wasn't the only favor she'd called in. My eyes traveled over her shoulder and through the front window. Across the street, a construction crew was wrenching down the boards from the theater window and painting a new sign above the marquee: "All Hours Cinema."

"It actually took all of my powers of persuasion to convince the Elder Seat to skip the fade on you lot," Lina said. "I'm only sorry I could not do the same for your parents."

Dex grinned. "I'm pretty sure this latest Jedi mind trick isn't working on my dad. He keeps talking about 'smoking' his enemies. Like, some guy cut him off on the road the other day, and he was all, 'I will *smoke* you!' through his windshield. Plus, I caught him in the barn the other day doing some kind of Krav Maga moves with the broken end of a broom handle."

Everyone laughed except Poe, who only sighed.

"I wish they *had* erased my memories. The Reginald-shaped ones."

I reached over to take Poe's hand in mine. At least I had been able to say goodbye, and I knew in my gut I would see my brother again when the time was right. But for Poe, Reg's sudden departure had left only loose ends, the frayed edge of a relationship unfinished. Maybe that meant their story wasn't quite over yet.

But I didn't want to give Poe false hope, so I said nothing and only squeezed his hand tight, sharing his pain. Just as I let go, I noticed a flash of movement—barely a shimmer—and felt a small disturbance in the air around us.

In my lap, an envelope sat where there had been nothing a moment ago. It was made of delicate parchment and addressed to me in Reg's unmistakable calligraphy. I looked at Lina, my heart bursting with hope, but she gave me a tiny headshake and an apologetic smile.

"Only a messenger," she said.

With a shaking hand, I turned the envelope over in my lap to see the seal holding it closed, the symbol of House Drake pressed into the wax. I knew then that Reg would never be very far away, and I hoped wherever he was, he would someday understand that I had not left him and that I didn't blame him for leaving me. Maybe the courier who had delivered this letter would tell him how happy I looked among my friends. I tucked the letter into the backpack at my feet to read later, when I was alone.

Then I noticed the wooden box, open to Reg's photo just seconds ago, was now closed. Heart thumping, I reached down to flip up the lid.

All of the pictures inside were gone.

I smiled to myself.

Maybe the photos, when they reached Reg, would trigger a memory—something buried too deep for the Elders to remove.

As for me, I had plenty of time to take more photos, create new memories. And this time, the memories were mine to keep.

ACKNOWLEDGMENTS

It takes a lot of truly amazing humans to launch a book into the world. The following people claim to be mere mortals, but their superhuman feats say otherwise.

I am endlessly grateful to my husband, Matt; my parents, Michael and Holly; and my in-laws, John and Donna. This book would not be possible without their constant support.

Jennifer Laughran, my agent for more than a decade, thank you for your unflinching honesty and for having my back as I veered into a new genre. Whichever way my publishing path turns, I feel confident because you are with me. And thank you to Taryn Fagerness, for spreading my stories around the world.

I won the lottery getting to work with Tara Weikum. Her editorial expertise, combined with the insights of Sarah Homer, made this story deeper and richer. Thank you, both, for caring about this quirky cast of characters and for bringing their world to life.

This book could not have found a better home than with HarperTeen. I deeply appreciate the collaboration and communication at every step of the publishing process. Thank you to Gweneth Morton, Mikayla Lawrence, Chris Kwon, Jenna

Stempel-Lobell, Arwen Rosenbaum, James Neel, Lisa Calcasola, Anna Ravenelle, and the entire team at HarperCollins.

Thank you to Amy Dominy, Amy Nichols, and Tom Leveen, for letting me bring chapters of the same book to writing group for two years. I never would have finished without you, and the book is so much better for your brilliant feedback.

I also want to give a shout-out to every young reader growing up in the cornfields of Middle America. I am so proud to be from the heartland, and I hope you know that magic happens *everywhere*.

Finally, and above all, I am grateful to Grace and Harper. Thank you for the daily inspiration and the belly laughs. Thank you for giving me purpose and for showing me a whole new depth to love. You are forever my two favorite humans.